... For a moment, there was a faint ghost of the old pride...it didn't last.

—from "The Band Played On."

ABOUT LESTER DEL REY...

Born in Saratoga, Minnesota in 1915, del Rey was a natural story teller, often times embellishing his own personal history and laying claim to a number of different (very long) birth names. He was a notable writer and most recognizable editor. A momentous accomplishment during his very long and active career was the initiation of the Sci-Fi division for Ballantine Books in 1977, aptly named "Del Rey Books." His legacy still stands today as publisher of adult "Star Wars" novels and a series of novelizations of the "Spider Man" films. Lester del Rey passed away in May of 1993.

TABLE OF CONTENTS

MASTERS OF SCIENCE FICTION

Volume 7

LESTER DEL REY: "THE BAND PLAYED ON" and other stories

ARMCHAIR FICTION
PO Box 4369, Medford, Oregon 97504

The original text of these stories first appeared in *Science Fiction Quarterly, Future Science Fiction, Infinity, Fantastic Universe, Worlds Beyond, Galaxy, Dynamic Science Fiction, and Space Science Fiction.*

Cover suggests a scene from *Forgive Us Our Debts*

For more information about Armchair Books and products, visit our website at…

www.armchairfiction.com

Or email us at…

armchairfiction@yahoo.com

The Band Played On

The Heroes' March was fitting for most spacemen. Somehow, though, it just didn't apply to a space-borne garbage man!

CHAPTER ONE

INSIDE the rocket grounds, the band was playing the inevitable *Heroes' March* while the cadets snapped through the final maneuvers of their drill. Captain Thomas Murdock stopped at the gate near the visitors' section, waiting until the final blatant notes blared out and were followed by the usual applause from the town kids in the stands. The cadets broke ranks and headed for their study halls, still stepping as if the band played on inside their heads.

Maybe it did, Murdock thought. There had been little parade drill and less music back on Johnston Island when his group won their rocket emblems fifteen years before; yet somehow there had been a sense of destiny, like a drum beating in their brains, to give them the same spring to their stride. It had sent most of them to their deaths and a few to command positions on the moon, long before the base was transferred here to the Florida coast.

Murdock shrugged and glanced upwards. The threatening clouds were closing in, scudding across the sky in dark blobs and streaks, and the wind velocity was rising. It was going to be lousy weather for a takeoff, even if things got no worse.

Behind him, a boy's voice called out. "Hey, pilot!"

He glanced about, but there was no other pilot near. He hesitated, frowning. Then, as the call was repeated, he turned doubtfully toward the stands. Surprisingly, a boy of about twelve was leaning over the railing, motioning toward him and waving a notebook emphatically.

"Autograph, pilot?"

Murdock took the book and signed the blank page automatically, while fifty pairs of eyes watched. No other books were held out, and there was complete silence from the audience. He handed the pencil and notebook back, trying to force a friendly smile onto his face. For a moment, there was a faint ghost of the old pride as he turned back across the deserted parade ground.

It didn't last. Behind him, an older voice broke the silence in disgusted tones. "Why'd you do that, Shorty? He ain't no pilot!"

"He is, too. I guess. I know a pilot's uniform," Shorty protested.

"So what? I already told you about him. He's the garbage man!"

There was no vocal answer to that—only the ripping sound of paper being torn from the notebook.

MURDOCK refused to look back as the boys left the stands. He went across the field, past the school buildings, on toward the main sections of the base—the business part, where the life-line to the space station and the moon was maintained. A job, he told himself, was a job. It was a word he would never have used six ships and fifteen years before.

The storm flag was up on the control tower, he saw. Worse, the guy cables were all tight, anchoring the three-stage ships firmly down in their blast deflection pits. There were no tractors or tankers on the rocket field to service the big ships. He stared through the thickening gloom toward the bay, but there was no activity there, either. The stage recovery boats were all in port, with their handling cranes folded down. Obviously, no flight was scheduled.

It didn't fit with predictions. Hurricane Greta was hustling northward out to sea, and the low ceiling and high winds were supposed to be the tag end of that disturbance, due to clear by mid-day. This didn't look that way; it looked more as if the weather men on the station had goofed for the first time in ten years.

Murdock stared down the line toward his own ship, set apart from the others, swaying slightly as the wind hit it. Getting it up through the weather was going to be hell, even if he got clearance, but he couldn't wait much longer, Greta had already put him four days behind his normal schedule, and he'd been counting on making the trip today.

There was a flash bulletin posted outside the weather shack, surrounded by a group of young majors and colonels from the pilot squad. Murdock stepped around them and into the building. He was glad to see that the man on duty was Collins, one of the few technicians left over from the old days on the Island.

Collins looked up from his scowling study of the maps and saluted casually without rising. "Hi, Tommy. How's the hog business?"

"Lousy," Murdock told him. "I'm going to have a hungry bunch of pigs if I don't get another load down. What gives with the storm signals? I thought Greta blew over."

Collins pawed the last cigarette out of a pack and shook his head as he lighted up. "This is Hulda, they tell me. Our geniuses on the station missed it—claimed Hulda was covered by Greta until she grew bigger. We're just beginning to feel her. No flights for maybe five days more."

"Hell!" It was worse than Murdock had feared. He twisted the weather maps to study them, unbelievingly. Unlike the newer pilots, he'd spent enough time in the weather shack to be able to read a map or a radar screen almost as well as Collins. "The station couldn't have goofed that much, Bill!"

"Did, though. Something's funny up there. Bailey and the other brass are holding some pow-wow about it now, over at Communications. It's boiling up to a first-class mess."

One of the teletypes began chattering, and Collins turned to it. Murdock moved outside where a thin rain was beginning to fall, whipping about in the gusts of wind. He headed for the control tower, knowing it was probably useless. In that, he was right; no clearances for flight could be given without General Bailey's okay, and Bailey was still tied up in conference, apparently.

He borrowed a rain cape and went out across the field toward his ship. The rain was getting heavier, and the *Mollyann* was grunting and creaking in her pit as he neared her. The guying had been well enough done, however, and she was in no danger that he could see. He checked the pit gauges and records. She'd been loaded with a cargo of heavy machinery, and her stage tanks were fully fueled. At least, if he could get clearance, she was ready to go. She was the oldest ship on the field, but her friction-burned skin covered sound construction and he had supervised her last overhaul himself.

Then he felt the wind picking up again, and his stomach knotted. He moved around to the more sheltered side of the ship, cursing the meteorologists on the station. If they'd predicted this correctly, he could have arranged to take off during the comparative lull between storms. Even that would have been bad enough, but now...

Abruptly, a ragged klaxon shrieked through the air in a series of short bursts, sounding assembly for the pilots. Murdock hesitated, then shrugged and headed out into the rain. He could ignore the signal if he chose, since he'd been on detached duty for years, except when actually scheduled for flight; yet it was probably his best chance to see Bailey. He slogged along while the other pilots trotted across the field toward Briefing on the double. Even now, covered with slickers and tramping through mud, they seemed to be on parade drill, as if a drum were beating out the time for them.

MURDOCK found a seat at the rear, separate from the others, out of old habit. Up front, an improvised crap game was going on; elsewhere, they were huddled in little groups, their young faces too bright and confident. Nobody noticed him until Colonel Lawrence Hennings glanced up from the crap game. "Hi, Tommy. Want in?"

Murdock shook his head, smiling briefly. "Can't afford it this week," he explained.

A cat could look at royalty; and royalty was free to look at or speak to anyone—even a man who ferried garbage for the station. At the moment, Hennings was king, even in this crowd of self-determined heroes. There was always one man who was the top dog. Hennings' current position seemed as inevitable as Murdock's own had become.

Damn it, someone had to carry the waste down from the station. The men up there couldn't just shove it out into space to have it follow their orbit and pile up around them; shooting it back to burn up in Earth's atmosphere had been suggested, but that took more fuel in the long run than bringing it down by ship. With nearly eight hundred men in the doubly expanded station, there was a lot of garbage, too. The job was as important as carrying the supplies up, and took just as much piloting skill. Only there was no band playing when the garbage ship took off, and there could never be a hero's mantle over the garbage man.

It had simply been his bad luck that he was pilot for the first load back. The heat of landing leaked through the red-hot skin of the cargo section, and the wastes boiled and steamed through the whole ship and plated themselves against the hull when it began to cool, until no amount of washing could clean it completely; after that, the ship was considered good for nothing but the carrying of garbage down and lifting such things as machine parts, where the smell wouldn't matter. He'd gone on detached duty at once, exiled from the pilot shack; it was probably only imagination, but the other men swore they couldn't sleep in the same room with him.

He'd made something of a joke of it at first, while he waited for his transfer at the end of the year. He'd finally consented to a second year when they couldn't get anyone else for the job. And by the end of five years of it, he knew he was stuck; even a transfer wouldn't erase his reputation as the garbage man, or give him the promotions and chances for leadership the others got. Oh, there were advantages in freedom, but if there had been anything outside of the service he could do…

The side door opened suddenly and General Bailey came in. He looked older than his forty years, and the expression on his face sobered the pilots almost at once. He took his time in dropping to the chair behind the table, giving them a chance to come to order. Murdock braced himself, watching as the man took out a cigarette. Then, as it was tapped sharply on the table to pack the end, he nodded. It was going to be a call for volunteers! The picture of the weather outside raced through his mind, twisting at his stomach, but he slid forward on his seat, ready to stand at once.

"At ease, men." Bailey took his time lighting the cigarette, and then plunged into things. "A lot of you have been cursing the station for their forecast. Well, you can forget that we're damned lucky they could spot Hulda at all. They're in bad shape. Know what acrolein is? You've all had courses in atmospherics. How about it?"

The answer came out in pieces from several of the pilots. Acrolein was one of the thirty odd poisons that had to be filtered from the air in the station, though it presented no problem in the huge atmosphere of Earth. It could get into the air from the overcooking of an egg or the burning of several proteins. "You can get it from some of the plastics, too," one of the men added.

Bailey nodded. "You can. And that's the way they got it, from an accident in the shops. They got enough to overload their filters, and the replacements aren't enough to handle it. They're all being poisoned up there—just enough to muddle their thinking at first, but getting worse all the time. They can't wait for Hulda to pass. They've got to have new filters at once. And that means—"

"Sir!" Hennings was on his feet, standing like a lance in a saddle boot. "Speaking for my crew, I ask permission to deliver whatever the station needs."

Murdock had been caught short by Hennings' sudden move, but now he was up, protesting. His voice sounded as hollow as he felt after the ringing tones of the younger man. "I'm overdue already! And by all rights—"

Bailey cut him off, nodding to Hennings. "Thank you, Colonel. We'll begin loading at once, while Control works out your tapes. All right, dismissed!" Then finally he turned to Murdock. "Thanks, Tom. I'll record your offer, but there's no time for us to unload your ship first. Afraid you're grounded for the storm."

He went out quickly, with Hennings following jauntily at his heels.

THE OTHERS were beginning to leave, grumbling with a certain admiration at Hennings' jumping the gun on them. Murdock trailed along, since there was no chance for him to change the orders now. He wondered what excuse would have been used if he'd been first to volunteer and if his ship had been empty. The choice of pilot had probably been made before the token request for volunteers, and he was certain that his name hadn't been considered.

The storm seemed to have let up when he started across the field, but it was only a lull. Before he could reach the shelter of the weather shack, it began pelting down again, harder than ever. He stopped inside the door to shake off some of the wetness. Collins was intently studying one of the radar screens where a remote pickup was showing conditions, alternately working a calculator and yelling into a phone. He looked up, made a desperate motion with his fingers for a cigarette, and went back to the phone.

Murdock shoved a lighted smoke toward him, then pulled a stool up to the window where he could watch the field. By rights, he should be heading back to his farm, to do what he could there; but he had no intention of leaving before the take-off. Lifting a ship in this weather was mostly theory. It had been done once on the Island, but the big ships were still too unstable to make it anything but a desperate emergency measure. He'd discussed it with the pilot after that trip and he'd spent a lot of time trying to work out a method in case he had to try it, but Hennings had his sympathy now. It took more than courage and confidence to handle this situation.

He studied the storm, trying to get the feel of it. During his first two years back here, he'd spent a lot of his free time flying a light plane, and some of the weather had been fairly bad. It gave him some idea of what Hennings had to face; he wondered whether the younger pilot realized what was coming.

Sodium lights were blazing on the field, he saw, clustered about Hennings' *Jennilee*, and men were slipping and sliding around in the mud, getting her ready and loading the filter packs. Two men were being run up on a lift to the crew entrance; Hennings carried both a co-pilot and a radio man, though many of the pilots now used only a single crewman.

Collins looked up from the phone. "Fifteen minutes to zero," he reported.

Murdock grunted in surprise. He'd expected the take-off to be two hours later, on the next swing of the station. It must mean that orders for loading the ship had been given before Bailey came into Briefing. It confirmed his suspicion that the pilot had been picked in advance.

A few minutes later, Hennings appeared, marching across the field toward the lift in the middle of a small group. Several of them rode up with him. As the lift began creaking backward, the pilot stood poised in the lock, grinning for the photographers. Naturally, the press had been tipped off; the service had learned long before that maximum publicity helped in getting the fattest possible appropriations.

When the lock was finally sealed and the field cleared, Murdock bent over the counter to study the radar screens. The storm was apparently erratic, from the hazy configurations he could see. Zero would be a poor choice for the take-off, though, from what he could estimate. Hennings would be smarter to delay and make manual corrections on his tape.

Then the klaxon went on, signaling the take-off. The last man on the field was darting for cover. From the blast pit, a dull, sickly red began to shine as the rockets were started. Murdock swore. The fool was taking off on schedule, trusting to his tapes!

The smoky red exhaust ran up the spectrum to blue, and the ship began to tremble faintly. The sound rose to crescendo. Now the *Jennilee* started to lift. Wind hit it, throwing it toward the side of the pit. The wings of the top stage caught most of the force, and the whole ship was tilting—the worst thing that could happen. They should have swiveled the ship around to put the wings parallel to most of the storm, instead of bucking it.

Murdock heard Collins' breath catch harshly, but suddenly the worst danger was over. A lull for a second or so gave Hennings his chance. He was at least riding his controls over the automatics. The blast deflection vanes shot the blue flame sidewise, and the ship shifted its bottom, righting itself. It was beginning to make its real climb now. The wings near the top literally vibrated like the arms of a tuning fork, and the blast trail was ragged. Yet she rose, her blast roar rising and falling as the wind altered, blowing some of the sound away from the watchers.

Now the Doppler Effect began to be noticeable, and the sound dropped in pitch as the *Jennilee* fought her way up. The overcast of scudding clouds hid all but the bright anger of the exhaust.

Murdock turned with the technician to another radar screen. Unlike those in Control, it wasn't set properly to catch the ship, but a hazy figure showed in one edge. "Right into some of the nastiest stuff blowing!" Collins swore.

CHAPTER TWO

HE WAS right. The timing had been as bad as possible. The blob of light on the screen was obviously being buffeted about. Something seemed to hit the top and jerk it.

The screen went blank, then lighted again. Collins had shifted his connections, to patch into the signal Control was watching. The blip of the *Jennilee* was now dead center, trying to tilt into a normal synergy curve. "Take it up, damn it!" Murdock swore hotly. This was no time to swing around the Earth until after the ship was above the storm. The tape for the automatic pilot should have been cut for a high first ascension. If Hennings was panicking and overriding it back to the familiar orbit...

As if the pilot heard him, the blip began rising again. It twisted and bucked. Something seemed to separate from it. There was a scattering of tiny white dots on the screen, drifting behind the ship. Murdock couldn't figure them. Then he forgot them as the first stage let go and began falling backward from the ship, heading on its great arc toward the ocean. Recovery would be rough. Now the second stage blasted out. And finally, the ship was above the storm and could begin to track toward its goal.

Abruptly the speaker in the corner snapped into life, and Hennings' voice sounded from it. "*Jennilee* to Base. Cancel the harps and haloes! We're in the clear!"

Collins snapped his hand down against a switch, killing the speaker. "Hotshot!" he said thickly, and yet there was a touch of admiration in his voice. "Ten years ago, they couldn't build ships to take what he gave it. So that makes him a tin god on wheels. Got a cigarette, Tommy?"

Murdock handed him the package and picked up the slicker again. He'd seen enough. The ship should have no further trouble, except for minor orbital corrections, well within the pilot's ability. For that matter, while Collins' statement was true enough, Hennings deserved a lot of the credit. And if he had to boast a little—well, maybe he deserved credit for the ability to snap back to normal after the pounding his body and nerves must have taken.

IN THE recreation hall, some of the pilots were busy exaggerating the dangers of the take-off for the newsmen, making it sound as if no parallel feat had been performed in all history. Murdock found a phone where he had some privacy and put through a call to let Pete and Sheila know when he'd be back—and that he was returning without a load. They'd already heard the news, however. He cut the call short and went out across the soggy field, cursing as his shoes filled with water. From the auditorium of the school, he could hear the band practicing; he wondered for a moment whether the drumbeat could make the cadets feel like heroes as they moved through mud with shoes that squished at every step. It had no such lifting effect on him.

The parking lot beyond the drill grounds was almost deserted, and his big truck seemed to huddle into the wind like a lonely old bull buffalo. He started the turbine and opened the cab heater, kicking off his sodden shoes. The dampness in the air brought out the smell of refuse and pigs from the rear, but he was used to it; anyhow, it was better than the machine-human-chemical stench of the space station.

Driving took most of his attention. The truck showed little wind-sway and the roads were nearly deserted, but vision was limited and the windshield kept steaming up, in spite of the silicone coating. He crawled along, grumbling to himself at the allocation of money for tourist superhighways at the expense of the back roads.

A little ways beyond the base, he was in farm country. It was totally unlike the picture of things he'd had originally. He'd expected only palm trees and citrus groves in Florida, though he'd known vaguely that it was one of the major cattle producing states. This part wasn't exactly like the Iowa section where he'd grown up, but it wasn't so different, either.

Pete Crane had introduced him to it. At the time, Pete was retiring after twenty years of service and looking for something to do. He'd found a small farm twenty miles from Base and he approached Murdock with the hope of getting the station garbage for food for the hogs he planned to buy. The contractor who took care of the Base garbage wouldn't touch the dehydrated, slightly scorched refuse, and disposal had always been a problem.

They ended up as partners, with permanent rights to all the station wastes. Pete's sister, Sheila, joined them to keep house for them. It beat living in hotels and offered the first hope for the future Murdock had. Unless his application for Moon service was accepted—which seemed unlikely, since he was already at the age limit of thirty-five—he had no other plans for his own compulsory twenty-year retirement. The farm also gave some purpose to his job as garbage collector for the station.

For two years, everything went well. Maybe they grew over-confident then. They sank everything into new buildings and more livestock. When the neighboring farm suddenly became available, they used all their credit in swinging the mortgage, leaving no margin for trouble. And trouble came when Pete was caught in front of a tractor that somehow slipped into gear; he was hospitalized for five weeks, and his medical insurance was only enough for a fraction of the cost. Now, with Hulda cancelling the critically necessary trip to the station…

THE TRUCK bumped over the last half mile and into the farmyard. Murdock parked it near the front door and jumped out. He let out a yell and made a bee-line for the kerosene heater, trying to get his feet warm on the floor near it. The house was better built than many in Florida, but that wasn't saying much. Even with the heater going, it was probably warmer in their new pig sty.

Sheila came through the dining room from the kitchen, spotted his wet feet, and darted for his bedroom. In a second she was back with dry clothes. "Change in here where it's warm. I'll have lunch ready in a couple of minutes," she told him, holding her face up for a kiss.

Sheila wasn't a beautiful woman and apparently didn't care. Murdock's mother would probably have called her plain good looks "wholesome," and referred to her slightly overweight body as "healthy." He only knew that she looked good to him, enough shorter to be comfortable, eyes pleasantly blue, and hair some shade of brown that seemed to fit her.

He pulled her to him snugly, but she wriggled away after a brief kiss. "Pete's in town, trying to get help. He'll be back any minute," she warned him.

He grinned and let her go. They'd gone through the romantic binge of discovering each other long enough ago to be comfortable with each other now, except for the occasional arguments when she didn't want to wait. Mostly, though, she had accepted their agreement. In eight more months he'd be thirty-six and too old for assignment on the Moon; if he didn't make that, they'd get married. But he had no intention of leaving her tied to him if he did leave, since the chance of taking her along was almost nil. Pete had backed him up on his decision, too.

He slipped into coveralls and dry boots and went out to the dining room, where a hot meal was waiting. At least their credit was good at the local grocery between paydays. He filled her in on what had happened while they ate. At the hour mark, he switched on the television to the news. It was filled with the station emergency and rescue, of course. Most of it seemed to be devoted to pictures of Hennings entering the ship and a highly colored account of the flight. But at least he learned that the flight had been completed. It made good publicity for the service. A sound track of a band playing the *Heroes' March* had been spliced into the movies. Maybe that was good publicity, too. He had to admit that Henning fitted the music better than he could have done.

For a moment, the racket of the wind outside died, and another sound reached his ears. The hogs knew it was past feeding time and were kicking up a fuss, Murdock grimaced. He shoved away from the table, feeling almost guilty at having stuffed himself, and dug rain clothes out of the back closet. He hated going out in the weather again, but the animals had to be pacified.

They heard him coming and set up more of a racket. He bent against the wind and made a dash for it, getting his feet wet again in a puddle. But the inside of the building was warmer than the house, as he had expected. He lifted the cover of the mash cooker and began ladling out the food into the troughs. His pail was scraping the bottom of the cooker, while the sleek Poland China hogs fought and shoved toward the spot where he was emptying it. They'd been on half rations since yesterday, and they were obviously hungry.

He stopped when he had used half of what was in the cooker and headed for the next building. On the way, he paused for a futile look in the big storage shed, but he knew the answer, Pete had used the last bag of grain in cooking the day's food. They'd exhausted the last of the waste from the station earlier and had to fall back on the precious commercial feed usually only used as a supplement. Damn Greta and double damn Hulda! If the weekly predictions had been right, he could have wangled clearance for a flight ahead of schedule, before the storms, and they wouldn't be in this mess.

It was worse in the brooder house. The sows seemed to know that milk for their sucklings depended on their feeding. They received a somewhat larger portion, but it disappeared from the troughs as he watched. The animals fought for the last scraps and then began rushing about looking for more. They were smart enough to know he was the source of it, and they stared at him, expressing their demands in eloquent hog language. They weren't like other animals. Cows were too stupid to realize they'd been gypped, sheep were always yelling even when things went well. But hogs I could pretty nearly swear in English when they felt robbed, as these did. Even the sucklings were squealing unhappily in sympathy with their mothers.

MURDOCK heard the door open behind him and turned to see Pete coming in, drenched to the skin. He looked worn out, and his back was still stiff from the accident, though he'd made a fine recovery. "Hi, Tom. Sis told me what happened at the field. Good thing, too. This stuff's no good for flights. How long till it clears?"

"Five days!" Murdock told him, and saw the older man flinch. The hogs might not starve to death in that time, but they'd suffer, as well as losing weight that would be hard to put back. He had no idea of how it would affect the milk supply for the little pigs, and he didn't want to guess.

They left the squealing hogs and slogged back to the house to change before Pete would report on his luck in town. It seemed to be all bad. They could get a loan against the mature hogs or they could sell some, but with the weekend coming up they would have to wait for money until they would no longer need it. Their credit at the only feed and grain store was used up.

Murdock frowned at that. "You mean Barr wouldn't let us have enough to carry us over in an emergency like this? After all our business with him?"

"Barr's gone north on some business," Pete reported. "His brother-in-law's running things. Claims he can't take the responsibility. Offered to lend me twenty bucks himself if I needed it, but no credit from the store. And he can't locate Barr. Darn it, if I hadn't had to get in front of that tractor—"

"If!" Sheila snorted. "If I hadn't insisted you two pay the hospital in full, or if I hadn't splurged on spring clothes… How much can we get for my car?"

Pete shrugged. "About half enough, but not till maybe Tuesday or Wednesday, after title transfer. I already asked at Circle Chevy. How about getting the weather reports, Sheila? With our luck, the center of Hulda might pass right here!"

There seemed no immediate danger of that, though, Hulda was following Greta, due to swing out to sea, and they'd miss the worst of her. Anyhow, Murdock knew that Bill Collins would call them if the farm was in danger. But with predictions gone sour from the station, they couldn't be sure. The new buildings were supposed to be hurricane proof, but…

They spent the afternoon trying to play canasta and listening to the rain and wind, until Pete slapped the cards back in the drawer in disgust. They ate early, dawdling over the food to kill time. Finally, the two men went out reluctantly. This time they scraped the bottom of the cookers dry. There was no sense in trying to spread the little food further and thinner.

How would a hero feel when a hog looked at him with hungry eyes? Or would the band playing destiny in his head drown out the frantic squealing of the animals? Murdock sighed and turned sickly back toward the house, with Pete at his heels.

Sheila met them at the door, motioning for silence and pointing to the television set. More news was finally coming through on the rescue flight by Hennings. And there was a picture on the screen showing the little third-stage rocket as seen from the station. It was obvious without the announcer's comment that the wings had been nearly wrenched from it and that it was in no condition for the return flight. Murdock's respect for Hennings' courage went up another notch. After a buffeting like that, it was a wonder he'd been able to make the effort of speaking to Base at all.

Then the rest of the news began to penetrate, and even the carefully chosen words couldn't make it sound too good, "…loss of filters when the airlock was sprung open on take-off was considerable, but it is believed that the replacements will be adequate until another flight can be made. Dr. Shapiro on the station reports that the men seem to be bearing up well, except for the two children. Plans are being made to isolate them in a special room, with extra filtration…"

Commander Phillips' kids, Murdock thought. The man had no business keeping them up there, anyhow. But the business about the sprung airlock…

Then he remembered the smaller blips on the radar screen that had separated from the *Jennilee*, before the first stage broke away. He frowned, trying to figure things more carefully. Just a few filters couldn't have made that much trace on the radar! But with the hasty packing, as he'd seen it, and the ship beginning to turn so the airlock was down, enough could have spilled to account for the trace—nearly the whole cargo, in fact!

He started for the phone, then shook his head. This would be better in person. He grabbed for the zipper on his coveralls and headed for his bedroom, while Pete frowned in slow comprehension.

"Tom, you can't do it!"

"I can try," he called back. "Warm up the truck, Sheila."

The zipper stuck. He swore at it, then forgot it. He wasn't dressing for parade drill. He dragged on his uniform cap, slipped into boots that might give some protection from the mud on the field, and stuffed his necessary papers and cards into the pockets of the coveralls. The service slicker was dry now, and he used it to hide most of his appearance.

"Any word of another flight planned?" he called out. It would be a sorry mess to reach the field just as some young pilot was taking off, ending any chance he had.

"None." Pete had the door open, and one of his big hands slapped against Murdock's shoulder. "Luck, you idiot!"

CHAPTER THREE

MURDOCK jumped out and into the open door of the truck. He started to shove Sheila out of the driver's seat, but she shook her head and began gunning the turbine. "I can handle this as well as you can. Tom, I won't have you starting *that* after wearing yourself out driving in. And stop looking at me like that! I'm not going to say what I'm thinking about this!"

He settled back in the passenger seat, reaching one hand out to touch her briefly. "Thanks, Hon," he said, as the truck swung out of the driveway and picked up speed on the road. She'd never been the kind to talk about worrying over his life, as some of the wives of the pilots did. She took it as part of him, and accepted it, however she felt. Now she was pushing the big truck to the maximum safe speed, as if sharing his eagerness.

After a second, she caught his hand in hers and smiled, without taking her eyes from the road. He relaxed on the seat, letting the swish of the wipers and the muffled storm sounds lull him into a half trance, resting as much as he could. He should be thinking of what he'd say to Bailey, but the relaxation was more important.

He was half asleep when the truck stopped at the guard house. He began fumbling for his papers, but the guard swung back after flashing his face and called out something. A corporal darted out of the shack and into the truck, reaching for the wheel. "General Bailey's expecting you and the young lady, sir," he said. "I'll take care of your truck."

Murdock grunted in surprise. Pete must have managed to get through to Bailey. It might make things more difficult, but it would at least save time; that could be important, if he were to take off while the station was in optimum position.

Bailey's aide met them at GHQ, escorting them directly to the general's private office, and closing the door behind them. Bailey glanced at Murdock's appearance, frowned, and motioned them to chairs. His own collar was unbuttoned and his cap lay on the desk, indicating that formality was out the window. He lifted a bottle toward three waiting glasses. "Tom? Miss Crane?"

He seemed to need the drink more than they did. His face was gray with fatigue and his hand was unsteady. But his voice was normal enough as he put down the empty glass. "All right, Tom, I know what you're here for. What makes you think I'm crazy enough to send another ship up in this weather?"

"A couple of kids who may be dying up there," Murdock answered. He saw the general flinch and knew he'd guessed right; the service wouldn't want the publicity of their deaths without further effort to save them, and the pressure on Bailey must be terrific by now. "How many filters got through?"

"Two bundles—out of thirty! But losing a man and ship won't help anything. I've turned down about every pilot here already. I'd need at least three good reasons why you're a better choice before I'd even consider you, in spite of the hell Washington's raising. Got them?"

He should have been thinking of them on the ride here, Murdock realized. "Experience, for one thing. I've made almost a thousand flights on the run I was assigned," he said, making no effort to conceal the bitterness that crept into his voice. "Has any of your hotshots made a hundred yet?"

Bailey shook his head. "No."

"How about ability to operate solo without help from the automatic pilot? You can't trust machinery in unpredictable situations, and there's no time for help from a crew." The combination of improved ships and the difficulty of getting a crew for the garbage run had resulted in Murdock's operating solo most of the time for nearly five years now. He saw two of Bailey's fingers go up, and groped for something that would finish his case. Again, he heard the bitterness in his voice. "Third, expendability. What's a garbage man and an old ship against your bright hopes for tomorrow?"

"I've thought of the first two already. They're valid. The third isn't." Bailey filled a second glass halfway, his eyes on the liquor. "I can get plenty of pilots, Tom. So far, I haven't been able to find one other reliable garbage man, as you call it—after fifteen years! You'll have to do better than that."

Sheila's heels tapped down on the floor sharply. "After fifteen years of doing a job nobody else will take, don't you think Tom has any right to a favor from you? Isn't that good enough a reason?"

Bailey swung his gaze to her, surprise on his face. He studied her for half a minute, nodding slowly. "My God, you're actually willing to have him go," he said at last. "I thought... Never mind. If you're willing to trust his ability, it's no reason I should. Or maybe it is. Maybe I want to be convinced. All right, Tom, we'll unload your ship and get the filters in. Want me to pick a volunteer crew for you?"

"I'll take it solo," Murdock told him. The fewer lives he was responsible for, the better; anyhow, there would be no time for help through the critical first few miles. "And leave the machinery in. Your filters are all bulk and no weight. She'll pitch less with a full load, from what I saw today. I'll be better off with that ballast."

BAILEY reached for the phone and began snapping orders while Murdock turned to say goodbye to Sheila. She made it easier than he'd expected.

"I'll wait here," she told him. "You'll need the truck when you come down." She kissed him again quickly, then shoved him away. "Go on, you don't have time for me now."

She was right in that, he knew. He started for Control at a run, surprised when a covered jeep swung beside him. Lights came on abruptly, showing the *Mollyann* dimly through the murk, with men and trucks pouring toward her. He sent the driver of the jeep after them with orders to see about turning the base so the wings of the third stage would be edge on to the wind. In Control, he found everything disorganized, with men still dazed from sleep staring at him unbelievingly. But they agreed to set up the circuit that would give him connection through his viewing screen to the weather radar. Over the phone, Collins' language was foul and his voice worried, but he caught onto what was wanted almost at once.

The *Mollyann* was shaking against her guy cables as the jeep took him out to her; removal of the cables would be the last thing before take-off. Half a dozen tractors were idling nearby, and Bailey came running toward him, waving toward the top and yelling something about turning her.

Murdock shrugged. He hadn't expected things to be smooth in this last-minute rush; if he had to take her up wrong, he had to. "Okay, forget it," he said. "So you can't turn her. I'll manage."

"Take a look," Bailey told him, pointing up again, a tired grin on his face. "The way the wind is now, she's perfect. We finally checked, after getting all set, and there she was."

It was true, and Murdock swore hotly at his own stupidity in not checking first. The big wings were parallel to the wind already, saving them precious minutes. It still left the steering vanes on the upper stage at the mercy of the wind, but they were stubbier, and hence considerably sturdier.

The portable lift was running up the filter packs. He climbed on as a flashbulb went off near him and began going up. He heard some sort of cry from the photographer, but there was no time for posing now, and he couldn't have looked less suitable for pictures, anyhow. There'd be time for that on his return, he hoped.

He checked the stowing of the packs and made sure that they were lashed down well enough to ride up, even if his airlock broke open. The technician in charge pointed out the extra dogs they were installing on the lock, swearing it would hold through anything. It looked right. The ship was swaying and bobbing noticeably up here, and he could hear the creak of the cables. He tried to close his ears as he crawled up the little ladder to the control cabin and began the final check-out. There was a yell from the speaker as he cut on connections to Control, but he paid little attention to it. After fifteen years, he had little need of them to tell him the exact second of ideal take-off. He found the picture of the weather on the screen as he settled into the acceleration couch under the manual control panel, designed to swivel as a unit under changing acceleration.

The weather image was his biggest hope. Here, his study could payoff and give him the advantage he needed. It might look showy to take off on the split second and fight whatever the weather handed out; he preferred to pick his own time, if possible. With luck, he could spot a chance to ride up without being tipped for the first few seconds.

He glanced at the chronometer and began strapping himself down, while trying to absorb the data on the storm Collins was sending into his earphones. The weatherman had several screens to work from, and could give a better general picture than the single one Murdock was able to watch.

He began to get the feel of it. The wind this far from the center of the hurricane, was erratic; there were moments of comparative quiet, and some measure of prediction was possible from the pattern on the screen. The real trick of taking off was to take advantage of every break. Once he began ascension, he'd have to trust to the automatic reflexes he'd developed and the general plan he'd worked out over the years as pure theory, with little help from reasoned thought. But until then, he could use his brains to make it as easy as it could possibly be.

He had no desire to take what was coming as a personal challenge. The kids in the station and the pigs on the farm were interested in results, not in his show of bravery.

COLLINS' VOICE cut off as Control interrupted to notify him that loading was complete and that the lifts, trucks and men were all clear.

He put one hand on the switch that would unlock the guy cables simultaneously. With the other, he started the peroxide pump for the fuel and threw the switch to ignite the rockets. He could hear the whine of the pump and feel the beginnings of power rumble through the ship, but he kept it at minimum. His eyes were glued to the weather picture on the screen that indicated his best chance coming up. Control was going crazy. With their count-off already finished, they wanted him off! Let them stew! A few seconds' difference in take-off was something he could correct for later.

Then his hand depressed the main blast lever all the way, a split second before he released the cable grapples. The *Mollyann* jumped free and began to walk upstairs on stilts, teetering and yawing in the wind. But his choke of take-off time had been correct. For the first hundred feet, she behaved herself, though the wind was driving him away from the blast deflection pit.

Then hell began. Acceleration mauled him backwards until only muscles toughened by a thousand previous flights could stand the power he was using. His fingers and arms would barely move against it. Yet they had to dance across the controls. The ship twisted and tilted, with every plate of her screaming in agony from the torsion and distortion of the pressures. Somehow, automatically, his fingers found a combination that righted her. His ears were clogged with the heavy pounding of his blood, his sense of balance was frozen, and his eyes could barely manage to focus on the dials in front of him.

He had stopped normal thinking and become a machine. The ship spun crazily in the twisting chaos of pressure differences. Unaccountably, she stayed upright as his hands moved with an unwilling life of their own, while fuel poured out at a rate that should have blacked him out from the acceleration. It was wasteful, but his only chance was to get through the storm in the shortest possible time and hang the consequences. If he could make the station at all, there would be fuel there for his return kick-off.

He was making no effort to tilt into a normal curve. A red light on the controls sprang into hazy existence before his eyes. The ship was going too fast for the height, heating the hull. He had to risk that, though.

Then surprisingly, the ship began to steady. He'd climbed over the storm.

He cut power back to normal, feeling a return of thought and hearing, and began tilting slowly to swing around the Earth toward his destination on the other side and a thousand miles up. It would make a rotten imitation of a synergy curve, but he'd survived! He felt the big first stage let go, followed by a brief moment with no pressure, until the second stage roared out. Only a little over a minute had passed in the storm, in spite of the hours of torture he had felt.

A voice started shouting in his phones, but he paid no attention to it. Now was his chance to say something heroic, to make the jest that was the ultimate in braggadocio!

"Shut up, damn it! I'm all right!" he screamed into the microphone. How could he figure out a proper saying for the papers when they wouldn't let him alone? Then slowly he realized he'd already answered, and it was too late for pretty phrases.

The second stage kicked off finally, and the third stage went on alone. He set up the rough corrections for his atypical takeoff, hoping he hadn't missed too much, while the second hand swept around until he could cut off all power and just drift. Then he lay back, welcoming weightlessness. He was trembling now, and his whole body seemed to be a mass of bruises he couldn't remember getting. Sweat poured from his forehead and goose pimples rose on his arms. He barely made it to the little cabinet in time to be sick without splattering the whole cabin.

He made a lousy hero. The only music in his head was the ringing in his ears and the drumming in his heart!

Yet the trip up was by far the easier part of his job. He still had to bring his cargo down in its unpowered glide through a storm that would be closer to its worst, or the whole trip would be useless for him, no matter how many lives it saved.

He was feeling almost himself again, though, when he finally matched orbits with the station. As far as he could determine, his wings and stabilizers were still sound, and air pressure in the cargo space indicated nothing had sprung there. He even had a few drops of fuel left after making his final corrections. At least he'd done an adequate job of piloting on the ascension.

With luck, he'd get the *Mollyann* down again intact. But he'd need that luck!

CHAPTER FOUR

THE BIG multi-tube affair into which the station had grown looked normal enough in the sunlight. But the men who came out in the little space ferry showed the hell of slow poisoning they'd been through, even over their jubilation at the sight of the filters. When they made seal-to-seal contact and he released the lock, the smell of their air was positively foul. They must have been reporting their plight as a lot better than it really was.

Commander Phillips came through first, almost crying as he grabbed Murdock's hand. He seemed at a complete loss for words.

"Hello, Red," Murdock greeted him. Phillips had been part of his own class, fifteen years before. "How are the kids?"

"Shapiro says they'll be okay, once we get some filters that aren't plated with contaminants. Tommy, I'd invite you over for champagne right now, but our air would ruin it. Just figure that anything I've got..."

Murdock cut him off. "I'll call it quits if you'll get this cargo out and my usual load in here on the double, along with some fuel. And you might have one of your engineers look over my wings for signs of strain. I've got to ride the next orbit back, two hours from now."

"Go back into that! You're crazy!" Phillips' shock drove everything else from the man's face. "You can't do it! I won't clear you!"

"I thought you were just offering me anything you had," Murdock pointed out.

It took five minutes more of heavy arguing to arrange it, and he might not have succeeded even then if he'd waited until the commander had recovered from his first burst of gratitude, or if the man hadn't been worn down by the poisons in the air and the fatigue of their desperate fight for survival. Phillips was hoarse and sick when he finally gave in and stumbled back to the loaded ferry. He croaked something about idiocy and grateful humanity and took off. Murdock tried, idly, to untangle it in his mind, but at the moment he was again more concerned with hungry pigs.

It was too busy a stretch for him to have time to worry. The square magnesium cans of dehydrated garbage began to come out, along with fuel. Sick men were somehow driving themselves to a final burst of energy as they stowed things carefully to preserve the trim of the ship. From outside, there was a, steady tapping and hammering as others went over the skin of the controls with their instruments.

At the end, there was another visit from Phillips, with more arguing. But finally the man gave in again. "All right, damn it. Maybe you can make it. I certainly hope so. But you're not going it alone. You'll take Henning along as co-pilot. He volunteered."

"Send him over, then," Murdock said wearily. He should have expected something like that—Hennings apparently reacted to the smell of glory like a warhorse to gunpowder.

He took a final look at the cargo, nodding in satisfaction. There was enough waste there to keep the farm going until they were over the hump. If Barr got back and they could enrich it with commercial food on temporary credit, Pete and he would be in clover. He pulled himself about and up to the control cabin, to see the ferry coming out on its last trip.

A minute later, Hennings came through the connecting seal and dogged it closed. "Hi, Tommy," he called out. "Ah, air again. How about letting me run her down for you? You look beat."

"The automatic pilot's disconnected," Murdock told him curtly. It had begun misfunctioning some twenty trips back, and he'd simply cut it out of the circuits, since he seldom used it.

Some of the starch seemed to run out of the younger man. He halted his march toward the controls and stared down at them doubtfully. Actually, little automatic piloting could be done on the down leg of a flight, but pilots were conditioned into thinking of the automatics almost reverently, ahead of anything else on the ship. It dated from the days when the ascension would have been physically impossible without such aid, and Murdock had felt the same for the first five years of piloting.

"Better strap in," he suggested.

Hennings dropped into the co-pilot couch while Murdock ran through the final check. The ship began swinging slowly about as the gyroscopes hummed, lining up for the return blast. "Ten seconds," Murdock announced. He ran a count in his head, then hit the blast lever gently. They began losing speed and dropping back toward Earth, while the station sailed on and away.

Then, with power off, there was nothing to do but stare at what was coming. It would still be night at Base, and even the sodium flares and radar beacons wouldn't be as much help as they should be in the storm. This time, they'd have to depend on lift, like a normal plane landing. It would be tough for any plane, for that matter, though possible enough in fully powered flight. But they had to come down like a glider. If there were any undetected strains in the wings…

"You came up *without* a tape?" Hennings asked suddenly.

Murdock grimaced, resenting the interruption to his brooding. He liked Hennings better as a cocky hero than as a worried young man. "A tape's no good for unpredictable conditions."

"Okay, if you say so," the younger man said doubtfully at last. He sat staring at the controls with an odd look on his face. Then surprisingly, he laughed and settled back loosely in his seat. "I guess maybe you don't need me, then."

He was snoring five minutes later. Murdock scowled at him, suspecting it was an act at first. Finally he shrugged and turned back to his worrying. He knew there'd been a good measure of luck to his take-off, in spite of all his careful efforts. He couldn't count on luck for the landing.

HE COULD still put in an emergency call and ask to land at some large airfield out of the storm, in theory. But it would do no good. Hulda was blanketing too great an area; any other field would be so far from the farm that trucking the garbage back would be out of the question. He might as well have remained at the station. Besides, he was already on a braking orbit that would bring him near Base, and changes now would involve risks of their own.

He watched the thin haze of the upper atmospheric levels approach, trying to force his muscles to relax and his nerves to steady. The worst part of the return was the chance for nervousness to build up. Hennings went on snoring quietly, floating in the co-pilot's couch. His relaxation didn't help Murdock any.

It was almost a relief when they finally hit the first layers of detectable air, where the controls became effective again, and where he could take over. The ship had to be guided steadily now, its dip into atmosphere coordinated with its speed to avoid the dangers of skipping out or of going low enough to overheat. Murdock eased her down, watching his instruments but depending more on the feel of the *Mollyann.* A feeling of weight began to return along with noise from outside, while the hull pyrometer rose to indicate that friction was working on them, turning their speed into heat. This part of the descent was almost a conditioned reflex to him by now. Outside, he knew, the skin of the ship would be rising slowly to red heat, until they could lose enough speed to drop into the lower layers of air where they could cool off.

The heat in the cabin rose slowly. The *Mollyann* was an old model among the ships; her cabin was less completely insulated and airtight than most of the others. But for the brief period of high heat, she was safe enough. Slowly the air picked up a faint odor that grew stronger as the hot hull radiated into the cargo space. He hardly noticed it, until Hennings woke up sniffing.

"Garbage," Murdock told him. "There's still enough water in it to boil off some. You get used to it."

They were dropping to denser air now, and he could feel perspiration on his palms. He dried them hastily. His head felt thick, and his stomach began to knot inside him. "Contact Control and have them shoot me the weather," he told Hennings.

When the pattern of it snapped onto the screen, he felt sicker. There was going to be no area of relative calm this time, and he couldn't wait for one to appear. He tried to get the weather pattern fixed in his mind while their descent flattened and they came closer to the storm area. He'd have to turn and follow the course set by the wind, heading into it; it meant coming down on a twisting curve, since there was some local disturbance near the field.

Then the first bumpiness registered. The ship seemed to sink and skid. There was no pressure of acceleration now, but his fingers felt weighted with lead, almost too slow to adjust the controls. The *Mollyann* dipped and tilted, and his stomach came up in his throat. He heard Hennings gasp, but he had no time to look at the other. The top of the storm was a boiling riot of pockets.

Things were getting worse by the second now. The last few miles were going to be hell. Lift wasn't steady, and eddies in the driving storm shook and twisted the ship. Her wing-loading wasn't bad, but she lacked the self-correcting design of the light planes he'd flown. The wings groaned and strained, and the controls seemed frozen. He was on the weather map now, a white blip that scudded along the edge. It gave him orientation, but the sight of his course offered little reassurance.

They hit a larger pocket and seemed to drop a hundred feet. The wings creaked sickeningly, and something whined from the rear controls. The elevators abruptly bucked back at him, catching him unaware, and he had to brace himself and fight against them, putting his muscles into it. Obviously the servo assist had conked out. Probably something had happened during take-off. He was left with only his own strength to buck the currents now, operating on the mechanical cable. If that couldn't hold…!

He was sweating as he fought the buffeting. In spite of his best efforts, they were pitching more now. Another violent swoop came, and was followed by a thump and scraping from the cargo section. The ship lost trim. Some of the cans had come loose from their fastenings and were skidding about!

HE SAW Hennings jerk from his couch and fight his way to the hatch. He yelled angrily, knowing the fool could get killed by something grinding into him down there. Then he had no time to worry as the heavy odor told him the boy had already gone through the hatch. He fought to hold the ship steady, but there was no predicting its behavior. His muscles were overworked and unable to handle the controls as smoothly as they should. Now the field was only a few miles away, and he had to buck and twist his way through the wind to arrive within the limits of the landing strip. To make things worse, the wind velocity must have been higher than he had estimated, and he had lost more speed than he could afford. It was going to be close, if he made it at all.

Then the ship began steadying as he could feel the trim restored. He had only time for a single sigh of relief before Hennings was up, dripping with sweat and garbage odor as he groped his way back to the couch. Murdock tried to call his thanks, knowing the courage it had taken to risk the cargo hold. But Hennings' whole attention was focused sickly on the weather map.

The field was coming at them, but not soon enough. Too much speed had been lost to the wind resistance. Murdock tried to flatten the glide, but gave up at once. They were already as near a stall as he dared risk in this stuff, and they'd still miss the field by a mile! They'd land

and go crashing into trees, rocks and maybe even houses down there!

Murdock swore and grabbed for the blast lever. There was no time to warm up properly, but he had to have more speed.

He heard Hennings' voice yell a single shocked word before his hand moved the lever. Behind them, sound roared out for a split second and the ship lurched forward. Power such as that wasn't meant for minor corrections in speed, and there was no way to meter it out properly, yet it was the only possible answer. He cut the blast, then threw it on again for a split second. Then he had to snap his hand back to the elevator controls, fighting against them to regain stability.

He couldn't risk more speed. If they undershot, they were lost. And if their speed were too high, there would be no second chance to try a landing. They couldn't turn and circle in the storm. They were only getting through by heading straight into the wind, jockeying to avoid cross currents. Beyond the field was the ocean, and these modern ships weren't designed for water landings—particularly in the seas they'd find running now.

A glint of yellow caught his eye. The field markers! And he was too high. He threw his weight against the sloppy controls and felt the ship beginning to go down. He'd picked up too much speed in the brief burst of power, but he had to land somehow at once.

He could make out some of the flares now, and he had to aim between them. He kicked out the landing wheels and fought her down savagely. He was already past the near edge of the field. Too far!

Suddenly the wheels hit. The ship bounced as the wind caught it from below and began slewing it around. Then it hit again, while he fought with brakes and controls to right it. It staggered, skidded, and went tearing down the runway. Ahead of them, the crash fence loomed up in the yellow light. Ten feet—another ten—

Murdock felt the ship hit and bounce. He was just feeling his relief that their speed was too low to crash through when his head struck against the control panel, and his mind exploded in a shower of hot sparks that slowly turned black.

HE HAD a vague period of semi-consciousness after that when he realized Hennings was carrying him out of the ship, with rain pelting on him and the sound of the gale in his ears. Something bright went off, and he had a vision of the photo they must have taken: Hennings carrying a body from the *Mollyann*—Hennings, immune to all accidents, standing poised and braced against the storm, marching straight toward the photographers, smiling…

There was another vague period when he seemed to hear the voices of Sheila and Bailey. The prick of a needle…

He swam up from a cloud of dark fuzz at last. There was a dull ache in his head and a bump on his scalp. The light hurt his eyes when he opened them, and he clamped them shut again, but not before he saw he was on a couch in the recreation hall. At least that must mean no concussion; it had been just an ordinary bump, on top of the strain and nervous fatigue.

From outside, there was a confused mixture of sounds and a hammering that seemed to be against the building. He started to pull himself up to look for the cause, but it was too much effort for the moment. He started to drift off into a half doze, until he heard steps, and Hennings' voice.

"…absolutely magnificent, Miss Crane! I'll never forget it. He didn't even try to kid around to keep his spirits up. He just sat there without a sign of worry, as if he was doing a regular milk run. He didn't bat an eyelash when he had to decide to use power. So help me, he was like one of the heroes out of the kids' serials I used to watch. And that lousy reporter writing that *I* brought the ship down. If I find him—"

"Forget it, Larry," Sheila's voice said quietly.

"I won't forget it! It was bad enough they cut him down to a quarter column on the take-off and had to call it a lull in the storm! But this time I'm going to see they print the facts!"

"That should give them another column on how you're modestly trying to give credit to someone else," Sheila answered quietly. "Let them print what they want. It won't change the facts that we all know. And Tom won't mind too much. He's used to the way things are."

Murdock opened his eyes again and sat up, cutting off their conversation. He still felt groggy, but after a second his vision cleared. He smiled at Sheila and pulled her down beside him.

"She's right, Hennings. Let them print what they like. It's good publicity for the service the way they probably have it. Besides, you did your share." He reached out a hand for the younger man's arm, conscious that he couldn't even do that with the right flourish. "It took guts, trimming the cargo when you did. I meant to thank you for that."

Hennings muttered something awkwardly, and then straightened into his old self as he marched out the door to leave them alone. Sheila smiled after him with a mixture of fondness and amusement.

"What happened to the *Mollyann* and her cargo? And how's the farm making out?" Murdock asked her a moment later.

"The farm's safe enough, from the latest reports," she told him. "And the ship's a little banged up, but nothing serious. General Bailey sent the cadets out to load the cargo into our truck. He said a little garbage smell should be good for them." She smiled again, then glanced at her watch. "He should be back now, for that matter."

Murdock grinned wryly. It was a shame the hogs would never know the attention their food was getting. It must have been something to see the cadets practicing being heroes while unloading the smelly cans. He glanced out the window but the storm was still too thick for clear vision. Someone scurried past, just outside, and there was more banging and a flurry of activity beyond the door, but apparently it had nothing to do with Bailey's return.

It was five minutes more before the general came in, walking over to stare at Murdock. "Your truck's outside, Tom. And don't bring it through the gates again until you're wearing a proper uniform!" He chuckled. "With eagles on the collar. I've been trying to wrangle them for you a long time now. Congratulations, Colonel! You earned them!"

Murdock pulled Sheila closer as he accepted Bailey's hand, feeling the strength of her against him. There were other strengths, too—the words he'd heard Hennings saying, the recognition and security the new rank offered, the awareness that he hadn't failed his job. But he still found himself awkward and unable to rise to the occasion.

He didn't try, but silently let Bailey guide them toward the door.

Then he turned. "There's one other thing. That application for Moon service—"

He felt Sheila stiffen briefly and relax against him again, but his words brought the general to a complete standstill.

Bailey's head nodded, reluctantly. "All right," he said at last. "I hate to let you go, Tom, but I'll put it through with a recommendation."

"Don't!" Murdock told him. "Tear it up! I've got a lot of hogs depending on the garbage run."

He threw the door open and saw the loaded truck waiting outside. He started toward it, drawing Sheila with him. Then he stopped, his mouth open in surprise, seeing what had caused all the banging he had heard.

There was a wide, clumsy plywood canopy built over the doorway now, running out to the truck. Lined up under it were all the pilots, with Hennings at the front, moving forward to open the door of the truck with a flourish. Precisely as Murdock's foot touched the ground, the band struck up the notes of *Heroes' March.*

Feeling like a fool, Murdock stumbled forward, awkwardly helping Sheila in and getting into the driver's seat, while fifty pairs of eyes remained zeroed in on him. Hennings shut the door with another flourish and stepped back into the ranks.

And suddenly Murdock knew what to do. He leaned from the window of the truck as Sheila settled into position beside him. He grinned at the pilots, raised his hand, placed his thumb against his nose and wriggled his fingers at them.

Hennings' face split into a wide grin and his arm lifted in the same salute, with fifty others following him in the gesture by a split second.

Murdock rolled up the window, and the big truck began moving across the field, heading toward home and the hogs.

Behind him, the band played on, but he wasn't listening.

Operation Distress

Explorers who dread spiders and snakes prove that heroism is always more heroic to outsiders. Then there's the case of the first space pilot to Mars who developed the itch—

BILL ADAMS was halfway back from Mars when he noticed the red rash on his hands. He'd been reaching for one of the few remaining tissues to cover a sneeze, while scratching vigorously at the base of his neck. Then he saw the red spot, and his hand halted, while all desire to sneeze gasped out of him.

He sat there, five feet seven inches of lean muscle am bronzed skin, sweating and staring, while the blond hair on the back of his neck seemed to stand on end. Finally he dropped his hand and pulled himself carefully erect. The cabin in the spaceship was big enough to permit turning around, but not much more, and with the ship cruising without power, there was almost no gravity to keep him from overshooting his goal.

He found the polished plate that served as a mirror and studied himself. His eyes were puffy, his nose was red, and there were other red splotches and marks on his face.

Whatever it was, he had it bad!

Pictures went through his head, all unpleasant. He'd been only a kid when the men came back from the South Pacific in the last war; but an uncle had spent years dying of some weird disease that the doctors couldn't identify. That had been from something caught on Earth. What would happen when the disease was from another planet?

It was ridiculous. Mars had no animal life, and even the thin lichen like plants were sparse and tiny. A man couldn't catch a disease from a plant. Even horses didn't communicate their ills to men. Then Bill remembered gangrene and cancer, which could attack any life, apparently.

He went back to the tiny Geiger-Muller counter, but there was no sign of radiation from the big atomic motor that powered the ship. He stripped his clothes off, spotting more of the red marks breaking out, but finding no sign of parasites. He hadn't really believed it, anyhow. That wouldn't account for the sneezing and sniffles, or the puffed eyes and burning inside his nose and throat.

Dust, maybe? Mars had been dusty, a waste of reddish sand and desert silt that made the Sahara seem like paradise, and it had settled on his spacesuit, to come in through the airlocks with him. But if it contained some irritant, it should have been worse on Mars than now. He could remember nothing annoying, and he'd turned on the tiny, compact little static dust traps, in any case, before leaving, to clear the air.

He went back to one of the traps now, and ripped the cover off it.

The little motor purred briskly. The plastic rods turned against fur brushes, while a wiper cleared off any dust they picked up. There was no dust he could see; the traps had done their work.

Some plant irritant, like poison ivy? No, he'd always worn his suit—Mars had an atmosphere, but it wasn't anything a man could breathe long. The suit was put on and off with automatic machine grapples, so he couldn't have touched it.

The rash seemed to get worse on his body as he looked at it. This time, he tore one of the tissues in quarters as he sneezed. The little supply was almost gone; there was never space enough for much beyond essentials in a spaceship, even with the new atomic drive. As he looked for spots, the burning in his nose seemed to increase.

He dropped back to the pilot seat, cursing. Two months of being cramped up in this cubicle, sweating out the trip to Mars without knowing how the new engine would last; three weeks on Mars, mapping frantically to cover all the territory he could, and planting little flags a hundred miles apart; now a week on the trip back at high acceleration most of the way—and this! He'd expected adventure of some kind. Mars, though, had proved as interesting as a sand pile, and even the "canals" had proved to be only mineral striations, invisible from the ground.

He looked for something to do, but found nothing. He'd developed his films the day before, after carefully cleaning the static traps and making sure the air was dust-free. He'd written up the accounts. And he'd been coasting along on the hope of getting home to a bath, a beer, and a few bull sessions, before he began to capitalize on being the first man to reach another planet beyond the Moon.

He cut on full acceleration again, more certain of his motors than of himself. He'd begun to notice the itching yesterday; today he was breaking out in the rash. How long would whatever was coming take? Good God, he might die—from something as humiliating and undramatic as this!

It hadn't hit him before, fully. There was no knowing about diseases from other planets. Men had developed immunity to the germs found on Earth; but just as smallpox had proved so fatal to the Indians and syphilis to Europe when they first hit, there was no telling how wildly this might progress. It might go away in a day, or it might kill him just as quickly.

He was figuring his new orbit on a tiny calculator. In two days at this acceleration, he could reach radar-distance of Earth; in four, he could land. The tubes might burn out in continuous firing. But the other way, he'd be two weeks making a landing, and most diseases he could remember seemed faster than that.

Bill wiped the sweat off his forehead, scratched at other places that were itching, and stared down at the small disk of Earth. There were doctors there—and, brother, he'd need them fast!

Things were a little worse when the first squeals came from the radar two days later. He'd run out of tissues, and his nose was a continual drip, while breathing seemed almost impossible. He was running some fever, too, though he had no way of knowing how much.

He cut his receiver in, punched out the code on his key. The receiver pipped again at him, bits of message getting through, but unclearly. There was no response to his signals. He checked his chronometer and flipped over the micropages of his *Ephemeris*; the big radar at Washington was still out of line with him, and the signals had to cut through too much air to come clearly. It should be good in another hour.

But right now, an hour seemed longer than a normal year. He checked the dust tray again, tried figuring out other orbits, managed to locate the Moon, and, scratched. Fifteen minutes. There was no room for pacing up and down. He pushed the back down from the pilot seat, lowered the table, and pulled out his bunk; he remade it, making sure all the corners were perfect. Then he folded it back and lifted the table and seat. That took less than five minutes.

His hands were shaking worse when the automatic radar signals began to come through more clearly. It wasn't an hour, but he could wait no longer. He opened the key and began to send. It would take fifteen seconds for the signal to reach Earth, and another quarter minute for an answer, even if an operator was on duty.

Half a minute later, he found one was. "Earth to Mars Rocket I. Thank God, you're ahead of schedule. If your tubes hold out, crowd them. Two other nations have ships out now. The U. N. has ruled that whoever comes back first with mapping surveys can claim the territory mapped. We're rushing the construction, but we need the ship for the second run if we're to claim our fair territory. Aw, hell—congratulations!"

He'd started hammering at his key before they finished, giving the facts on the tubes, which were standing up beyond all expectations. "And get a doctor ready—a bunch of them," he finished. "I seem to have picked up something like a disease."

There was a long delay before an answer came this time—more than five minutes. The hand on the key was obviously different, slower and not as steady. "What symptoms, Adams? Give all details!"

He began, giving all the information he had, from the first itching through the rash and the fever. Again, longer this time, the main station hesitated.

"Anything I can do about it now?" Bill asked, finally. "And how about having those doctors ready?"

"We're checking with Medical," the signals answered. "We're… Here's their report. Not enough data—could be anything. Dozens of diseases like that. Nothing you can do, except try salt water gargle and spray; you've got stuff for that. Wash off rash with soap and hot water, followed by some of your hypo. We'll get a medical kit up to the Moon for you."

He let that sink in, then clicked back: "The *Moon?*"

"You think you can land here with whatever you've got, man? There's no way of knowing how contagious it is. And keep an hourly check with us. If you pass out, we'll try to get someone out in a Moon rocket to pick you up. But we can't risk danger of infecting the whole planet. You're quarantined on the Moon—we'll send up landing instructions later—not even for Luna Base, but where there will be no chance of contamination for others. You didn't really expect to come back here, did you, Adams?"

He should have thought of it. He knew that. And he knew that the words from Earth weren't as callous as they sounded. Down there, men would be sweating with him, going crazy trying to do something. But they were right. Earth had to be protected first; Bill Adams was only one out of two and a half billions, even if he had reached a planet before any other man.

Yeah, it was fine to be a hero.

But heroes shouldn't menace the rest of the world.

Logically, he knew they were right. That helped him get his emotions under control. "Where do you want me to put down?"

"Tycho. It isn't hard to spot for radar-controlled delivery of supplies to you, but it's a good seven hundred miles from Lunar Base. And look—we'll try to get a doctor to you. But keep us informed if anything slips. We need those maps, if we can find a way to sterilize 'em."

"Okay," he acknowledged. "And tell the cartographers there are no craters, no intelligence, and only plants about half an inch high. Mars stinks."

They'd already been busy, he saw, as he teetered down on his jets for a landing on Tycho. Holding control was the hardest job he'd ever done. A series of itchings cropped out just as the work got tricky, when he could no longer see the surface, and had to go by feel. But somehow he made it. Then he relaxed and began an orgy of scratching.

And he'd thought there was something romantic about being a hero!

The supplies that had already been sent up by the superfast unmanned missiles would give him something to do, at least. He moved back the two feet needed to reach his developing tanks and went through the process of spraying and gargling. It was soothing enough while it went on, but it offered only momentary help.

Then his stomach began showing distress signs. He fought against it, tightening up. It did no good. His hasty breakfast of just black coffee wanted to come up—and did, giving him barely time to make the little booth.

He washed his mouth out and grabbed for the radar key, banging out a report on this. The doctors must have been standing by down at the big station, because there was only a slight delay before the answering signal came: "Any blood?"

Another knot added itself to his intestines. "I don't know—don't think so, but I didn't look."

"Look, next time. We're trying to get this related to some of the familiar diseases. It must have some relation—there are only so many ways a man can be sick. We've got a doctor coming over, Adams. None on the

Moon, but we're shipping him through. He'll set down in about nine hours. And there's some stuff to take on the supply missiles. May not help, but we're trying a mixture of the antibiotics. Also some ACS and anodynes for the itching and rash. Hope they work. Let us know any reaction!"

Bill cut off. He'd have to try. They were as much in the dark about this as he was, but they had a better background for guessing and trial and error. And if the bugs in him happened to like tachiomycetin, he wouldn't be too much worse off. Damn it, *had* there been blood?

He forced his mind off it, climbed into his clothes and then into the spacesuit that hung from the grapples. It moved automatically into position, the two halves sliding shut and sealing from outside. The big gloves on his hands were too clumsy for such operations.

Then he went bounding across the Moon. Halfway to the supplies he felt the itching come back, and he slithered and wriggled around, trying to scratch his skin against his clothing. It didn't help much. He was sweating harder, and his eyes were watering. He manipulated the little visor-cleaning gadget, trying to poke his face forward to brush the frustration tears from his eyes. He couldn't quite reach it.

There were three supply missiles, each holding about two hundred pounds, Earth weight. He tied them together and slung them over his back, heading toward his ship. Here they weighed only a hundred pounds, and with his own weight and the suit added, the whole load came to little more than his normal weight on Earth.

He tried shifting the supplies around on his back, getting them to press against the spots of torment as he walked. It simply unbalanced him, without really relieving the itching. Fortunately, though, his eyes were clearing a little. He gritted his teeth and fought back through the powdery pumice surface, kicking up clouds of dust that settled slowly but completely—though the gravity was low, there was no air to hold them up.

Nothing had ever looked better than the airlock of the ship. He let the grapples hook the suit off him as soon as the outer seal was shut and went into a whirling dervish act. Aches and pains could be stood—but *itching!*

Apparently, though, the spray and gargle had helped a little, since his nose felt somewhat clearer and his eyes were definitely better. He repeated them, and then found the medical supplies, with a long list of instructions.

They were really shooting the pharmacy at him. He injected himself, swallowed things, rubbed himself down with others, and waited. Whatever they'd given him didn't offer any immediate help. He began to feel worse. But on contacting Earth by radar, he was assured that that might be expected.

"We've got another missile coming, with metal foil for the maps and photos—plus a small copying camera. You can print them right on the metal, seal that in a can, and leave it for the rocket that's bringing the doctor. The pilot will blast over it—that should sterilize it—and pick it up when it cools."

Bill swore, but he was in his suit when the missile landed, heading out across the pumice-covered wastes toward it. The salves had helped the itching a little, but not much. And his nose had grown worse again.

He jockeyed the big supply can out of the torpedo-shaped missile, packed it on his back, and headed for his ship. The itching was acting up as he sweated—this made a real load, about like packing a hundred bulky pounds over his normal Earth weight through the soft drift of the pumice. But his nose was clearing again; it was apparently becoming cyclic. He'd have to relay that information back to the medics. And where were they getting a doctor crazy enough to take a chance with him?

He climbed out of the suit and went through the ritual of scratching, noticing that his fever had gone up, and that his muscles were shaking. His head seemed light, as if he were in for a spell of dizziness. They'd be interested in that, back on Earth, though it wouldn't do much good. He couldn't work up a clinical attitude about himself. All he wanted was a chance to get over this disease before it killed him.

He dragged out the photo and copying equipment, under a red light. It filled what little space was left in his cubbyhole cabin. Then he swore, gulping down more of the pills where they were waiting for him. The metal sheets were fine. They were excellent. The only thing wrong was that they wouldn't fit his developing trays—and they were tough enough to give him no way of cutting them to size.

He stuffed them back in their container and shoved it into the airlock. Then his stomach kicked up again. He couldn't see any blood in the result, but he couldn't be sure—the color of the pills might hide traces. He flushed it down, his head turning in circles, and went to the radar. This time he didn't even wait for a reply, let them worry about their damned maps. They could send cutting equipment with the doctor and pick up the things later. They could pick up his corpse and cremate it at the same time, for all he cared right now.

He yanked out his bunk and slumped into it, curling up as much as the itching would permit. And finally, for the first time in over fifty hours, he managed to doze off, though his sleep was full of nightmares.

It was the sound of the bull-throated chemical rocket that brought him out of it—the sound traveling along the surface through the rocks and up through the metal ship, even without air to carry it.

He could feel the rumble of its takeoff later, but he waited long after that for the doctor. There was no knock on the port. Finally he pulled himself up from the bunk, sweating and shaken, and looked out.

The doctor was there—or at least a man in a spacesuit was. But somebody had been in a hurry for volunteers, and given the man no basic training at all. The figure would pull itself erect, make a few strides that were all bounce and no progress, and then slide down into the pumice. Moon-walking was tricky until you learned how.

Bill sighed, scratching unconsciously, and made his way somehow out to his suit, climbing into it. He paused for a final good scratch, and then the grapples took over. This time, he stumbled also as he made his way across the powdery rubble. But the other man was making no real progress at all.

Bill reached him, and touched helmets long enough to issue simple instructions through metal sound conduction. Then he managed to guide the other's steps; there had been accounts of the days of learning spent by the first men on the Moon, but it wasn't that bad with an instructor to help. The doctor picked up as they went along. Bill's legs were buckling under him by then, and the itches were past endurance. At the end, the doctor was helping him. But somehow they made the ship, and were getting out of the suits—Bill first, then the doctor, using the grapples under Bill's guidance.

The doctor was young, and obviously scared, but fighting his fear. He'd been picked for his smallness to lighten the load on the chemical rocket, and his little face was intent. But be managed a weak grin.

"Thanks, Adams. I'm Doctor Ames—Ted to you. Get onto that cot. You're about out on your feet."

The test he made didn't take long, but his head was shaking at the conclusion.

"Your symptoms make no sense," he summarized. "I've got a feeling some are due to one thing, some to another. Maybe we'll have to wait until I come down with it and compare notes."

His grin was wry, but Bill was vaguely glad that he wasn't trying any bedside manner. There wasn't much use in thanking the man for volunteering—Ames had known what he was up against, and he might be scared, but his courage was above thanks.

"What about the maps?" Bill asked. "They tell you?"

"They've left cutters outside. I started to bring them. Then the pumice got me—I couldn't stand upright in it. They'll pick up the maps later, but they're important. The competing ships will claim our territory if we don't file first."

He knocked the dust off his instrument, and wiped his hands. Bill looked down at the bed to see a fine film of Moon silt there. They'd been bringing in too much on the suits—it was too fine, and the traps weren't getting it fast enough.

He got up shakily, moving toward the dust trap that had been running steadily. But now it was out of order, obviously, with the fur brushes worn down until they could generate almost no static against the rod. He groped into the supplies, hoping there would be replacements.

Ames caught his arm. "Cut it out, Adams. You're in no shape for this. Hey, how long since you've eaten?"

Bill thought it over, his head thick. "I had coffee before I landed."

Doctor Ames nodded quickly. "Vomiting, dizziness, tremors, excess sweating—what did you expect man? You put yourself under this strain, not knowing what comes next, having to land with an empty stomach, skipping meals and loading your stomach with pills—and probably no sleep! Those symptoms are perfectly normal."

He was at the tiny galley equipment, fixing quick food as he spoke. But his face was still sober. He was probably thinking of the same thing that worried Bill—an empty stomach didn't make the itching rash, the runny nose and eyes, and the general misery that had begun the whole thing.

He sorted through the stock of replacement parts, a few fieldsistors, suit wadding, spare gloves, cellophane-wrapped gadgets. Then he had it. Ames was over, urging him toward the cot, but he shook him off.

"Got to get the dust out of here—dust'll make the itching worse. Moon dust is sharp, Doc. Just install new brushes… Where are those instructions? Yeah, insert the cat's fur brushes under the… *Cat's* fur? Is *that* what they use, Doc?"

"Sure. It's cheap and generates static electricity. Do you expect sable?"

Bill took the can of soup and sipped it without tasting or thinking, his hand going toward a fresh place that itched. His nose began running, but he disregarded it. He still felt lousy, but strength was flowing through him, and life was almost good again.

He tossed the bunk back into its slot, lifted the pilot's stool, and motioned Ames forward. "You operate a key—hell, I *am* getting slow. You can contact Luna Base by phone, have them relay. There. Now tell 'em I'm blasting off pronto for Earth, and I'll be down in four hours with their plans."

"You're crazy." The words were flat, but there was desperation on the little doctor's face. He glanced about hastily, taking the microphone woodenly. "Adams, they'll have an atomic bomb up to blast you out before you're near Earth. They've got to protect themselves. You can't..."

Bill scratched, but there was the beginning of a grin on his face. "Nope, I'm not delirious now, though I damn near cracked up. You figured out half the symptoms. Take a look at those brushes—cat's fur brushes—and figure what they'll do to a man who was breathing the air and who is allergic to cats! All I ever had was some jerk in Planning who didn't check my medical record with trip logistics! I never had these symptoms until I unzipped the traps and turned 'em on. It got better whenever I was in the suit, breathing canned air. We should have known a man can't catch a disease from plants."

The doctor looked at him, and at the fur pieces he'd thrown into a waste bin, and the whiteness ran from his face. He was seeing his own salvation, and the chuckle began weakly, gathering strength as he turned to the microphone.

"Cat asthma—simple allergy. Who'd figure you'd get that in deep space? But you're right, Bill. It figures."

Bill Adams nodded as he reached for the controls, and the tubes began firing, ready to take them back to Earth. Then he caught himself and swung to the doctor.

"Doc," he said quickly, "just be sure and tell them this isn't to get out. If they'll keep still about it, so will I."

He'd make a hell of a hero on Earth if people heard of it, and he could use a little of a hero's reward.

No catcalls, thanks.

The Deadliest Female

Angered or thwarted, the normal female of the species can be deadly enough, Lord knows...and Lee was no ordinary female—in fact, she belonged to no ordinary species!

MARK TAYOWA groaned as the jeep went over a bump in the road across the spaceport, and his eyes lanced upward to the lanky bulk of the driver. The man chuckled, and Mark turned away, nursing his aching head in silence. Damn the smugness of these Normals!

All right, so he was a freak. He'd come into the world without tonsils; adenoids, sinuses or appendix; he weighed a hundred pounds even, and barely topped four feet of stocky, heavy-boned height. He had a nerve current speed of thirty-two hundred feet a second instead of eleven hundred, and he could take eight gravities of pressure, upright. But none of that made his hangover more pleasant.

"Wipe it off!" he told the driver, infuriated by the man's grin.

The grin widened. "You're *cute,*" the driver said, in a reedy falsetto, "I know Maisie! Some mouse. And that's some mouse you got on the eye."

For a second, Mark's arm tautened with sheer hunger to drive a fist into the other's soft-muscled belly. Then he collapsed into a sick slump on the seat. Yeah, Maisie. He'd picked her up somewhere along the line, celebrating his graduation from Spaceman special flight training and his simultaneous assignment to his first ship—in only nine months out from the crèche, too. She'd gotten him drunk, calmly picked his pocket, and then yelled for help.

Naturally, the Normals stuck together against a freak. He fingered his blackened eye, then cupped his thin, strong hands around his head and groaned.

Women! It was bad enough to be brought up in the hothouse atmosphere of a crèche, raised with a few other Spacemen by Normals who were entirely too blasted "understanding," without even seeing a girl; but then to get out into the world and find the females of your own species were as flat-chested as men, and the Normal girls either wanted to pet you like a dog or roll you!

The driver nudged him. "We're here, Peewee. All out. End of the line."

Mark climbed out, lifting his thin bag of possessions. The *Venture* was an old ship, he saw, but a sound one. And it was obviously near blast-off. He should have been there an hour before, but he'd slept through the alarm. Then he saw the big Normal on the ramp carrying triple stars on his shoulder, and snapped into salute. "Mark Tayowa, lieutenant assigned to *Venture*, sir."

The man turned and shouted inside, "Hey, Lee—it's here. Blast at three-oh-seven." Then he nodded toward Mark, and jerked a thumb inward. "Okay, you and Lee Tanming have it. And you'd better report in—you're graduated now; you don't have to stand here saluting all day."

Mark went up the little ramp, and a muffled voice came down the tiny communication shaft from control. "Seal up, Tayowa. We blast in one minute."

He triggered the seals, watched the ramp come up and sink into place, and went through the inner lock; checking to make sure it also sealed properly. Then he hesitated, while a rumbling came from below, and the sudden punch of acceleration hit him. They were lifting at five gravities, headed out for nine months to Pluto; and he was on his first actual trip into space—the work for which he'd been destined through eight generations. He sampled it, while he began climbing up to the control room, and even the hangover was no longer important.

Starting now, he was free of the Normals, out where he belonged—where his body was no freak, but something tailored ideally for its purpose.

Then he stopped. The figure stooped over the controls was unmistakable. Stringy hair was caught back in double braids, and the shoulders had a female slope to them, while the rest of the three-foot-eight figure showed the stringy, neuter angularity of the females of his race. As he looked, Lee Tanming turned, her narrow body jerking about with a total lack of grace. For nine months he had to be cooped up with a female!

She gave him one disgusted glance before she swung back to reset the controls. "My last trip before they ground me for good," she said bitterly, "and they give me a green kid who hasn't got the brains to stay away from those grinning spaceport tramps. Where's your luggage, Romeo?"

He doubled his fists, then shrugged wearily. "Okay, Okay, I guess the whole field knew about it. Maisie got my supply money. Go ahead, laugh."

"You'll have to get funnier than that, Bobo. I don't give a damn how dumb you are ashore. But since you have one suit to your name, you'll wash it every night, or I'll throw it in the incinerator." She turned for another quick glance at him. "We'll have to live together, sonny—and I don't like it any better than you. Get some aspirin from the galley stock, toss your duffle in cabin two—mine's number one, with the lock—and then get below. Takes someone in the engine-room eventually."

He looked at her insignia, knowing Spacewomen were never promoted higher than lieutenants—his own rank—since they were automatically retired at thirty-five. That was about to happen to Tanming, evidently, and she was sore about it. "Yessir, *Captain!*"

"Seniority, sonny," she said. "I've been running the Pluto jump eleven years. *And* the fact I can stand three more gravs than you can, from practice. Get below!"

To demonstrate, she began jockeying the controls, increasing and decreasing the acceleration pressure. He stood it a few seconds, until his stomach gave in. Then he lurched away, hunting for the latrine. He found it barely in time.

It was going to be a great trip.

There was the smell of coffee when he came to; and he was surprised to find himself in a hammock. Some of the ache was gone, and his stomach felt better. He eased to the deck, dreading what he'd see when he picked up his suit; but it had been cleaned. Then Lee's fist banged on the door, and her voice reached him, "Come and get it, sonny. And better grab that aspirin on the way."

Mark shook his head, and regretted it. But maybe he'd misjudged her. He owed her an apology for not tending ship, at least; he knew she must have had hell until speed built up, running both control and engines. He'd been cross-grained from the Normals, and it must have been tough on her, nearing thirty-five and about to be grounded...whereas he was good for fifty years' service, and they both knew it.

He climbed to the galley, where a plastube of coffee waited, and headed for the medicine kit on the wall, his hands shaking. From above, an alarm sounded, and then there was a muttered damn from Lee. The ship leaped suddenly and the medicine chest came down under his clutching fingers, bottles and supplies breaking under heavy acceleration as they hit the floor.

Moments later, she was at the door. "Nice work, sonny. Well, no medical supplies, not even a fever thermometer now. If you get space chills, all I can do for you is stuff you out the airlock. We're running a library and supplies to Pluto, not a nursery, but I guess the brass on Earth can't tell the difference. Normal administrators!"

"There must be medical supplies in the cargo—" he began.

Her laughter cut him off. "When Pluto's supercold hi-vac labs are the source of our top medicals, system wide? We're shipping out plutonium, sonny—pure energy, practically. Scared?"

He knew what she meant. With plutonium in its insulating wraps as cargo, they'd need just one good pea-sized meteorite through the hull to blast them into nothingness. But he shook his head.

"Liar," she remarked coldly. "Incidentally, I cleaned up this time for you. Don't mention it. From now on, you do *all* the cooking and washing aboard, I'm turning in. Take over, sonny. And when you get me up, I'll expect these clothes clean, my eggs scrambled lightly, and no damn-fool nonsense with the controls."

She swung down to Cabin 1, and the lock clicked. Mark picked up his coffee—which was lousy, saccharine-sweet—and apologized to himself for any good ideas of her he'd had. It looked as if she'd spent her life building up resentment at being female and not a Normal, and now meant to take it all out on him. She'd probably get worse.

She did. Lee had imagination enough to vary the beat; she went from synthetic sympathy to biting arrogance, and followed it by long lectures on what would happen if she wrote up his default on takeoff. She told him the rumors about him and Maisie among the port attendants before takeoff. And she refused to lend him even one of her books.

That was the worst of all. Once blast-off is made, most of the trip is pure monotony, and the microcard books are almost a psychological necessity. He should have brought his own—but Maisie's theft had ruled that out. Mark fought it out past Mars and well towards Jupiter, and at times even welcomed the menial duties of cooking and cleaning. But there was still too much time left over.

He broke half a day's silence, finally. "What sort of a library do we ship, and where's it stowed?"

Lee looked up from a book she was too obviously enjoying and shook her hair, filling the air with the perfume she'd found that he couldn't stand. "Technical. The hold marked with the big 'Entry Illegal' sign. And that sign means you."

He'd already noticed it and wondered. Well, technical books were better than nothing, and nobody needed to know he'd borrowed them. Of course, the hold was sealed with the official tape and slug, but he knew how to work them well enough to stand all but the most careful inspection. He'd learned that trick in flight training, where the older boys passed the trick down to the younger.

For the next few watches, he noticed her frequent sudden appearance when he was near the hold. He grinned, carefully avoiding any further examination of the seal, until it seemed finally that she'd given up and decided he wasn't going to try it. He waited out two more watches, and then moved suddenly, hastily stripping away the seal and throwing the hatch back.

"I could shoot you, you know."

He jerked around to find her standing casually on the landing above him, with a gun in one thin hand. "You know the rule against breaking into the room of a suspended Normal; this is worse."

He'd already seen the gelatin with which the room was filled, and guessed the answer. Apparently, it took less room to ship out a full Eidetic who could remember everything on a page forever from a single tenth-of-a-second glance. Eidetics were rarer than Spacemen, and breaking one out of suspended animation, where he could stand the acceleration, would more than justify shooting.

Mark began resealing with hands that were sweating. "You could have told me," he muttered.

"More fun this way, sonny. If I enter this on the log—along with the picture I just took—well, you figure what happens when we land... Better think it over."

She bent over, running her hand around the rim of the landing. "Filthy. See that it's clean when I wake up."

Mark tried unsuccessfully to retain some dignity as he climbed down to the engine room, but his hands were shaking. Blackmail now—and she could make it stick, apparently. He brooded over a picture in his mind of her neck between his hands, mentally listening to the snap of her vertebrae. Then he got out his chem-cleaning set and began scrubbing the shaft walls and landings.

But there's a limit to anything. He reached it just beyond Jupiter, when Lee objected to the lack of seasoning in the soup. He took the bulb silently back to the galley, located the red pepper and used it generously, together with a bit of mustard and some dehydrated horseradish to make sure. Maybe she'd grown too confident; she squeezed the bulb for a generous sip.

When she came up, yelling, her gun was still clipped to the back of the chair, and Mark was on it in a single pounce. He tossed it into the shaft, put a hand on her shoulder and shoved her down again. "Eat it, you witch. I want to see you eat every damned drop of it. After that, you do the cooking and cleaning around here—and while I'm at it, I'll take that camera of yours."

"Sure of yourself, sonny?"

"Dead sure. Start eating!"

"You wouldn't strike a woman," she suggested, but she was beginning to glance about, and a worried line appeared on her forehead.

"No," he agreed. "Not a woman. But if *you* don't eat every drop of that soup, I'll shove your nose through the—"

Something that might have been a cross between lightning and a battering ram came up from the chair and knocked him crossways. And then she was free of the little table-shelf, and moving in, a sudden grin on her face.

"Big mistake, sonny." A fist came out, changed to a hard-edged palm, and chopped down on the bridge of his nose. "Never hit a woman—" She was lifting him then, over one shoulder, and in a twist that brought him slamming down against the deck, "—who has lived in hi-grav acceleration fourteen years." One foot was on the small of his back, and her arms were dragging his arms backwards, until he could feel the vertebrae begin to snap. "Better scream."

He held out for a moment longer, and she upped the pull. "I can hold it for an hour," she mentioned, hardly breathing harder. "It's worse than space chills. Better scream."

But the advice was needless. She'd increased the tension again, and the scream ripped out of his throat. She kicked him with casual efficiency, hoisted him over her shoulder, and carried him down to his cabin.

"You'll be all right in an hour, sonny. Only, when you come out, stick a *sir* after anything you say to me—or *madam*—I'm not particular. And smile, damn you…um-hmm. I think I'm going to like this trip!"

Then she located a slip of cloth in a pocket and held it out. "'Sall right, sonny. Go right ahead and cry it out. A good cry is good for you. Here."

Maybe it was the power of suggestion; Mark felt tears running hotly into his eyes, and all his determination couldn't hold them back.

He had stopped feeling sorry for himself a few minutes later, and something in the back of his mind had recognized that things could get no worse. With that decision, even the pain couldn't keep his thoughts back. He was remembering everything he knew of space chills, and grimly checking over the details of the ship in his head. The fever thermometer was broken, and the only other temperature gauge was on the thermostat.

His head reeled as he slipped out of the room and down to the engine room. There he worked quickly and surely, assembling what he needed. And he was back in the cabin when she knocked.

"Your watch. Hit the deck."

He plastered a smile on his face, and came out. "Yes, ma'am. I relieve you, ma'am."

After her door clicked, he lost no time. It was easy to clip the bearing on the thermometer needle, and to solder it onto the figure 72°. His watch gave him a timer, and the other little contacts went into place, one by one. Finally, he nodded in satisfaction. He'd have to readjust it every so often, beginning gently and working up. But it was a good job.

And the sleeping tablets hadn't been among the bottles broken, fortunately. He'd slipped them out and had been using them to help sleep away what time he could, but there were still almost a thousand in the bottle.

It should be plenty.

At that, she held out better than he expected. It was two weeks before she mentioned it, though that might have been because the beginning was so gradual. But space chills, a violent reaction of the body to radiation that couldn't all be shielded out from space, were the worst thing that could happen to any space-voyager—even a Spaceman.

They were near Saturn when it finally happened, the final stage he'd been waiting for. He'd left her coffee half an hour before, spiked with a sleeping pill, and the temperature cycle had gone into high. Now he stopped to wipe his face and hands carefully with astringent, and stepped into the control room.

She shook her head groggily, and ran sweating fingers over her forehead. And this time, finally, she got up from the chair and motioned him down. "Mark—I got 'em again. The fever, this time. Here, feel."

She'd dropped the feud a week before, and he'd let it seem to die. Now he put his hand—still cool from astringent—to her head, and shook his own. "If we only had some medicine… How long since you thought you were freezing? Two hours, wasn't it?"

She nodded unhappily. She'd stopped studying the thermometer, convinced that the fault was her own, since he seemed to feel no change in the temperature.

"Mark, I'm scared. We can't go on—I can't. There's medicine for it down there—down on Titan. Mark, you've got to set down at Gilead!"

He debated it, his face carefully showing doubt—some of which was real. Making a landing on a crude port without two fully competent Spacemen was tricky. But her hand clutched at his arm. "Mark, I'll help all I can. And—I'll do all the cooking, every bit of washing. I'll say sir all the way to Pluto and back. I've got to finish this trip—it's my last. And I need the medicine."

Finally he nodded, and reached out for the controls, refiguring the course. She looked her gratitude, and was gone, wiping perspiration from her forehead. He pulled out his astringent, and made sure his face still seemed cool, in spite of the heat of the air. He was fresh again when she came back, bringing him coffee and a bottle of cognac—the only liquor aboard the ship.

It was a long, weary business, fighting down the velocity they'd built up all the way from Earth and jockeying the ship down to Titan; but he was proud of his landing, and she was full of praise. It hadn't been bad for a first major landing, at that. He accepted the double slug of cognac she poured, and let her refill the glass before he got up.

"The doctor's house is up there, just over the hill," she said. He nodded, buckled on a jacket, and headed out.

Sure, he'd get the doctor. He grinned as he saw the distant figures of two Spacemen coming across the field toward the ship. She could take care of explanations, until he got back with the doc. And while they had the right to go aboard, he knew the Spacemen here wouldn't—there was still enough fear that space chills were contagious. When the doctor was working on her, he could remove the tricks on the thermostat.

And then let her yelp when the medico said she had nothing but blue funk from plain fear of carrying plutonium to Pluto. They'd pull her back Earthside, and he'd get someone else to carry on the rest of the trip with him—someone junior to him!

Then, as he crossed to the other side of the hill, it hit him: drowsiness, like a numbing drug poured into his veins… He was getting groggier by the minute as he fought down toward the doctor's little dome. He felt someone helping him inside the dome, and then he collapsed.

"Drunk," he heard a man's heavy voice say. But he couldn't protest.

It seemed only moments later when the voice came again, repeating, "Drunk."

"Yeah." It was a woman's voice. "Yeah, scared of the Pluto hop. Lee had a lot of trouble with him. How's he now?"

"About ready to come to, I shot enough stimulant into him."

A door opened and shut then, and Mark opened his eyes, with an effort. But his head was clearing rapidly now. And it was a Spacewoman who stood there.

She looked at him in disgusted silence as he staggered to a wash basin and began ducking his head. When he was finished and fully clothed, he started out the nearest door, but she motioned to another. It was a back exit, and he noticed that she stuck to dimly lighted ways, still moving in silence. Finally she swung around.

"All right, I suppose I'll have to get used to you. I'm Pat Runyon, I run the satellite freight here—and from now on, brother, you're my helper. It's tough—you'll wish you were back on the Pluto hop—but you'll run it with me. And you won't go running to a doctor before I can open the port whenever we land, either. Give me those lieutenant bars!"

"Eh?"

"You heard me. Message from Earth to demote you when Lee got authority to replace you with my helper—a nice guy, *he* was, too. Then they stick me with you for the rest of his contract. Well, stop staring at me, you'll get to know me in three years. But, brother, don't get cold feet on me. I'm not soft-hearted like Lee, I can't stand a yellow Spaceman. Here, she told me to give you this."

It was a little bundle of wires and relays, with his watch in the middle of it. He looked at it slowly. Then he looked up at the sky where Pluto should be, thinking of three long, back-breaking years ahead of him...three years, to give Lee Tanming plenty of time to laugh about the way she'd ground a raw kid's face into the dust—time to tell the story of that kid's clumsy trick with a thermostat, and her own cleverness with the cognac, until it grew stale—time enough even to forget the thing had ever happened.

But Mark knew that he wouldn't forget.

The same slow, bitter surge of hatred was in Mark Tayowa three years later as he dropped the freighter down, unconscious of the dozen gravities that were hitting her deck. It burned in his eyes as he passed from Spaceman's bar to hotel and on to another city. Nobody laughed at him now—long. He had chain-lightning reactions now, and muscle sheaths that almost rang when hit; he also had his lieutenant's bars back and the right to name his own next job, but those were unimportant. What counted was that he had three months' free time coming.

It took him just three weeks to track her down. She wasn't Lee Tanming, any more; she was Mrs. Ivan Aiello. Interestingly enough, Aiello was the man she'd picked up from Titan to replace him—and he was currently off to Mercury, which left things nicely uncomplicated. Mark smiled thinly and ran his tongue over his lips.

He was vaguely grateful to the builders of his race, who'd put no nonsense about chivalry into his makeup. As it was, he could beat hell out of her and enjoy every minute of it.

He punched the bell, noting that this community system for the Spacemen beat the old crèche and community halls in every way. The houses were neat, the yards attractive, and here and there the skinny, big-eyed children seemed happier and healthier.

Then someone threw open the door, and he looked up to see a Spacewoman standing there. He blinked, and changed the words in his head. Not a Spacewoman…a Space angel. She was unmistakably of his race—her height, just under his own; the hint of the Oriental in her black eyes and ivory skin; her slender frame. But there was nothing angular about her. She glowed. She was utterly, disarmingly beautiful.

She frowned at his stare, and then suddenly laughed. "Mark!" she said. "Mark Tayowa. And how wonderful you're looking! Pat must have done you good. Come in, let me get you some coffee." She paused, stricken by a sudden thought. "You're not mad any more, are you? Here, Herbie, get that top out of your mouth. And you, Hank, stop pulling Fido's tail. Meet the twin brats, Mark."

Mark followed her in, still dazed. It *couldn't* be Lee. He remembered the scrawny, neuter figure as well as if he'd had her picture pasted into his helmet these long three years. He started forward, then stopped as she came out of the kitchen, carrying cups and a pot of coffee, and looking completely domestic.

For want of anything else to do, he sat down and tried awkwardly to look interested in the twins. But they were normal enough Spaceman children. And she still had that glow that drew his eyes to her.

"You're beautiful," he said finally, and his voice was harsh. "I didn't recognize you."

"Oh, that!" She laughed at him. "You, Herbie. Stop it! Just wait'll your father comes back from Mercury. He'll give it to you. Mark—you didn't expect me to stay neuter after the change, did you? Silly kid! I'll bet you never saw a Spacewoman over thirty-five before, did you? Though Pat Runyon must be about thirty-four, come to think of it. We—well; we develop."

It was too magnificent an understatement. Mark couldn't think of any way to handle it. He stood up slowly, awkwardly, feeling like a fool.

"Oh, come on, you're not mad? I've thought about it lots of times. (*Her-bie!*) I was so damn mad at having to quit space to be some Spaceman's wife. I used to have the craziest ideas—I actually hated the idea of going through puberty, at my age… And you were an awful infant, I've often wondered what happened to you, you know. Ivan and I've had more fun guessing about that."

He nodded. "Yeah, I had fun, too. I guess maybe I'm still a little green around the ears."

"No-o." She considered him, smiling. "No, Mark. You've grown up. Mm-hmm. (Hank, let the dog *alone!*) But sit down, Mark, have some coffee. For old time's sake. We've got a lot to talk over, haven't we? (*Herbie!*) And I'm awfully lonesome—Ivan won't be home for another week."

Mark put his hands in his pockets slowly, and turned to the door. He took them out again, looked at Lee thoughtfully. Then he stared down at the two children. His shoulders drooped as he thrust his fists deep into his pockets.

She could never stand three gravities now, judging by the soft femininity of her.

"Sorry," he mumbled. "Like to, but I've got to report back. Just thought I'd drop in, say hello."

"Oh, but Mark…(Hank, if you don't stop that!) Mark…"

But he was already down the steps, moving toward the waiting cab, letting her voice die out behind him.

Three years of sweating, driving his body until it ached every night, goading Pat Runyon to throw the book at him, picking a fight with every Spaceman he ran into…and now a soft, female form and a couple of kids had made it all useless. He doubled up a fist, trying to imagine Lee's neck inside his grasp. But it wouldn't come as a picture now—the old straight neck with its boyish tendons was gone, and the softly rounded throat he'd seen wouldn't replace it.

He cursed. "Take me to the nearest bar," he ordered the driver curtly.

Then slowly he reconsidered. "Make it the spaceport. And step on it."

He saw the driver throw him an odd look, but he didn't care what Normals thought now. There was still time to ask for his old job back, out on Titan, freighting around the satellites. He took a deep, slow breath and leaned back against the cushions.

In another year, Pat Runyon would be thirty-five-and the change would begin. Pat wasn't a bad person, come to think of it. Not bad at all. A good person to know…

Imitation of Death

Councilman Curtis would never cooperate with Max Fleigh's plans for overthrow. But a duplicate of Curtis, a simulacra, which could not be distinguished from the real man, would follow Fleigh's orders to perfection. And one man, Jeremiah Greek, knew the secret of making the duplications...

MAX FLEIGH'S heavy jowls relaxed and he chuckled without humor as he examined the knots that bound the man at his feet. Quite impersonally; he planted the toe of his boot in Curtis' ribs, listened to the muffled grunt of pain, and decided that the gag was effective. For once, Slim had done a good job, and there was nothing wrong. It was probably unnecessary, anyway, but there could be no bungling when the future of the Plutarchy was at stake.

Incompetence had cost them an empire once, and there would be no third opportunity. The stupid democracies that had called themselves a World Union had colonized the planets and ruled them without plan. And when Mars, Venus, and the Jovian Worlds had revolted and set up a Planet Council, all that Earth could do was to come crawling to it, begging polite permission to join what they should have owned!

But that had been before practical realists had kicked out the dreamers and set up the Plutarchy under an iron discipline that could implement its plans. Now, they were heading back toward their lost empire, colonizing the asteroids and establishing claims that gave them a rough rule over the outlaws who had retreated there. With the Council softened up by years of cautious propaganda, they were in a position to ask and receive a Mandate over the scattered planetoids.

It was the opening wedge, and all they needed. Once the asteroids could be given spurious independence to seek a Council seat, they would be ready to strike at the Jovian Worlds. With proper incidents, propaganda, and quislings, plus the planetoids to separate Jupiter from Mars, there could be no question of the outcome. Earth would gain a majority of three votes, and the Council would be the basis of a new and greater Plutarchy.

Fleigh gave the bound body of Curtis another careless kick and went forward to the cabin, where the lanky form of his companion was hunched dourly over the controls of the little space-craft. "How's it going, Slim?"

"So-so." Slim ejected a green stream of narcotic juice and grinned sourly. "But I still say we been crowdin' our luck too hard!"

"Rot! Layout the right moves, cover all possibilities, outmaneuver your enemies, and you don't need luck! Ever play chess?"

"Nope, can't say I did. Played the horses on Mars, though, time we h'isted the *Euphemeron.* Won, too—after I bought my lucky ghost charm; been in the chips ever since!" Slim's grin widened, but his face remained stubbornly unconvinced.

Fleigh chuckled. If the planetoid outlaws depended on magic, while the Council visionaries spouted sentimental twaddle, so much the better for the realists. "Charms don't work in politics, Slim. We have to anticipate resistance. And you saw what happened to our fine Martian Councilor Curtis when he decided to expose us and ruin the Mandate!"

"Yeah," Slim's yellow teeth chewed thoughtfully on his cud. "S'pose he'd stood on Mars, though?"

"We'd have dropped hints of just the information he needed on Ceres and trapped him there—as we did. Checkmate!"

"Or check-out! So when he don't come back, they smell a rat—an' I ain't plannin' on bein' around to chew rat-poison. My grandpappy killed a Councilor once—poor grandpappy…! Hey, there's the rock!"

THERE was no outward sign of life on the barren little planetoid. But as the ship came to a grinding stop in a narrow gorge, a concealing shield snapped over them, and a crudely painted sign blazed out in phosphorescent gaudiness on one rocky wall: *SIMILACRA, LTD. Jeremiah Greek, Prop.* (A line in Greek characters.) Specialist: (Another line in Greek characters.)

Fleigh came out of the lock first and paused while he waited for Slim to shoulder the tarpaulin-covered Curtis and follow. He grinned and pointed at the Greek characters in the sign, "*Magician and wonderworker; specialist in imitation and mockery*," he translated. "I looked it up on Mars, so don't go thinking it's some kind of spell… Now if the old fool will open up…"

Max remembered his own preconceptions of Greek's process, pictured various impressive-looking apparatus, which included a large tube through which some sort of lightning zigzagged, and a beautiful woman taking form from a stream of transmuted elements streaming from the top. It was nothing like such cinematic legerdermain, of course.

"Why ain't English good enough for him?" complained Slim. "I don't go for that magic stuff, Max. We been…"

But the Sigma was already swinging back on its tips to reveal a passage through the rock. A little, shriveled man in tattered shorts and thick-lensed glasses stood motioning them in impatiently, and the door closed silently when they obeyed his summons. They headed down a side passage toward a ramp and the sound of busy humming.

Greek threw open a door and pointed to a table where the duplicate of Councilor Curtis lay, with a duplicate Jeremiah Greek fussing over it and humming through his nose. The guide dropped to a bench and began removing his chest and inserting a fresh power pack between two terminals.

Slim's mouth dropped open and his burden slipped from his back to the floor with a sodden thump, while he stared from one Greek to the other, and back to the first. His fingers were stretched in the ancient sign of the horns as he watched the changing of accumulators, and his voice was hoarse and uncertain, "A damned robot!"

"Not a robot—a similacrum," denied the owl-eyed man who must have been the original of the metal creature. "I'm a mimesist, not a creator. A robot has independent life, but that's only a limited copy of my memories and habits, like this phony Curtis. And those tapes you brought me, Fleigh—they stink!"

He gestured toward the spools of the marvelous wire that could record electromagnetic waves of any type of frequency up to several million megacycles. In one corner, a stereo-player was running one off, but the vision screen was fuzzy, and the voice part was a mass of gibberish.

Fleigh scowled at it, and turned back suspiciously to Greek. "Sure you know how to use them? Those were made by—"

"By a fool who had a shield leak in his scanner! Only a few were any good. I was using pancyclic tape before you ever saw a stereo-record. Where do you think I impress my similacrum's memory—on a real brain? It takes miles of tape to feed the selectrons! I did the best I could, but… Here, take a look!" He reached into the false Curtis' mouth and did something that made the figure sit up suddenly.

Max went over and muttered into the thing's ear, but after the first few answers it lapsed into sullen silence, and he swung back toward Greek. "I told you Curtis had to be perfect! This wouldn't fool a Jovian!"

"And I told you I wasn't Jehovah—I specialize in mechanical imitations," Greek answered shortly. "Bum tape, bum similacrum! If you brought me some decent reels, I'll see what I can do, though."

FLEIGH grunted and yanked the tarpaulin off the real Curtis. At the sight, new interest appeared on Greek's face, and he came over to examine the Councilor, but stopped after a cursory look had shown that the man was still alive.

He nodded. "That's more like it, Fleigh. I'll set up an encephalograph and ideoform analyzer and record directly off his mind—it's better than feeding impressions from tapes, anyway, though I always used an editing circuit before. Okay, you'll get something his own mother would swear was perfect."

"When?"

"Depends. Narrow-band analysis would take a couple weeks, but it'd be permanent. If I run an all-wave impressor in, the tapes will be barely affected. I can do it in ten—twelve hours, but your similacrum will begin to fade in a week, and wash out completely in a month."

"Suits me," Fleigh decided. "We won't need him more than a few days; any place where Slim and I can catch up on our sleep while you finish?"

Greek's double came to life at a signal and led them down a series of rock corridors to a room that lacked nothing in comfort, then went silently out and left them alone. To Fleigh's relief, Slim tested the bed in sour displeasure, pulled a blanket' off, and rolled up on the floor, leaving the flotation mattress unoccupied. He had as little use for such luxuries as his boss had for his presence in the same bed. Max climbed in and adjusted the speegee dial to perfect comfort with a relaxed grunt of pleasure.

He had no intention of sleeping, though, while things that concerned him were going on. Three hours later, he heaved out and slipped silently down the rocky halls on sponge-rubber slippers. But his training had covered the stupidity of spy-stereos, and there was nothing stealthy about his entry into the laboratory. Greek looked up from a maze of wires and gadgets with faint surprise but no suspicion.

"Couldn't sleep," Fleigh volunteered apologetically. "I was wondering if you had any barbiturates?"

A few minutes later he took the tablet from Greek's double and turned back down the hallway with a muttered thanks. He had learned all he wanted to know. Both Greeks and Curtises were present and accounted for, where they belonged, and the mimesist was busy about his work; there was no funny business involved. Actually, he had expected none, but it never did any harm to make sure of such things when dealing with men who were outside the law of either the Plutarchy or the Council.

Slim was snoring and kicking about on the floor when he returned, and he grinned as he plopped back onto the mattress. The outlaws were useful enough now. But once Earth took over the Mandate, something would have to be done about them; too many were the wrong sort to fit into the Plutarchy. Fleigh stretched with a self-satisfied yawn, and slipped into well-earned sleep.

GREEK'S similacrum wakened them in the morning and led them back to the laboratory, where the scientist was waiting beside the imitation Curtis. The real Councilor must have been drugged, for he lay unconscious on one of the tables. Fleigh wasted only a casual glance at him, and then turned to the new similacrum as Greek flipped it on.

This time his tests were longer, and there were no sullen silences from the imitation. Its response was quick, sure, and completely correct; the real Curtis could have done no better, and Fleigh stepped back at last and nodded his approval. He'd demanded a perfect similacrum, and it had been delivered.

"You're sure it has a good strong desire to live?" he asked briefly as he fished into his bag for the little prepared relay that was ready.

Greek smiled faintly. "They all have that—they couldn't pass as normal men without it. And if your dimensions were correct, you should have no trouble installing your relay."

He stripped aside the blouse, to reveal a small cavity in the back of the similacrum, with a bundle of little wires which Fleigh hooked onto the relay. It slipped in, and locked firmly. Greek unclipped the tiny switch from inside the machine's mouth. The animation within the similacrum disappeared at once, to snap back again as a switch on Fleigh's bag was pressed. A little circle of the pancyclic strip moved over a scanner inside the bag, sending out a complex wave, while a receiver in the similacrum's back responded by closing the relay. Then the animation was cut off again, and came back at once on a second pressure of the switch.

"Attempted removal of the relay will destroy all circuits, just as you ordered," Greek assured the operative. "Well?"

Fleigh's face mirrored complete satisfaction. "You get the fire emeralds, as promised!"

He reached into the bag and came out with a little bundle, a grin stretched across his face. It stayed there while Greek moved forward quickly, to stagger back with a chopped-off scream as the slugs poured into his face and exploded his head into a mangled mess of blood and grey tissue.

For a second, the Greek double moved forward, but it turned with a shriek and went down the hall at a clumsy run as Fleigh ripped the smoking gun from the package. He let it go. Curtis' head dissolved under a second series of slugs, and only the similacrum of the Councilor was left in the laboratory with the two men.

Slim closed his mouth slowly and reached for his green narcotic, but he made no protest. The other moved about, gathering up combustibles and stacking them in a corner, then setting fire to the pile.

"Which takes care of almost everything, Slim," Fleigh said calmly. They headed out and down the hall toward their ship, with the imitation Curtis moving quietly along behind. Another slug from the gun destroyed the lock on the big Sigma, and they pushed through, out into the rocky gorge. "Nothing left to chance, and a perfect red herring to cover up Curtis' disappearance."

SLIM DUCKED into the lock and went forward to the controls. "Uh-huh. Grandpappy'd sure of admired you, Max! Used to look just the same when he drilled somebody he didn't like. All set for takeoff?"

"Forgetting anything, Slim?"

The outlaw looked up in puzzled surprise, while Fleigh shook his head and went over to the receiver. There was no sense in trying to teach the fool anything, apparently, but at least he might have learned elementary caution from his mode of life. The Plutarch operative ripped out the tape from the illegal all-wave recorder and slipped it into a playback slot, while slow comprehension crossed the other's face.

But everything was in order, with the usual hash of faint signals on various frequencies. There were no signs of a strong response, such as would have been made by any attempt on Greek's part to double-cross him with a call to the outside. He set the receiver to record, and went toward the rear cabin and the similacrum, while the ship blasted off and headed toward Mars.

The false Curtis was already at a table, and groping through a bag of notes the original Councilor had carried. It looked up as Fleigh came in, grimaced, and went on organizing the papers before it. The operative dropped to a chair with his familiar humorless chuckle.

"You realize your life is dependent on obedience, uh—Curtis?"

"Would I have let you kill myself otherwise?" the thing asked grimly. "Leave that control gadget of yours where I can get it, and you'll feel the difference between my hands and mere flesh ones! But meantime, I'll cooperate, since I have no choice; I suppose you intend helping me with my speech before the Council?"

Fleigh's appreciation for the peculiar genius of Greek went up several points, as he assented tersely. The thing was perfect, or so nearly so that it seemed to consider itself the real man. There would be no trouble on that score. As for the control bag—he had no intention of letting that out of his hands until the similacrum was turned off.

It gestured toward the notes with a motion peculiar to Curtis. "You'd only ruin anything you edited, Fleigh. I'm perfectly capable of writing the thing myself, and it'll sound like me. But if I'm going to give you a clean sheet and not make the whole Council suspicious, I'll need more information than I have. I must have the whole picture, so that I can take care of all objections without running counter to what some other Councilors may know already. Also, I think you'd better learn to address me as *Councilor* Curtis."

"Quite so, Councilor," Fleigh agreed, and this time the amusement in his laugh was genuine. "Now, if you'll tell me what you know of our plans and methods, I'll fill in the blanks. But I want to see that speech, when you're finished."

IT WAS amazing, the amount of evidence Curtis had managed to accumulate in a brief week; or perhaps much of it had been in his hands before, and only needed organizing against what they had let him find on Ceres. It was enough to have ruined all hopes of Earth's getting the Mandate, and seriously endangered her relations with the Planet Council in addition. Fleigh made a mental note to press for an investigation of some of the outland operatives as he began filling in the missing links in the other's information.

Curtis took the facts down in a notebook, grim-faced and silent, checked them back, and reached for thc typewriter. The first part of the speech he had meant to deliver needed but slight modification, and Fleigh read it over the similacrum's shoulder as it operated the machine. Then the going grew tougher, and there were long pauses while the thing considered, revising a word here, or changing a paragraph there. It disregarded Fleigh's suggestions with the same disdain that would have been on the real Councilor's face, and the operative began to realize that it was justified. When it came to writing speeches, he was only an amateur, and this$ was professional work.

He was beginning to regret that the thing could have a life of only from a week to ten days, when it finished; Earth could have used such a propagandist, particularly one accepted on the Council as Mars' chief representative! Curtis' speeches had always been good, but he had never realized that the man's talents would have been equally good on propaganda. It was hard to believe that this was fiction, as he listened to the calm, assured voice running through it, apparently reciting only the simple truth, and yet coloring every word with some trick of oratory that seemed to make it glow with virtue and integrity.

"Perfect!" he commented when it was finished. He cut off the relay signal, watched the similacrum slip to the floor, and went forward to the control cabin with a full measure of satisfaction. Earth could not fail!

And already the red disc of Mars was large and close on the viewplate. Fleigh hadn't realized the time the writing of the speech had taken, but he did not regret a second of it as Slim began nursing the ship down through the thin atmosphere toward the Solar Center.

THE TASTE of coming victory was strong in Max Fleigh as he waited outside the Martian House the next day, but Slim was still glum and morose. Part of that was probably due to his orders to stay out of the usual outlaw haunts on the planet, where the police might have picked him up and ruined the whole plan. The rest, Fleigh decided, was just his natural fear of what he could not understand.

The outlaw was grumbling and turning his lucky ghost charm over and over in his palms. "Leavin' the thing run around this way! We been lucky, Max, but tain't reasonable to figger it'll hold! You shoulda let me tail him!"

"Sure, Slim. People expect him to go around with you at his heels, no doubt!" Fleigh spat dango seeds out of the open car window, and took another bite of the cool fruit before going on. "We have to let him circulate; no Councilor just back from a two-week trip would hole up before this meeting, when he had instructions to pick up and last minute details piling in. Besides, we're not dealing with Curtis now, but with a machine. And it knows who its master is. The minute I cut the relay, or it gets ten miles away from me—no life."

He spotted the similacrum coming down the steps and jumped out to open the car door. Slim grunted dourly, pulling his chauffeur's cap further down over his forehead, but he took the curt order from Curtis with no other protests and headed the big car toward the Council Chambers. The Councilor passed over two slips of elaborate pasteboard and leaned back against the seat.

"Passes for the two of you. Are you sure Slim knows what he's to do?"

There was a disgusted sound from the front, but Fleigh ignored it. "He'd better; we've been over it often enough. But go ahead and make sure."

The similacrum ticked off the points with incisive authority. The Council Chamber was radiation proof, and since Curtis would not be trusted with the relay signal, the success of the whole thing depended on Slim's behavior. Max had secured a duplicate of his signal generator which the outlaw was to use outside the Assembly, while Fleigh went inside with his and waited. The operative had developed complete confidence in the ability of the false Curtis, and he was sure of his own part. It was all up to Slim, but there was no reason for him to fail, and he had always taken orders well enough before.

Actually, it all went off with perfect smoothness. The guards passed him in after a careful scrutiny of his permit, and he carried the briefcase that held the generator up to the gallery and turned it on. Seconds later, the similacrum came through the big doorway, with only a slight flicker of uncertainty as the anti-radiation shield touched him and he passed from one generator to the other.

Curtis walked along the aisle with the proper confidence and attention to his friends, presented his credentials for the purely perfunctory examination, and turned off into one of the little council-rooms. Two of the other Martian Councilors followed him, and passed out of Fleigh's field of view, but he was not worried about that. Slim came slouching down the gallery stairs and dropped into a seat beside the operative, putting the duplicate generator between his feet.

"Satisfied?"

"Perfect," Fleigh assured him.

They would reverse it going out. After that, Curtis would announce that he was leaving on a long trip to

Ganymede, and they would be able to dispose of the similacrum without any parts left to show what he was.

THEN CURTIS came back into the main chamber. Apparently the Council had been waiting for his return, for the Sergeant-at-Arms waved for order, and the meeting began, with almost no preliminaries. Earth brought up the subject of the Mandate, and the head of the Venus Council began to come to his feet. But Curtis was up first, and the Chair recognized him.

Fleigh relaxed completely as the familiar words of the speech began to come to him, while the Venusians glanced about in surprise, and then began to listen. A moment later they were under the sway of his oratory. The single speech should do it, since the question had been tentatively decided in favor of Earth at the last meeting, pending Curtis' investigation. By night, the Mandate should be a *fait accompli*, and Earth could begin moving out her mercenary legions in the squat "mining" freighters.

Fleigh had a pretty good idea of who would lead them. He'd been in line for promotion for some time already, and the Plutarch had dropped hints of the outcome of success. It would be good to leave the dubious position of operative and become a legally recognized governor of the mandate planetoids, to settle down and begin organizing his own private little plans for the Plutarch's job!

Slim nudged him with a bony knee, but Fleigh was too wrapped in his own thoughts to bother until the other seized his elbow and hissed at him. Then he came out of his daydreams. Something was going on—the Councilors were paying too careful attention, and the Earth Delegation didn't look right! In a second, his mind was back on the speech, and the words came to a chilling focus in his ears.

"...found the organization inconceivably complex. And yet the basic pattern is old—old as the barbarism that prompted it, Gentlemen. I have only my word as evidence now, but I can name names and give exact locations that will enable our Planetary Police to confirm every word of it before night falls on this meeting. The Plutarch of Earth, on the twentieth of April, forty-two years ago, gave the following orders, which I quote..."

Fleigh grabbed for Slim's generator, and yanked the button savagely; but still the damning words went on, detail piling on exact detail, while Secret Servicemen moved forward to cut the speaker off from the Earth Delegates. Their rudeness was an open declaration that Earth was immediately severed from the Council. Max ripped out the generator, crushing the delicate tubes in his hands. He was stamping on his own device at the same time, but the voice went on unchecked!

Down on the floor, Curtis looked upwards without pausing in his detailed list of evidence, found the operative's eye, and grinned. Then he resumed his normal gravity and went on.

Slim's hands were trembling and fumbling over his charm. Fleigh practically carried him to the aisle, and dragged him along as he made his way up the infinite distance to the gallery door. Every step was made with the expectation of a shouted order from Curtis that would send the big explosive slugs tearing through him, but it did not come. Instead, there was only the quiet continuance of the speech, and Slim's hoarse prayers to the ghosts of the charm to save them.

Surprisingly, the doors opened in the hands of the courteous guards and the hall was before them, with no police in sight. Max cut Slim's babbled relief off with a crisp whisper, "We're not out of it, you fool! Ten to one, it's cat and mouse, with us the losers. But if we're going to make use of the tenth chance, shut up! Walk, damn it, and *grin!*"

THERE WAS another flight of stairs leading down, a long hall, and a second door that opened promptly and politely as they neared it. Then the main steps led down to the street. It was impossible that the similacrum could have given no orders for their arrest; as impossible as that the relay could be tampered with! But the big car waited at the curb, and there were still no police.

Reaction left Slim drooling narcotic juice over the hands that were caressing and kissing the charm. Fleigh yanked him savagely into the car and gunned the electros. It went tearing out into the street under full power, while a wild yell of despair ripped out of the outlaw's throat.

"My ghost charm!" He was pawing frantically at the door lock, with his face swiveled around toward the bright receding twinkle of the metal piece on the sidewalk behind. "Max! Max!"

"Shut up and stay put! There must be a hundred more of those things you can buy if we get out of this." Fleigh freed a hand and forced the cringing fool back into the seat, where he relaxed woodenly, terror fading out to sullen despair that gradually mingled with doubt.

"Then let's get out quick, Max! Once we hit Earth, I know a guy's got another. Tain't as good a ghost with it as mine, but it ain't no fake, neither! You gotta give me enough to get it, Max!"

Fleigh hid his thin grin from the other. They'd need more than a ghost charm or even planning if they ever went to Earth! He'd seen what happened to failures there, and he knew that it would be better to walk into the nearest Planet Police Bureau. But he reached over soothingly and patted the outlaw's shoulder. "Sure, Slim. We'll get you another, maybe before we leave here."

It shouldn't be hard to find one of the charm peddlers, and dope up a story. There was a place on Venus where they could hide, once Slim worked up his nerve to pilot them there—and provided that their luck held long enough to keep the police from impounding the little craft. But the hideout would take money, and that had to come first. Planning took care of that; he'd always been careful to avoid tying his personal fortune up in the Earth Operative strongholds.

He swung the car around a corner, glanced up at a jeweler's sign, and cursed without slowing down. The red light was on, warning that it had been raided. One of his secret quarters gone!

He stopped obediently for a through highway, and roared on. But the second was no better. There was sweat on his forehead, and his hands were slippery with it when he headed out Mars Center Canal into the suburbs. Damn Curtis! It was impossible for him to have found the hideout—or should have been!

But there was no warning light in the window of the third and last place. The lawyer's faded sign swung in the thin wind, and everything was serenely peaceful. Fleigh jerked Slim out of the car, set its automatic chauffeur, and let it go rolling off.

Then he moved up the steps with the outlaw at his heels, listened cautiously at the door, and nodded. The steady click of a typewriter indicated that the scrawny little secretary was doing the routine office-work, and Sammy must have been undisturbed. He opened the door eagerly, to a louder clicking from the typewriter.

ABOVE IT, Curtis looked up with an assured smile, and waved the grandfather of all hand weapons at him in genial greeting.

"Come in, Max," he said cordially. "Like my double's speech?"

Slim's trembling hand fumbled out automatically in the sign of the horns. His blanched mouth worked furiously, but the words refused to come until Curtis turned to him. Then jerked back, waving his fingers. "He couldn'ta… We'd of beat him… *Max!* He's dead! He's a ghost!"

Fleigh's hand groped for him, and missed. Another apparition came into the room from the inner office. This one was a shriveled, little man, with owl-eyes that blinked at them out of thick-lensed spectacles. Jeremiah Greek picked up a pencil with a contented grin, drew it across the bare flesh of his arm; and held the red mark that rose on the skin out toward the outlaw.

"In the flesh," he stated.

But Slim was no longer listening. Slowly, as if moved by worn-down clock-works, he slid down the wall and his dead-faced head bent forward to meet the knees that drew upwards. There he stayed, motionless.

"If that's catatonic return to the fetal position, it's an all-time record for speed," Curtis commented with quiet interest. "Sit down, Max. You seem to have overestimated your companion's moral fiber, and underestimated your opponent's. Never count on luck! It takes planning to get anywhere in this universe… By the way, Jeremiah Greek is the original inventor of pancyclic tape: you should have checked up on him before you trusted him, and found out the way your Plutarchy gypped him out of his invention.

He wasn't the sort of man who'd cooperate very well with Earth. In fact, he was the sort who could and would fake a tape for your recorder to cover up the call he put in under my code to the Martian Council!"

Fleigh moved toward the chair as the gun commanded, only half conscious of the words. He sank into a sitting position, his mind churning savagely and getting nowhere. *Play along! Keep your eyes open! If you let the other guy make the moves he'll slip up somewhere.* It was basic training to operatives, though there was uncertainty in even that logic now. But there was nothing else to do.

Greek picked up the account, "With a promise of secrecy from Councilor Curtis, and a chance to do legitimate research here, I felt quite free to drop my very doubtful loyalty to my native planet, Mr. Fleigh. Those two similacra you shot were crude, and the brain and blood imitation was quite poor, I thought. But fortunately, you didn't investigate thoroughly."

"I didn't think the relay control could fail. So you simply let the similacrum collapse and took its place?" Fleigh was forcing himself to casualness, while his brain hashed over all the rules for upsetting a trap. But it returned inevitably to the basic need of stalling for time, and keeping them talking.

"Not at all," Curtis corrected him. "We were late returning, so they simply used an all-wave receiver to record your control signal on pancyclic tape, inserted it into a generator, and the similacrum had his freedom in his pocket two minutes after you turned on your control in the Council Chamber. You really didn't think I'd leave my speech in the middle to chase you, when I had a perfectly good double, surely?"

FLEIGH'S eyes darted to Slim, but there would be no help from that quarter. Not a muscle had moved since the outlaw had collapsed onto the floor.

He forced himself to relax deliberately. Relax! As long as he was tensed up in the chair, they'd watch him, but they'd be less cautious if he seemed to abandon hope. And he was younger and faster than they were, in spite of his fat.

Greek's amused cackle broke his chain of thought. "So simple a solution, Max! But of course, an involute brain would miss just that... That's fine, relax. And when you start anything, you'll be surprised to find how quickly and efficiently a couple of sentimental visionary fools can shoot! Or do you think, Councilor, that we're really such fools?"

"I doubt it," Curtis answered, with the same hard amusement in his voice. "As I see it, a reactionary is simply unable to adapt to new conditions; he's filled with a blind, stubborn dependence on the rude past. And brute force is an admission of that intellectual poverty, Max, you should have studied history better. The addle-pated idealists have a peculiar habit of winning."

They stood there, grinning and studying their captive with the one thing in the universe he had never encountered—open contempt. Fleigh wet his lips, glancing from one to the other, and considering the hopeless distance to the door.

And suddenly the beginnings of an idea permeated through the hard knot of fear in his brain. They didn't believe in brute force! They wouldn't kill him without provocation; and they couldn't turn him in to the police!

He swung back to Curtis, and this time there was a grin on his own lips. "You said you promised Mr. Greek secrecy, Councilor. Not immunity, because the old law against making robots is too strong; and similacra would be considered robots. Well, just how do you figure you can turn me over to the authorities without breaking that promise and having him strung up beside me?"

"I never meant to turn you in," Curtis answered.

"And you said yourself that brute force was stupid!"

"Quite true." It was Greek who answered this time. "But the rules of justice sometimes invoke it. The penalty for treason, like that for robotry, is still death, though we've abandoned most other reasons for capital punishment."

"Then turn me in or kill me yourselves—and you'll find that brute force really is stupid on Mars! The police here are the best in the system, which is why I always preferred to do my little jobs elsewhere. You amateurs wouldn't have a chance. Well?"

But he knew that he had them, and the taste of freedom in his mouth was sweet after the fear and hopelessness of their gloating power. He did not wait for an answering nod from them, but turned from his chair in calm assurance, and headed for the door.

GREEK'S voice interrupted his exit. "Just a minute, Max. You really should know *all* your mistakes, and there's one we forgot… Never use a perfect similacrum. It can't be perfect without thinking exactly like its original; the same mind must operate the same way. Your similacrum was limited only by the time it could exist—and it knew that, as well as knowing it was useless among real men!"

"So what?" Fleigh asked jauntily, and reached for the door. "And so long!"

Steel hands grabbed him, and a pair of arms with inhuman strength picked him up and turned him around to face the two men. Curtis dropped his gun onto the table with a slow, deliberate motion, holding the struggling operative with a single hand, while he stretched the other out to Jeremiah Greek. Then he turned toward the door, dragging the fat body of Fleigh along without effort.

"So when you're found dead in your house, killed by the robot you were having built in some fiendish plot against Councilor Curtis, I don't think the police will worry—beyond seeing that both you and the robot are thoroughly beyond repair."

There was bitterness in the voice of the similacrum, but it was resolute and determined bitterness. "When the real Curtis replaced me in the Council Chamber, he meant to make my few days of existence as pleasant as possible. But even a limited similacrum likes to be useful. Come along, Max."

Max Fleigh went along; there was nothing else he could do, as the duplicate of Curtis tossed him into a small car and began driving back toward the town and the house that had been his Martian home and would soon be his tomb. He couldn't even think straight, for his head insisted on dwelling on nonsense.

Slim had been right, after all, and his ghost charm had brought him luck, even after he lost it. But for the man who had refused to believe in it, there was no hope for such insane oblivion. There was simply no hope of any kind.

Absolutely No Paradox

If time-travel is possible, then why haven't we been visited by people from the future? Pete LeFranc found the answer to that.

THE OLD MEN'S section of the Arts and Science Club was always the best ordered. The robots somehow managed to avoid clanking there; the greensward beyond the veranda was always just right, and the drinks were the best for six counties. Old Ned Brussels touched his glass to his lips appreciatively, sighed in contentment, and waited for some of the other oldsters to break the silence.

Finally, Lem Hardy took the plunge. "He did it," he announced, referring to a conversation of weeks before. Then, at their puzzled looks, he amplified. "My grandson, damn it! He's got a time machine—it works. Sent a cat four days up, and it came through unharmed."

The glass fell from Old Ned's hand, bouncing on the floor, and spilling good liquor. A robot came forward silently to clean it up, but Ned didn't look at it. "Four days doesn't mean a thing. Lem—is that kid planning on trying it out?"

"He's going to try it next week."

"Then for the Lord's sake, stop him! Look, does it work like this?" His fingers slipped over the pencil smoothly, as they had always done when he worked, drafting robot bodies in the old days. A rude schematic seemed to grow almost instantly on the paper.

Lem took it, then stiffened suddenly. "Who told you?"

"A youngster named Pete LeFranc—and it was forty years...no, over fifty years ago. Lem, if you like your grandson, keep him out of the machine. Four days, four weeks—they don't mean anything. Time machines don't work, however well they seem to."

A bustle from behind them pulled their eyes around. One of the robots was quietly restraining a nervous young man who was trying to break free and join the group. His face was tense, excited, with an odd bitter fear behind it. His words were seemingly cut out of steel. "...told me I'd find him here. Damn it..."

"Sorry, sir. You'll have to wait." The robot's voice was adamant under its smoothness.

Ned grunted, and then impulse led him to look again. He'd seen the man somewhere. He hunted for it, then dismissed it, knowing that his memory was tricky these days. But he motioned the robot aside. "We don't allow interruptions for junior members," he told the man, letting his voice soften the words. "Still, if you want to sit down and listen—quietly—nobody'll stop you."

"But..."

"*Quietly,*" the robot stressed the word. The man looked at it, then swiveled to Ned Brussels. For a moment, the bitterness halted, as if frozen, then gave place to a sudden sharp amusement. His eyes searched Ned's, and he nodded, dropping into a chair.

Lem took up the conversation again. "It worked. And if it works for four days, it should work for four centuries. You're just scared of paradoxes, Ned—going back and killing your grandfather, or such rot. You've been reading too many stories on it."

"Fifty years ago, Pete LeFranc said the same thing. Young man, either sit down, or get out. This is the Old Men's section! He had answers for all the paradoxes, too—except one question."

NED HAD BEEN YOUNG, then, just getting started at synthanatomy drafting, and not rich enough for wine of the type Pete always kept. He sipped it with relish, and looked at the odd cage Pete was displaying. "All the same, it won't work!"

Pete laughed. "Reality doesn't mean a thing to an artist, does it? Be damned to your paradoxes—there's some answer to them. It did work; the dog appeared exactly four weeks later, just finishing his bark!"

"Then why haven't time machines come back from the future?" Ned shot at him. He'c been saving that as his final argument, and he sat back to watch the bomb explode.

For a second, Pete blinked. "You never figured that out yourself."

"Nope. I got it from a science fiction story. But why haven't they? If yours works, there'll be more time machines built. With more built, they'll be improved. They'll get to be commonplace. People'd use them—and someone would turn up here with one. Or in the past. Why haven't we met time travelers, Pete?"

"Maybe we have met them, but didn't know it?"

"Nonsense. You get in that machine and go back to Elizabethan England. Try to pass yourself off as being native to that time even an hour. No; there'd be slip-ups."

Pete considered it, pouring more wine. "An idea—but you're right, maybe. I haven't tried going back—if I'd sent the dog backwards. I couldn't have checked up on it, while I could be waiting in the future. Okay, you've convinced me."

"Then you're not going in the contraption."

Pete's laughter was spontaneous and loaded with amusement. "I'm going forward and find out why no one has come back! I've got a nice collection of rare coins I can trade off up there—should be more valuable—and I'll bring you back a working invention from the next century. With luck, I'll bring you the answer. And after that, maybe I can go back and kill an ancestor, just to see what happens."

"Don't be a fool!"

But Pete was grinning, and opening the door to the cage that rested in the middle of his laboratory. "Fifty years this trip," he said, spinning the dials. "And you won't have long to wait. I'll come back just about in no time."

Ned started to yell something, but there was a curious flicker, such as he'd seen when Pete sent the dog forward. The time machine blurred over, its surface seeming to stretch into infinity while contracting to nothing at the same time.

Then it was gone. Ned groped for the wine bottle, cursing, and drained the contents. Then he sat down to wait.

Three days later, the police came looking for Pete, on some mysterious tip, probably from a fellow worker. It was a pretty rough time, for a while, though they finally decided it was just another mystery, and that Ned's yarn of having been there only to keep an appointment was true. Ned had influential friends, even if he didn't have money, then.

For three years, he rented Pete's laboratory, before he made enough to buy it. For a decade, he lived in it; but by then he'd begun to know that Pete wasn't coming back.

THE BUILDING'S STILL there," Old Ned finished. "The diagrams of his machine are still in the drawers. But Pete never showed up. I tell you, keep your fool grandson out of time machines, Lem. They don't work. Too many paradoxes—if they'd work, you could steal a future invention, get credit for inventing it, and nobody would ever have to invent it. When things have that many angles that can't work, the thing itself can't work."

Lem shook his head stubbornly. "It worked; the kid got the cat back. Something just happened to your friend—maybe his power failed."

"Then he wouldn't have gotten all the way—and he'd have reappeared years ago. Pete measured things—and there was no displacement in space. If something had happened to him, the machine would have been there, anyhow. Besides, I had alarms wired to call the police in—told 'em it was to protect a safe—the minute he showed up. He never showed up; he never came back."

"So I suppose he just disappeared—time ate him up?" Lem's stubbornness was cracking a bit, though. His voice was higher than even an old man's should be.

"I don't know. But time machines don't work. Otherwise where are the time travelers from the future?"

They sat quietly for a second. Ned was remembering the years, up to the time he'd given up, disconnected the alarms, and come here to the Arts and Science Club to live. He'd been stubborn, maybe—a little bit—but Pete hadn't reappeared.

Behind him, the young man cleared his throat, and the robot moved forward. But there was no rule against intrusion when no one was speaking, and the robot came to a stop. Ned looked back, just as the man decided the robot wouldn't interfere. There was more amusement on the man's face now, but the bitterness still lay there.

He grinned at Ned, a familiar grin, and his voice was flat and positive. "Time machines work. And there are no paradoxes—absolutely no paradoxes!"

Lem stirred, craning back, and Ned bristled. But something about the younger man caught back the words, as he picked up the thin thread of memory.

The other grinned again, wryly.

"It's simple. Time machines work in one direction—they can't go back. Your time traveler found that out too late. No trips to the past, no return from the future—and no paradoxes, Ned Brussels."

He came to his feet, moving over to drop into the chair beside Ned. The older man nodded, stretching out his hand.

"I told you not to try the damned machine, Pete," Ned told him. Then he chuckled as the oldest cliché among old friends meeting again came to his lips. "Fifty years—and you haven't changed a bit, Pete LeFranc!"

Forgive Us Our Debts

A lesser culture can be murdered by the more advanced without war, without violence, without exploitation, without even the intent to harm…

FANE FELT the force of the *kral* fields slowing the ship before the sleep was out of his eyes, and the soft purring hiss of power that was only barely tapped, usually. It had been three generations since the fields had been used, except in the ritual tests.

"Closssse," the great integrating reactors hissed. "Closse."

In another day they would reach the planet they had selected, and the long Cruise might be over. Fifty generations, if the legends were right—eleven branchings—fifteen hundred of those mysteriously arbitrary divisions called years…and now they had found a world that might have been made for them.

Lissa still lay snoring faintly on the bunk, her red hair sprawled out over her pale shoulders, beautiful even in her sleep. Fane's eyes lingered a moment over the curves the thin sheet revealed. Perhaps, when this was over, and they had landed, he might ally himself with Lissa. He'd thought about it before—though, as a rule, only when another girl shared his cabin.

He shook her awake, grinning at the anger that always swept over her features at waking. This time, though, the sounds of surging power brought her out of the depths more readily. She half-opened her eyes. "What day?"

"Wednesday," he answered.

Lissa hated Wednesdays, when gravity was set for half over normal, and the air pressure and humidity were raised.

There had been no way of knowing what the world at Cruise-end might be like, and each day had been different.

But she made no comment now; instead, she reached for the *kofe* and wafers he had heated and wriggled rapidly into her kirtle and officer's halter. She giggled suddenly, and he realized he'd been standing with one arm in his tunic and the other hanging for the last few minutes. He pulled it on, just as the panel buzzed.

"Captain's meeting in fifteen minutes," the speaker announced. "Compulsory, not optional. Acknowledge."

Lissa pressed his button, and they went out into the hall, toward the nearest bank of teleports. The *Kraling* still had the mono-relay setup—one of the many disadvantages of a ship two branchings old and long outmoded—and they had to wait while other previous jumps were cleared. Then the light blinked, and they were in the Captain's observatory.

The star they were nearing was bright enough by now to need shields over it, and the tank had four planets showing around it—two huge ones, and two of habitable size. Even as they watched, another, smallest of all, came into existence, far to the side. Observers were checking, but locating planets was always a slow business.

They were nearing the second observed planet from the star, about a hundred million miles out. Fane set the tank for maximum magnification, and gasped faintly. There were clouds in the atmosphere, thick over much of the planet. Below, the markings showed what must be continents and seas. Fane had never seen a planet, but study of detailed reports about several hundred that the Cruise along this branch-line passed had made him generally familiar with them. This was unusually rich in evidence of air and water. He reached the key and dialed the tank for details.

Estimated pressure, fifteen pounds at the surface; gravity about normal; nitrogen and oxygen four to one, traces of carbon-dioxide; average temperature midway between equator and poles about right for comfort; estimated rotation around star one year; rotation on axis about twenty-four hours—generally an almost ideal world. There was an extreme tilt of the axis from the plane of rotation about the sun—which might make for a highly variable climate, but not beyond tolerable limits. And certain phenomena indicated that there was vegetation based on chlorophyll already on the planet!

LISSA shuddered ecstatically. "Ours, Fane—all ours! After all the generations, *we* are chosen. Discoveries, novelty, thrills, excitement—a whole world to bend to our desires—space unlimited to spread out for our children!"

"And a base," he added, more soberly. He caught a glimpse of his chiseled features, lean, tall body, and dark complexion beside her flame and ivory in the tank's plastic. For a moment, he felt some of her desires race through him, but he shook them back. "A place where we can build again—rear cities and increase, study and perfect ourselves. No more being little creatures in tiny worlds of metal, unnatural to the universe."

She made a mouth at him, but the warning bell cut it off. He started for the teleport, but Lissa dragged him back. "Fane, before you go—are you with us?"

He looked at her in surprise. "With you?"

"Do you want Cruise-end here? Will you vote for it? Even if your father wants to go on, along with the other old men who think because they were born in space their grandchildren should be born the same? Fane, are you on our side?"

It hadn't entered his mind to doubt, though he had heard talk among his father's friends that giving up the ships for a planet was like leaving a small, comfortable bed for a big room full of needles. He looked at the globe in the tank again. "I'm with you!"

* * *

His father was already seated at the head of the table where captains of the fifteen ships, their allies, or their companions with them, waited. Fane settled beside Lissa, conscious of the envious eyes on him. His father nodded, and picked up the ceremonial scrolls.

"It is customary," Commander Bran began, "when approaching a place where branching may be made—"

Lusato, of the *Volanyi* cut in quickly. "Branching? Are we to set down, build new ships for our surplus population, and then split off into two parties—to go off on the Cruise? Not By God and by Atom, we *stay* here. I've seen the world in the tank; it's Cruise-end!"

Bran turned to him, a faint smile on his face. "I was about to say that, in this case, the customary reading of our history seems unimportant, since you are all impatient to decide. Any objections?"

They stirred, and nodded quick agreement. Most of the history was half-legendary, anyway. A short-lived cult of fanatics had killed the custodians and destroyed most of the records after the second branching. They knew they had been sent from some world to find and colonize another solar system, and to report back—sent out in a ship so crude that it seemed impossible it had made the voyage at all—one that had taken eighty years to travel six-light-years. It had found no hospitable planet, and gone on, until finally the pressure of population and exhaustion of supplies had forced it down on a barren world. There, somehow, more ships had been built, and the expedition had split, each half going off independently, to cover more space. Since then, there had been ten other such branchings—and incalculable progress. Now the ships made better than three-quarters light speed, powered by engines that took energy directly from space, and reacting through the *kral* fields directly on space for their drive. They could take any matter—even the massive stuff from a dark star—to build whatever they liked.

Bran smiled again. "Very well. We have a decision; the world below can, perhaps, be Cruise-end. Or any of these worlds can lead to another branching—since most of our young men feel cramped by the necessary restrictions on having children in our space. But I feel I should point out that we have already achieved all that we could have done, had we found a planet long ago—and more. We represent inconceivable progress, meaningless figures of population, and innumerable cultures, if we assume even half of the branching parties have survived. We are not subject to the whim of a planet, but make our own conditions. And the world to which we are to report—it is lost, hopelessly. Why behave like grown men looking for a womb into which to retreat?"

Lissa looked at Fane, and he felt himself rising to his feet. Bran nodded for him to speak.

"We want Cruise-end," he said slowly, trying to find his reasons. "We've done well here—nobody questions that. But men belong on planets, father—where a billion people may work together, and where real progress can be made. You tell us we've gone far—but how far must the original world have gone? Suppose they come looking for us—and find us a bunch of primitives, living in what they consider hovels? Will we be happy in space then? By now they may have the very planets on which they live moving throughout space. They may travel faster than light—we know it is possible! They—"

"You want new adventures, unlike the old?" his father asked.

"Very well," Fane said; "we want new adventures. Is that wrong?"

Lissa jumped up beside him. "Vote!"

The younger men picked it up. Bran shrugged, and nodded, counting the hands. It was nine to six to make this Cruise-end. Bran noted it down on the scrolls, and rose. "That's all, captains—except that you can still change your minds. Look at your ships when you return, and imagine life on the planet. Then wonder if it may not already be inhabited, since it is so well adapted for life. Because—it is!"

He turned and went out. Lissa caught Fane's arm, and bent to his ear to whisper, but he jerked back making her wait, pouting, until the others had gone. "You needn't worry, Fane. I'm not trying to ally with you—not after what you called a speech. All I wanted to say was that it's already beginning! Just think, a primitive race to overcome. We'll live, Fane—really live! We'll be heroes, fighting, conquering…"

SOMETHING hit the ship, jerking it as if space had dropped out from under it. The air swooped past them, roaring down the corridor, until the slap of air-seals went on. From overhead, the scream of a siren sounded, and the speakers snapped on.

"Captains to stations! Ships are under attack! All officers at stations! Locators..."

Fane jerked past Lissa and hit the studs of the teleport savagely, to come out in the *Kraling's* observation-control room. He snapped orders, after a single glance at the tank, but saw that the screens had already dropped. The generators took up a heavier hum under the load.

Outside the ships, space seemed to swarm with tiny specks. The sister ships of the *Kraling* seemed monstrous hulks beside them, huge doughnuts with lumps instead of holes in their middles, lumbering along at a crawl as they continued to slow toward the planet below. The little specks darted here and there, leaving trails of fire behind them. They twisted and turned impossibly.

Fane focused on one. It was obviously a one-man vessel, open except for a narrow frame. The pointed nose with the power and control section led back across the swelling frame to a tail that belched added flame whenever the vessel turned—obviously a steering mechanism. He puzzled back in his memory for the drive being used, and finally came up with it—the distorter that buckled space slightly. It could serve as a shield as strong as metal walls, yet it was so instable that only a small vessel was possible. Even then, it kept breaking down and reforming, making the fiery trail of electrons around and behind it—built from the collapsing of space in the distorted field.

One came down against the *Kraling*, and the big ship lurched, while a gout of roaring flame danced off into space behind it, where its field had touched that of the ship.

Then Fane swore in sudden amazement. Inside it was a woman—as human as Lissa, though her face was set in a mask of concentration and hate as she tried to hold her field steady and bore back for another strike.

Men were running in answer to his orders, space-suited and heading for the outer guns along the rim of the *Kraling*. He saw the same maneuver going on at the *Spendat*, where fat old captain Monoi was probably letting Lissa run things. The other ships were all following suit, now.

Two of the little ships suddenly came into the field of the guns, and imploded. Where they had been, all metal ceased to be, and the unprotected figures of the male and female drivers of the little ships suddenly puffed up and died in open space.

Fane felt sick. He had heard the legends of battles with other races, but these present were human—or nearly so. And their cause was hopeless. They were gallant enough—they still came roaring in for the battle, though they could do no harm to the big ships now, and were sitting ducks—whatever ducks were—for the gunner. The fools! If they had no better than space distortion, the *Kraling* alone could blast the atmosphere off their planet, or set the inner core into atomic explosions that would rip it to shreds!

Suddenly he countermanded his orders to the gunners and went running toward the port, pulling on his spacesuit. "Give me a gig, invisible," he ordered over his helmet phone.

* * *

The small gig used for picking up specimens of rock—or with luck, for examining planets they might find—was waiting, just sinking into invisibility as he reached it. He tossed open the tiny port, and leaped to the controls. There were only two of the little ships left, and he had no time for caution. He ripped upward at full acceleration, jerked the gig toward the nearest, and opened the big cargo hatch. The little ship was swinging for a return at the *Kraling* as he matched course and surrounded it.

The cargo-hatch swung shut, and he adjusted his controls, damping out the space distortion as quickly as air could run into the hold. The girl driver let out a frightened screech, and fainted as she seemed to be exposed to empty space.

He went back to the hold, cutting off the power-consuming invisibility, and found her sprawling across the cushions of her tiny machine, but unharmed. So close, she looked even more human. The ghastly make-up on her face came off with a few quick dabs, revealing normal enough skin. He bent and jerked the brief costume off her, just as she came to.

The absence of clothes made no difference to her, but his presence was a shock second only to her expected death. She drew back, muttering strange words in a moaning monotone. Like her body, there was nothing inhuman about her voice or her reactions.

Then she was at him, clawing and scratching. He clipped her quickly on the jaw, and carried her to the control room, where he set the gig back toward the *Kraling.* "Kill the space warp drives and put in a small *kral* field, with invisibility," he told the men. "And take this to my cabin."

HE WENT at a full run to the control room, switching into the Commander's line. "Dad, there isn't anything non-human about my captive!"

Bran's voice was tired and weary, "I know—I had a tracer on you. This world must have been found by another branch and settled. It isn't our right to invade—we'll have to go on."

But there was a satisfaction to his final wards, Fane noticed. He started to protest, when another voice came on, that of Lissa. "Captain Lissa—Monoi had a heart attack. Commander Bran, we voted! That still stands! If they've sunk this far, or never gotten beyond the space distorter, they don't rate a world. We protest."

Once a vote was made, it took unanimous assent to change it. Bran's sigh indicated his failing hopes. "Very well. What now, Fane?"

"I'm going to follow the other ship—call off any attack on him. I'm taking an invisibility suit, and I'll riffle their records, somehow—enough to find whether it is a colony, and what they're like. They may have other weapons—sometimes a culture produces a single device out of keeping with the pattern—and that can be something completely outside our defensive knowledge. Your permission?"

"Granted."

* * *

Fane was gone again at a run, while excitement stirred in him. Lissa had been too high-handed—but she was right. He hated the killing, and yet something stirred in him. With a whole world before them, and a generation of making it wholly theirs, life would have zest that it could never have on the ship.

He spotted the retreating single tiny ship, and caught up with it easily, following it down. Others were patrolling below. They obviously had no test for invisibility.

* * *

Another ridiculous battle was going on when he returned, but he paid no attention to it.

He dropped onto the *Kraling*, throwing out a bundle, and began a report before he reached the control room, coupling in through his suit phone. "They have a dozen languages, father—but one of them is the same as the language of the old records! They pronounce it oddly, but on one island they seem to be trying to revive it—they call it English! I found some newspapers in it. I'm sending them over."

He cut off before the excited babble of the other ships could reach him. The fracas outside was dying down now, as the ships retreated before the power of the larger vessels. Fane took a look at the tank, nodded to his lieutenant, and went back to his cabin.

It seemed incredible; no culture could drop that far. He had found no clue as to the Branch that had settled this world, nor as to the time they had been there. But the population indicated it must have been many generations before.

Even to his unpracticed eye, there were people here who were mere property—owned by others, a few who lived in what must seem to them luxury. The papers confirmed it, reporting on the "slave" rebellion just put down in connection with this "invasion from space." There were indications that some section had slaves and some did not, but he couldn't be sure. Most of the mess he had found in the records and the current papers meant nothing to him—except that science was little more than witchcraft, and that human dignity seemed to be something talked about a great deal, with no understanding.

Any Branch that had so far lost their culture had no right to a planet!

"The captive is being washed and disinfected for possible disease," he was told, but he only half heard it. He muttered an order for her to be sent when it was finished and went into his cabin.

IT BECAME more incredible as he studied the duplicate records and papers he had kept for himself. Terms that were meaningless began to have meaning—and ugly ones. Money became a symbol for one man to own more than another, irrespective of right and contribution to humanity. Nation became a term that meant disunity and hatred. They fought savagely against this "invasion"—and no wonder! They'd been fighting for thirty years before among themselves, with only a prohibition against atomics and nucleonics—because those ruined the wealth and the wealthy.

One nation, he saw, was trying to get the practice of slavery banned—and to begin exploiting the planets they had discovered again. For a time it looked like sanity—and probably was, for them. But it was a unity which included mob hysteria, persecution of minorities—apparently smaller groups who disagreed or were somehow different—and incredibly inefficient controls. And they talked about a "Dark Age" a few centuries before!

He threw it aside in disgust, and went to look at the control room. When he came back, Lissa and the captive were in the cabin. Lissa was experimenting with a tiny nerve stimulator that sent the girl jerking and jumping, screaming faintly.

He jerked it from Lissa's hands. "*Bitch!*"

She grinned easily. "All right, Fane. I won't destroy your little plaything. I'll even let you have others, when we've captured these. But don't forget—I have my rights, too."

He looked at her slowly and for the first time, he really saw her. She'd fit, down there; she'd fit beautifully. Here, her future was clear enough—she'd try to become Commander by every trick she could—and the tardy, reluctant Psychometrists would decide that she must be given a mind-quieting, and a job of no importance; they'd hold off until the last moment, but the welfare of the Branch came before everything else.

He picked her up by one arm and a leg and threw her out into the hallway, where she went off, chuckling at what she thought lay behind his action.

The captive stared at him doubtfully. "*Bitch!* You speak English!"

Her accent was barbarous, but he could understand it.

"Of course. You're from that Island—"

"Slave there, yes. But I was going to be freed—I'm from Nioway, and we don't have slaves. We can speak English, most of us—once it was our language, too."

It was the most progressive of the savage communities there, covering one whole continent. He nodded, and she glowered at him. "England was going to free all its slaves—until you came along and we had to be used for war. England and Nioway are making a treating. Now—"

She slumped down onto the floor and began crying. With a sudden impulse, he pulled her up beside him, and tried to comfort her. One person didn't matter out of the billions that would be eliminated when they took the planet, and such savages hardly merited any consideration. Yet she seemed as normal and human as he was—there was nothing savage about her. The culture she came from was atrocious, but it seemed that the people in it could be simply normal humans in a crazy world. Now she was afraid, sick, and miserable, willing to find comfort even from a captor.

On that, he thought grimly, she'd probably had experience.

HIS FATHER'S voice awoke him. The Commander had come there in person. Sandra, the girl, darted back to the corner of the room, her face turning scarlet for some reason, but the Commander barely noticed her.

"They aren't a branch," Bran said wearily. "The planet is Earth—the world we all came from. This is the mother that sent us out—we've circled and come home. We have a map of the system from before, and we've charted the planets. This—this is what happens to a race on a planet. Every five hundred years, they change direction—they recognize it as being due to something about sunspots, but they still obey the planetary law. They reached a peak, once, and sent us out, like an egg producing life. They might do it again, for all I know—but..."

Fane shook his head, and the knowledge was something that had been nagging his mind. "Then—they sent us out, father, expecting us to come back with new frontiers for them. I've seen some of the records, though I didn't understand. And we didn't come back—there are no new frontiers. This is the only planet suitable for men." He shook his head. "They gave us life—and now we're bringing them death."

The older man shrugged. "I tried to have the decision changed, but Lissa refuses. The others—except you—have agreed, and I might even change your mind. But it doesn't matter; the psychodynamicists have worked out enough on the basis of the records to predict that. If we retreat now, they'll still know we could have taken them with a power they can't even dream of. And they'll give up, sick at their own little progress, to go back down the road to full savagery, or to die. Whenever one of their little backwaters of the Dark Ages has been found by the more advanced, its culture has died. This time, they will all be savages beside us."

He turned on his heel to leave. Then he stopped.

"In spite of the Covenant, Fane, thirteen of us are leaving—we have been enough of life on a planet. We know that man was born there, but that he evolved beyond it once he reached space. Those who remain behind or drop back to the old level are wasted. The future of man belongs to the universe, not to mythical Course-endings. You can come—or you can stay with Lissa."

Fane stared about, trying to avoid his father's eyes. "I'll stay!"

He sat miserably, thinking it over, and this time Sandra tried to comfort him. But he wanted none of it. One ship alone could ruin a planet—and it seemed that none would be needed to ruin this mother world which had borne offspring she could not follow.

***

Sudden, savage attack began again, and this time the ships were larger—two-man affairs, with one man fighting to control the instable field while the other used the full power of its waste to strike again and again at the interstellar vessels. Fane swore, and went into the control-room.

Some of the ships from Earth were dropping from their own failures. But they had courage.

Thirteen of the ships above began moving slowly away—their fields were lowered to keep from upsetting the instable drives of the tiny ships from Earth, and there were no guns firing from them. Bran and the other twelve captains were keeping their word.

"Fane!" Lissa's voice came over the communicator. "Fane, my darling, I knew you'd stick. Give them hell!"

Her ship was spouting guns, and dropping off the little craft, like a hot plate destroying drops of water.

The tiny craft suddenly came swooping down at him, as if detecting indecisiveness. He watched the harmless display of firc they set up from his screens impassively and reluctantly ordered out a few gunners to chase them back. In the tank, one of the ten ships moving away hesitated. *It's fine to watch such a nice clean sport*, Fane thought bitterly.

Beside him, Sandra had crept up and was watching with a white face.

SLOWLY, his hand descended on the controls. The little ships darted down again, and a shout came up from the engine pit speaker. "Captain Fane, strengthen your screen! It's too low! We're being pitted a little here."

"Something wrong," he shouted back hoarsely. "Do you detect new radiation?"

"No!"

"Neither do I—but we're losing screen power… All hands—evacuate ship!"

He waited tensely, watching the counter on the teleport click off each use as the men obeyed. A thousand drills had madc it automatic. And beside him, another counter indicated steadily dwindling power in the field around, though the generators still howled.

Somewhere below, power was running into huge batteries of accumulators, shunted across the control panel, and building up and up, far beyond overload. Fane grinned tensely. "Lissa!" he called. "I'm under some new attack. Can you cover me?"

She swung her ship toward him, stretching out her shield to the maximum, and drawing closer to make them meet. The tiny swarm of ships came at them savagely now. "Fane—what is it? Why—?"

The ships were almost touching now—and the accumulators were far beyond overload. Something like a small sun leaped suddenly from the *Kraling* toward her ship, and the shield vanished.

Fane heard her instinctive order to abandon ship, and knew that it was equipped with simultaneous teleports that would clear it in three seconds. Her call had been made without time to realize what had happened, but now she knew, and a burst of profanity poured from the speaker as she jerked her unmanned ship back under emergency manual and tried to reestablish control.

She might make it—if she could hold, she could call back the men. He had no illusions as to what would happen to him then—the overload's discharge had burned out every bit of power in the ship, and he was already falling toward Earth, with the little ships picking bits of him off every second.

Something flashed in the tank, and he saw the third ship lashing out with the maximum power of its beams. Lissa's ship seemed to fall apart under them.

IT WAS NO speaker that brought Lissa's words a second later. She stood behind him in the teleport booth, stepping slowly forward, with a hand-blaster held toward him. Her face was insane, and she strangled over the words. Obviously, she hadn't seen where the beams originated, and blamed him.

Sandra struck her down with a flying leap against her knees. Behind her, suddenly, the erect, proud form of Bran stood. He bent over, seized Lissa around the waist, and tossed her into the teleport, punching out a code rapidly.

"They'll take care of her in Psycho," he said quietly. "Good work, Sandra."

His fingers reached out for the teleport controls, and locked them, while Fane slowly realized that the third ship to drop back had been his father's. He grinned slowly, nodding, and the older man echoed his chuckle.

"We're not so much different, after all, son—we both thought of the same trick. You've still got the gig, complete with invisibility? Good. Let's leave your ship, along with mine and Lissa's, for those tiny bits of courage out there to break into shreds before they reach atmosphere. I think they'll be convinced by now that we put on a big fight, but that we couldn't match them for power—and they'll go home feeling victorious until they begin wondering if we were only the advance guard. That should cure their little fights, and get them moving toward some real progress."

Fane led the way to the gig, while Sandra pointed out Nioway to him. Suddenly he started to turn back, but Bran shook his head. "I brought enough jewels and other trinkets, Fane. We can be rich enough for what we'll need to do—if this girl you've found can keep quiet."

Fane grinned, and translated. Sandra nodded emphatically, and the older man chuckled again.

They'd lost their rightful domain, lost it almost at the moment they'd realized what was truly theirs, what they had become—star-man. Once man conquered space, planets were no longer for him; he belonged out there among the stars, to expand and take all the multiple courses of progress. Well…the others would know, sooner or later; the big ships would probably stop for a Branching at this system's outer planet, but they were forever beyond Fane's reach. He was through with space.

"We'll pay our debts," he said. "We came home unknowingly, and our coming almost wrecked it."

Home. A young man on an old world. But his son, or grandson at the latest, would go forth, perhaps on another ship seeking frontiers that didn't exist. Earth could produce one other child, at least. And what he and the other immigrants knew must never be told; Earth's children must find this truth for themselves.

He pulled Sandra closer, and headed toward Nioway.

Earthbound

He wanted above anything else to go into space. He had been waiting for it—a long time!

IT WAS hours after the last official ceremony before Clifton could escape the crowd of planetlubbers with their babblings, their eligible daughters and their stupid self-admiration. They'd paid through the nose to get him here, and they meant to get their money's worth.

The exit led only to a little balcony, but it seemed to be deserted. He took a deep breath of the night air and his eyes moved unconsciously toward the stars.

Coming back to Earth had been a mistake, but he'd needed the money. Space Products Unlimited wanted a real deepspace hero to help celebrate its hundredth anniversary. He had just finished the Regulation of Rigel, so he'd been picked. Damn them and their silly speeches and awards—and damn Earth! What was one planet when there were a billion up there among the stars?

From the other side of a potted plant there was a soft sigh.

Clifton swung his head, then relaxed as he saw the other man was not looking at him. The eyes behind the dark glasses were directed toward the sky.

"Aldebaran, Sirius, Deneb, Alpha Centauri," the voice whispered. It was a high-pitched voice with an odd accent, but there was the poetry of ancient yearning in it.

He was a small, shriveled old man. His shoulders were bent. A long beard and dark glasses covered most of his face, but could not entirely conceal the deep wrinkles, even in the moonlight.

Clifton felt a sudden touch of pity and moved closer, without quite knowing why. "Didn't I see you on the platform?"

"Your memory is very good, Captain. I was awarded publicly—for fifty years of faithful service making space boots. Well, I was always a good cobbler, and perhaps my boots helped some men out there." The old man's hand swept toward the stars, then fell back to grip the railing tightly. "They gave me a gold watch, though time means nothing to me. And a cheap world cruise ticket. As if there were any spot on this world I could still want to see." He laughed harshly. "Forgive me if I sound bitter. But, you see, I've never been off Earth!"

Clifton stared at him incredulously. "But everyone—"

"Everyone but me," the old man said. "Oh, I tried. I was utterly weary of Earth and I looked at the stars and dreamed. But I failed the early rigid physicals. Then, when things were easier, I tried again. A plague grounded the first ship. A strike delayed another. Then one exploded on the pad and only a few on board were saved. It was then I realized I was meant to wait here—here on Earth, and nowhere else. So I stayed, making space boots."

PITY AND impulse forced unexpected words to Clifton's lips. "I'm taking off for Rigel again in four hours, and there's a spare cabin on the Maryloo. You're coming with me."

The old hand that gripped his arm was oddly gentle. "Bless you, Captain. But it would never work. I'm under orders to remain here."

"Nobody can order a man grounded forever. You're coming with me if I have to drag you, Mr.—"

"Ahasuerus."

The old man hesitated, as if expecting the name to mean something. Then he sighed and lifted his dark glasses.

Clifton met the other's gaze for less than a second. Then his own eyes dropped, though memory of what he had seen was already fading. He vaulted over the balcony railing and began running away from Ahasuerus, toward his ship and the unconfined reaches of space.

Behind him, the eternal wanderer tarried and waited.

I am Tomorrow

A NOVELETTE OF DESTINY DENIED

His dream was to give people freedom—not to hand it to them on a platter, but give them the one weapon they needed to win it for themselves. But to do this, Thomas Blake had to get into a position of power, had to obtain the Presidency. That was his only motive for his ambition. But, as his aide, Gideon Pierce, said, "...once you have the power, and somebody bucks you—you know what will happen!" It wouldn't happen, Blake swore—but would it, after all?

CHAPTER ONE

IDIOCY wrenched at the mind of Thomas Blake; the television cameras, the fine old mansion, the people cheering, all seemed to vanish into a blankness. His mind was suddenly alien to his brain, his thoughts twisting against a weight of absolute blankness that resisted with a fierce impulse to live. Before him, light seemed to lash down; and a grim, expressionless face swam out of nothing, while an old man's voice dinned in ears that were curiously not his.

It passed, almost at once, leaving only the sureness that this was more than fancy. Blake caught a quick view of himself in a monitor, spotting the sagging muscles of his face, and carrying them back to a smile. His eyes darted to the face of Gideon Pierce, and he saw that the slip could only have been momentary; his campaign manager was still smiling the too-warm smile of a professional politician, creasing his fat jowls into false pleasantness.

The shouting behind him caught Blake's ears then, making him realize that his short speech was ended. He stood there, studying himself in the monitor. He was still lean and trim at forty, with the finest camera face in politics. To the women, he had looked like a man who was still boyish; to the men, like a man among men. And none of that had hurt, though it wasn't the only reason he had just been conceded victory as the youngest governor of the state, on his first entry into politics.

But under his attempt to appraise himself, Blake's mind was still trembling as if huddled down into the familiar pattern of his physical brain. Mice, with icy feet, sneaked up his backbone, and centipedes with hot claws crawled down. No man can ever *feel* another brain—and yet Blake had just experienced that very feeling—contact with a vague, mindless, inchoate brain that no dream, or attack of nerves, could have conjured up for him.

He reached for a glass of Chablis and downed it at a sudden gulp, before the wash of congratulatory handclasps could reach him. Gideon Pierce suddenly snapped to life and was at his side, sensitive to every deviation from the normal. "Nerves, Tom?"

Blake nodded "Excitement, I guess."

"Go on up, then; I'll take care of them here."

For a second, Blake almost liked the man, hollow though he knew Gideon to be. He let Pierce clear the way for him, not even listening to the man's explanations, and slipped out. Blake's room was on the fourth floor, where he had grown up as a boy, but with a private entrance and stairs that were a later addition. He slipped up to its quiet simplicity; there, in the soft light, with the big logs burning down to coals in the fireplace, seated in his worn leather chair before his desk, he should have been safe from anything.

He should have—but the wrenching came again. There was no light this time, but the same voice was droning frantically in the distance; and again he felt the touch of a brain, filled with stark idiocy, fighting to drive him out of its alien cells. He was aware of a difference this time, though—a coarser, cruder brain, filled with endocrine rage in spite of its lack of thought. It fought, and won, and Blake was suddenly back in his room.

For a second, his senses threatened to crack under hysteria, but he caught them up. In the small bathroom, he found a four-year-old box of barbiturates and swallowed two of them. He knew they wouldn't work for minutes, but the psychological relief of taking them meant something.

The idea of a strange attack on him hit Blake; at once, his fingers flew out to a knob on the desk, pressing it in a secret combination. A concealed drawer slipped out, and he grabbed at the papers inside—they were all there. His brother, James, had spent ten years—and fifty million dollars that had bankrupt and killed him, to get a few diagrams and instructions onto these papers.

Silas McKinley had postulated that some form of military absolutism was inevitable when the greatest weapons of the time required great means to use them—as had the phalanx, the highly-trained Roman Legion, the heavy equipment of feudal knights, or the atomic bombs, planes, and tanks of modern war. Contrariwise, when the major weapons could be owned and used by the general citizenry, then reasonably-peaceful democracy must result, as it had from the colonial muskets of the 18th Century, and would do from the use of James Blake's seemingly-impossible accomplishment.

Unless, Tom added to himself, it could be suppressed. Stealing the papers wouldn't be enough for that; he had them all completely memorized. He managed to grin at his fear, and closed the drawer, just as a knock sounded and Gideon Pierce came in.

WATCHING the man's public mask slip off and reveal a cynical, old face did more to stabilize Blake's emotions than any amount of barbiturates could have done. He motioned to another chair and poured whiskey and soda into a glass, adding ice from the small freezer in the little bar. "Rough down there?"

The older man shook his head. "No—not after we knew you won; I'm used to celebrations. But—my God, Tom—the last month—the way you were going, you didn't have a chance! Getting the nomination was miracle enough—you had no business winning with the stuff you were handing out! It's all right to promise things—but you have to be realistic about even that! When you can't deliver..."

"I'll deliver," Blake told him. "I've always delivered on everything I ever said I'd do; and I've always tried to give them what they really wanted. Now *I* want something—and they give it to me. The old principle, Gideon—cast thy bread upon the water and it shall return after many days."

"Yeah—soggy!" Pierce swirled the drink in his mouth and swallowed it without tasting it. "So what do you get out of it, if you *do* manage to keep some of your promises?"

Insanity, maybe, Blake thought, remembering the mind-wrenching; then he thrust it down. "I get to be President—where I can *really* do some good; where I can give them decent, honest, democratic peace and self-respect."

"Sure." Pierce dragged out a cigar and began chewing on it, shaking his head. "Tom, I'm beginning to believe you mean it. If you do, take the advice of a man who has been around longer; get out of politics! It's no place for you. You're too naive—too filled with bright ideals that are one hundred percent right—except that they neglect human nature. You'll find even the President has opposition, boy; once you *have* the power and somebody bucks you, well—well, you've seen it happen. And you get bitter. I was full of noble thoughts once myself; take a look at what you see on my face now. You don't belong in this racket."

Blake held out a lighter to the other, grinning. "They told me I didn't belong in the newspaper business, Gideon. When I inherited my foster-father's string of yellow, war-mongering journals and decided to build them into the honest, fighting group they are now, they told me I'd go broke. I doubled the circulation."

"Yeah—and probably convinced a few thousand voters to change their ideas—until they voted; then they cast their ballot for favors, and with the same selfish reasons they'd had before. You're as hopeless as your brother James, burning himself out and wasting a fortune on a perpetual motion machine. But you're going to break *my* heart when you find out the facts. Oh, hell! Good night, Governor."

Pierce got up and went out, grumbling before Tom could sputter the words that came to his lips. Then he shrugged; James Blake had deliberately built up a reputation as a crackpot while he went ahead turning a gadget out of the wildest of science fiction speculations into reality. He'd developed a hand-weapon which was equal to a cannon, for offense, and simultaneously protected the user from anything up to the first blast of a hydrogen bomb.

And now it was up to Tom Blake to get to a position where he could have this weapon produced in quantity, and released before it could be suppressed. As President, there would be ways he could do that; with it would come an end to war, once and for all, and the genuine equality of all men. Maybe this was idealism, perhaps even naive—but the Blakes got what they wanted.

He started to undress, and then flopped down on the bed with half his clothes on. It had been a hard day, and those two attacks hadn't helped any; they must have been caused by nervous strain, he thought...and knew he was only trying to deceive himself. But the barbiturates were working, finally, bringing a cloudy euphoria that kept him from pursuing his doubts.

He was reaching up for the light-switch when the third attack came.

CHAPTER TWO

THIS TIME, it was different; the first ones had been mere feelers; now the attack on his mental stability had the sure drive of power and firmness behind it.

The euphoria vanished, as if Blake's thoughts no longer had any relation to his body—which seemed to be the case. He tried to see, and found that there was jet darkness around him. He could no longer feel his arm raised toward the switch—though he was sure he hadn't dropped it, and that the light must still be on. There was no feeling of any kind.

That was wrong, though: he could feel a *pull*, but it bore no relation to anything he had experienced before, except in the two previous fantasies. It was as if immaterial tongs had clasped his thoughts and were lifting them, delicately, but with all the power of the universe. There was a snapping, and then only a wild, confused feeling of transition.

Everything seemed slower than before. Now the pressure guided him toward something—and there was a resistance, which the guiding force could overcome only partially. Streamers of emotion shot out at him—and his own wild desire for a locus and a point of stability met them and clashed in something, which managed to be agonizingly painful, yet without sensation!

Idiocy again!

The brain set against Blake's own mind resisted without thought, without the slightest trace of knowledge. He could sense the wild frenzy with which it collected data as it went and tried to find answers that were not there. Something that might have been a soundless scream of desperation went up from it, as the force guiding Blake managed to press it aside.

Blake felt the probing brain wrenched more wildly than he himself had been handled; again, there was a feeling of something snapping. Beside him, something tried to maintain itself, but without enough individuality to hold it began drifting into nothing, and then was gone. But where it had been, was a suction that dragged him toward it.

He settled suddenly, feeling the alienness of a new location. It wasn't either of the two other places where he *had* been—this was new. There was nothing here to contest with him for his place, but something tried to erase him into the emptiness that had been the idiot-thing before him. From somewhere outside, force and pressure seemed to descend, to mold Blake's new haven into the patterns of his thoughts, and make it accept him. The effort of holding his own, where he himself was still alien, became less; but it now fitted his mind. It was cramped, and without the warmth of his own body, but he was physically alive again.

The pressure vanished, and he relaxed back on the bed suddenly.

But this wasn't Tom Blake's own bed, any more than it was his own body. This was a hard pad under him, in place of the foam-rubber cushion—and this new body seemed to be quite unmindful of the bumpiness, which his own body would have found intolerable.

Blake shook himself, chasing away the final stages of the fantasy this had to be. He was probably half asleep, which made this one last longer; if he opened his eyes...

They seemed to work with difficulty, but they came open finally to show the contour of a body under a dingy, grey sheet—something that must have been black, before it faded. Blake moved his hand, glancing at it. His eyes focused slowly on a heavy, muscular arm, deep brown from sun and wind that ended in a hand covered with hair, and lacking a finger.

Blake tried to scream. He was hysterical inside, but no sound came out; the lack of physical response struck him like a second blow, snapping him out of it.

He wasn't in his own body, and this wasn't a dream. Somehow, something had picked up his thoughts and memories and planted them in the skull of an entirely different man. It couldn't be done, but Blake was here to prove it.

"Magic," came the memory of his brother's words from their adolescence, *"does not exist. It is only a distortion of what could be scientific facts, if properly understood. If poltergeists exist, then accept them, but remember they're natural phenomena obeying natural principles we don't fully understand. That's science."*

BLAKE CLUTCHED at the idea. Nobody had conjured him here, wherever here was; it was the work of intelligence, operating with natural laws—and that could never be fully horrible. He was only feeling horror because the cave-beast that feared the dark was part of his emotional and environmental heritage.

He put the cave-beast down enough to try to find where "here" was.

He found that his head was strapped down, and that webbing under the sheet restrained his new body. Inability to move more than his eyes limited his view to one end of this room. He could see monotracks over his head, with great machines that might have been anything from lamps, to over-sized routers sliding along them, under the cold glare of fluorescent tubes. The wall ahead of him was a featureless grey; the floor was out of his view. And along the wall was a single bench, covered with cots, each holding a body strapped down as Blake's was. Their heads were clamped, hiding them from him; but he could see that each had a hairy hand outside the sheet, and that all the bodies were about the same height and build—fairly tall, and uniformly solid in build. He supposed he fitted the same description, since there was so much uniformity.

As he watched, the machines travelled down the track, stopping in clusters over a few heads at a time, while odd lights glowed, and a whirring sound came from them. From each man under a cluster of machines, there would be a mutter, then a prolonged groan…and silence, until the machines moved on.

It wasn't an inspiring view, and it told Blake almost nothing. He seemed to have seen bits of it before in his first attack, but he couldn't be sure.

As he watched, a door opened in the wall, and a man came through, dressed in a smock that fell to the floor and was of shiny black material. He was tall and thin but wide shouldered, with a face that was frozen into complete lack of expression. A chill shuddered through Blake; this was the same face he'd first seen. Then, somehow, even that bit of familiarity made it easier to take.

He wasn't surprised to hear a mutter in the voice of an old man. It was a complaining sound, ending in a sharp question.

The smocked man shrugged. "I know, Excellency, but we're beyond even the borderland of familiar science here. If it works, it will be a miracle. I told you that then, and I still say it. Once we catch him, we can erase him. But the problem is to catch him—on fancy guesswork as to just what mind-pattern we're looking for, way back then."

"Something worked before." The figure coming through the door now looked at the rows of men, with a sharpness oddly in contrast with the voice. He was of indeterminate age—somewhere between sixty and eighty, Blake thought. But his body was reasonably straight, and with none of the fat or gauntness most older men have. His hair was steel grey—just a shade darker than the soft grey uniform he wore—and his movements were seemingly easy and sure. His face was handsome except for the expression there. The mouth was too straight, the eyes too cynical—and over the aura of power was a hint of repressed but seething fear.

He coughed, and turned to the nearer group of figures on the cots. His voice suddenly lost its touch of tremor, and became the firm, modulated tones of a trained speaker. "Well, don't you think it's time you asked where you are, young man?" he asked.

The nearer figure struggled to sit upright. *"Wahnsinnigkeit! Um Gottes Willen, wenn ich nur frei wachre…"*

"German," the man in the black smock said. "And you don't speak it."

"Never learned it," the older man agreed. He looked down the line, started toward another, and then shrugged; a sudden smile flashed over his face. "Tom Blake, you're the man we want; are you here?"

"Here!" The word ripped out of Blake with an explosive force of its own, while all his uncertainties gathered themselves together in expectation of the explanation that would now mercifully be forthcoming.

The other man beamed. "Good, Tom! Remember the desk combination? We have to be sure." His voice was almost young now.

"Right in, left in, left out, twice left," Blake repeated.

"That's it!" The old man beamed again, and was still smiling as he turned to the man in the black smock. "Okay, Sarnoff. Burn out his brain—and do a good job of it, because I'm watching!"

CHAPTER THREE

BLAKE SCREAMED as the machines suddenly swooped over him, and one began droning again. He had no way of knowing what it would do—but the result was obvious from the shouted words. Sarnoff climbed up and inspected it, giving it a sudden test. Something in Blake's mind slithered, and the force of the alienness grew stronger.

"Pure luck," Sarnoff said, his voice as emotionless as his expression. "Even with what we had to work with, guessing his resonant frequency range was just good luck. I didn't even know whether we could reach back forty years into the past. Excellency, I deserve that bonus—but chance deserves a bigger one."

"You'll get your bonus," the older man agreed, and some of the age crept back into his speech. "Double it. We've got his mind matrix here—here where we can work on it with the burner; that's all I care about. I want it eliminated permanently, Sarnoff."

The other nodded. The machine began to purr again, and Blake felt another scream come to his lips, and freeze there. Forty years into the future—to be eliminated! It wasn't science or magic—it was simply horror. There was no purpose…no right…no…

The slithering began in his brain again. This wasn't the same as the previous force; it was an erasing of himself. Tom Blake's memories began to blur, beginning with the earliest ones. His foster-father suddenly stepped before his mental eye, chuckling at a successful creation of trouble at a disputed border that would be constant headlines for his papers. Then his foster-father was gone, and Blake had no memory of anything before the age of ten.

His brother…what had his brother said? Funny, how he'd ever gotten the chain of newspapers? Someone must have given them to Tom. Then the election was gone, and all he had heard here.

He lay staring up at the pretty lights that glistened in the machine. A dim consciousness of self was left, but it seemed to be half outside his head—as if a funny part of him were trying to pull away and go back somewhere. He had no words, nor could he understand the words that were said in front of him.

His eyes moved whenever sudden motion brought them around by catching their attention. But it was all something interesting in a purely sensory way. He saw Sarnoff test him; he lay for hours in a big room with other bodies that stirred senselessly. He felt them carry him to a truck and place him inside. The motion of the truck was scary and exciting at first, but he went to sleep soon after. His bodily functions woke him, just as the truck came to a sudden halt and other men climbed into it and began carting the drooling creatures with him away somewhere. But then he went to sleep again.

Far away, a part of himself as bereft of words as Tom was, began to cry unhappily, as if conscious that this was wrong. But it didn't waken him.

There were the beginnings of words again, when he finally did begin to come out of his sleep. Slow, bit by tedious part, his mind seemed to be reaching back to its dimmest recesses and pulling facts up for him. Sometimes whole chains of thought would pop into his mind and fade back into his permanent memory. Again, it would take what seemed like years of concentration to root out one totally unimportant thing.

Blake was delighted when he discovered who he was. He mouthed his name to himself, soundlessly. The motion brought some attention; a sharp prick that he somehow identified as a hypodermic needle was thrust into his arm.

"Go to sleep," a soft voice whispered. "Sleep, Jed. We need you whole, and you'll come back better if you don't try too hard. That's it, honey!"

BLAKE WAS himself when he wakened—or rather, that other body with its alien brain which somehow had become himself. He was in a basement, from the smell and the dampness; lying on a cot across the dimly lighted room from a small, crude machine that resembled one he had seen in Sarnoff's place. Another of the men who had been on one of Sarnoff's cots sat near him, watching doubtfully, with some kind of a gun in his hand. And beside him, leaning over to kiss him as he opened his eyes was a girl with an intense, half-pretty face and eyes that could have drawn the damned from Hell straight through the pearly gates.

She held him, moaning softly against him as her lips burned on his. Blake wanted to push her aside for a moment, but the body and brain in which he now lived had a warmer endocrine balance than his own. Desire washed over him, yet with a strange mingling of gentleness and protective instinct. She drew away at last, her eyes misty and shining. "Jed! Oh, Jed."

From the other cot, the man chuckled. "Give him a chance, Sherry! The guy's been through plenty—*I* know!"

She blushed, and dropped her eyes. Blake's mind jerked at the archaic behavior. He studied her more carefully, waiting for hints from them. Obviously, they knew him as the person who had formerly inhabited this body. But beyond that, he had no clues.

Sherry was dressed in a dress that touched the floor and came high on her throat. Even the sleeves were fastened at her wrists. She blushed again, as he watched, and tried to pull the hem of the skirt—or rather, the floor-length, ballooning jodhpurs—down over a toe that was showing. "Jed!" she breathed indignantly. "Not here!"

The man chuckled again, not too nicely, and gave up trying to see the whole of the girl's shoe. He came over to drop on the cot beside Blake, tossing the gun at him. "Here, Jed, you'll need your statidyne. Lucky for you you'd had a light dose of mind-burning before; they really gave you the works that time. We thought there wasn't a trace of a memory left in your head, but Mark swore the brain can't be washed completely a second time. We put you under his restorer, on a chance—and here you are, good as new."

"Not quite." Blake knew he couldn't stay silent forever, and a little truth might help. "I'm not quite the same. I…"

"Blank spots," Sherry moaned it. "We had them with Herman, too… Rufe, can we put him back under the restorer?"

"Mark said he'd gone as far as he could," Rufe told her. "Jed, what's missing? The last few years? After you joined the movement, or before?"

"Not after, Jed," Sherry begged. But Blake nodded slowly.

Rufe motioned Sherry out. "This is going to be rough," he warned her. "No stuff for mixed company when we talk about *him* in a hurry. Even if you have been married three years."

She kissed Blake quickly, while he absorbed the fact that he was now officially married, and then she slipped out after an elaborate examination through small cracks in a doorway. Rufe came closer, squatting down.

RUFE'S TALK was a quick summary of why Blake had apparently joined a rebel movement against the dictator this world seemed to have. It was old stuff to anyone who had grown up in a world where Hitler and Mussolini had been daily fare in the papers, with only a personal element added. The Bigshot—obviously a swearword now—had taken over slowly, always with the velvet glove over the steel fist. He'd apparently had some sort of invincible weapon, since he'd united the whole world under his heel.

Then he'd begun reforming it. Criminals first—and then non-conformists had been treated to progressively more severe erasure of all memory and personality. The unfit had been sterilized. All labor had been handled through the State; all profits were "equalized", and the Iron Guard had grown up, using weapons that could not be overcome. Finally, the mind-burning and sterilization had gotten out of hand; complaints had added up until the rebels began to sprout under every tree—as Blake found he had rebelled after being pronounced unsafe, and receiving sterilization. Twice, they had tried to revolt, and twice they had been battered down. Now the third try was due, without any better chance against the invincible Bigshot.

But they had discovered from Mark, the spy in Sarnoff's laboratory who had built their restorer, that there was less time than they thought. A new rejuvenation treatment had been found: in two weeks, the eighty year old dictator would be restored to something like forty. From meaningless gabble with Blake in Sarnoff's laboratory, Rufe was sure the man was now in his dotage; however there wouldn't be any chance against him after he was restored to his age of greatest vigor.

"Playing jokes like that," Rufe finished shaking his head. "Used to burn us quick, but now he's making a big game of it, *drat*—no, by golly, darn him! You rest up a couple of days, Jed. We're going to need you!"

Blake didn't try to press Rufe for more details; this was an old familiar story in history, even though it seemed to be a burning new one to Rufe. But it puzzled Blake—here was exactly the events which he was hoping to end with his brother's weapon. He protested weakly, "I'm not that important to you, Rufe."

"You're not! You don't think they pulled a broad-daylight rescue for me, do you? No sir! Another week, when we get that entrance blasted, you're going to be the man of the hour—the man who can outshoot all of us, that's who. We can't go without our head executioner can we? Jed, when you get Mr. Bigshot Thomas Blake in your sights, I'd…Hey what's wrong?"

"Nothing," Blake managed.

But Rufe was already leaving. "I talk too much when you need sleep. You rest up, Jed, and I'll see you later."

CHAPTER FOUR

BLAKE SAT rigidly, trying to fit it into his knowledge, and finding it an indigestible lump. For minutes, he tried to convince himself he was suffering from delusions—but that explanation required such a degree of insanity that the question of "reality" wouldn't matter at all; he rejected it.

Blake decided to see what sort of order he could make by accepting the events and objects at their face value.

There was a sort of pattern. Someone had taken the trouble to fish Tom Blake's mind up through forty years, in the hope of eliminating it. That "someone" was Sarnoff, and Sarnoff was obviously working for—for the Bigshot; then the man behind what had happened to Tom Blake had to be Tom Blake himself, as he was in this later age—or, perhaps, someone near the throne who regarded the make of forty years ago a menace to the Blake of "now." Then, because of this man Mark, he—the younger Blake—had been saved, simply because the body in which the younger Blake's consciousness rested was the body of one of the rebels' chief tools.

Blake remembered a phrase he'd often heard, "A is not A;" here was an example of it, and with a vengeance!

Somehow, on all sides, he—young Tom Blake as he now was beginning to think of himself—was supposed to be a menace to his later self. Tom Blake A was presently embroiled in a war—a "future" war—where his sole purpose was to kill off Tom Blake N—the product of forty years of Tom Blake A's living.

He wanted to reject the proposition; he rebelled against it; every reaction shouted, "I am I; I am Tom Blake; I *won't* change!"

He put it into the back of his mind, as he had learned slowly to do with things that had no seeming answer, afraid to touch it further—consciously, at least. He picked up the gun Rufe had left him, and began examining it. A hinge on the top of the plastic case caught his eye, and a second later the case lay open.

It was the gun James Blake had invented—the gun that was supposed to end all strife, prevent war, and bring in eternal democracy!

Then Tom shook his head; this was only part of that gun. The original invention, which had taken years of work by "geniuses" under the "super-genius" leadership of James, was simply a selective stasis field. It surrounded a man with a bubble of force—or lack of force, depending on how you phrased it; that bubble was carefully adjusted on several levels, so that nothing material beyond a certain low speed, and no energy-particle beyond a certain level of energy, could travel through it. The further from the limits, the greater the resistance, on an asymptotic curve. Light could pass; soft x-rays were slowed and worked down to safe limits; gamma radiation was bounced back. Or, while something travelling only a few miles an hour, up to about fifty, met almost no opposition, anything having the speed of a bullet, or that of a concussion-wave from a bomb met an impregnable wall.

But all that was missing from this gun. There was only the offensive force—a simple means of projecting a beam of that static force at a variable speed, so that whatever it hit seemed to be moving toward it. At low speeds, it could knock over or stun; at light speed, it could blast a hole through a mountain, with absolutely no reaction against the user's hand. Theoretically, its range was infinite, limited only by the fact it travelled in a straight line. Since it wasn't a true force, it actually required almost no energy, and could run for years off a tiny dry-cell.

On the back was stamped the serial number—a figure over forty billion and the price—two dollars! Obviously, James' weapon was being used generally, but not as it had been intended; apparently only the Iron Guard had the whole mechanism—if anyone had.

Damn the dictator who could pervert it to such use!

TOM BLAKE stopped, realizing he was damning himself; it made less sense than ever. All the rest of the indictment against the Bigshot had more sides; there was justification for erasing the brains of criminals and for sterilizing the unfit—and he had heard only one side, which might actually be a criminal side. The uniting of the world under one rule was something he had long dreamed of, and was certainly justified.

But such perversion of the weapon was another matter; it was something Blake felt he could never rationalize to himself, even if he lived to be a hundred.

And the morality bothered him. Obviously, prudery had been reintroduced, and carried to an extreme. He'd been puzzling over it, without too much success. For an absolute ruler, it might have its advantages; it would both serve to occupy a good deal of time and thought on the part of the masses, and impose limits on them, which the ruler would not necessarily be compelled to admit for himself. It would make them more subservient to authority. But it wasn't the move of a man who wanted to improve the world.

Sherry came in, then, as if to prove his point . She drew a cot up beside him and lay down, fully clothed. He noticed that her garments were fastened with a great many buttons, and without a zipper anywhere. His own clothes, when he looked, were as intricately fastened.

"Jed," she whispered. "Jed, I'm sorry I—I kissed you—in front of Rufe. I'm so ashamed!"

He reached out a reassuring hand, flame leaping up in his body again. There was something about her eyes and the way she avoided showing even a trace of her feet; and wrists…

She caught his hand, then jerked her own back. "Jed—not here. Someone might come in!"

Someone did, shortly after she fell asleep, while Blake was still twisting and turning in his own mind—if even his mind was still his own. He pretended sleep, when Rufe led the other up to him.

"You're crazy, Mark," the man whispered, "do you think Sherry wouldn't know her own husband?"

Mark was a young man with a troubled face and eyes sunk in their sockets under scraggly brows. He looked like early pictures of Lincoln, except for the incongruity of a short, stubbed nose. Now he shook his head. "I don't know, Rufe. I didn't quite like his response when I got out to rebuild his brain patterns. Sarnoff's switching minds—it's the only answer I can get to all the machinery he's using. And I think he may have been trying to run in a ringer on us."

"A spy?"

"What else? Probably one of those other men was from the Guard, and they switched minds. But still…well, I can't see Sherry sleeping beside anyone unless she was sure it was Jed! And I don't see why a ringer wouldn't pretend to remember everything, instead of admitting his mind is partly numbed—as it should be, after what hit Jed!"

"So what do we do?" Rufe asked.

"We don't do anything. We can't test him by having him shoot—that's conditioned reflex, outside his mind. We take him along, making sure he doesn't meet anyone else until we break in. Then he either shoots the Bigshot—"

"Shh, Mark! Sherry's here."

"Sorry. Slipped. He either shoots, or we shoot him. With the only opening we can find, that first shot has to be good all the way across the chamber, before the automatics cut on the screen around *him*. Jed's got the only reflexes that can do it."

THEY WENT out, leaving Blake to his thoughts—which weren't pretty. He wasn't going to enjoy shooting himself on the amount of evidence he had; and he liked the idea of being shot at his present age even less.

They didn't sound like a criminal mob—not even like one of the possible radical malcontent segments that might grow up in any government. They sounded, unfortunately, like honest citizens getting ready for another Lexington and Concord—the very type of citizen he had hoped to develop with his own ideas and James' gun.

But Tom Blake still couldn't picture himself as a monster. He'd spent a good many years under every sort of temptation he could imagine, and he'd grown steadily more convinced that the world belonged to the decent, normal folk in it—not to any Bigshot, including himself. He felt he should be able to trust himself more than he could trust anyone else in this cockeyed age.

The trouble was that it was cockeyed—and there was no reason for it. It should have been a utopia; why hadn't the later Blake given the defensive part of the gun out?

Or was that one under the control of someone else—the old man who had been with Sarnoff, perhaps? The old man looked capable of anything, and he'd proved completely ruthless. If the real Thomas Blake of this period was simply a front, forced somehow to do the will of another other…

But how could he be forced when no weapon would hurt him?

* * *

Blake got up in the morning with his eyes burning from lack of sleep, and no nearer the answer than before. Under Sherry's urging, he began an hour of target practice, using the slowest "speed" of the gun; Mark had been right—his shooting was pure conditioned reflex, and hadn't been hurt by the change.

He'd reached only one emotional and one logical conclusion, and he mulled them over at breakfast. Emotionally, he wanted to get back to his own age somehow, to his own body—as he had to do sometime if there was ever to be an elder Blake. Logically, he knew he couldn't go, if he had the choice, until he found out the facts about what he had become.

But there were a number of questions that had come up as he lay tossing. He didn't believe in variable time—the whole theory of the stasis gun demanded a fixed, absolute cause-and-effect time-scheme in the universe, somehow; and the gun worked. That meant the elder Blake had been through all this before, and should know every move he would make. Why had he slipped through the fingers of the Sarnoff group? Also, if he did get back to his own time—as he had to, seemingly—how could he do anything about what he could become, even if the worst was true?

That night he was assigned permanent quarters—his old ones, apparently—with Sherry. There he found that some of her morality vanished, while some of his own got in his way, at first. And it didn't make it any easier to feel that she belonged to a crowd of criminals or crackpots when his emotions began to become solidly entrenched in his head.

He was obviously falling in love with a girl who believed his highest mission in life was to shoot his older self!

CHAPTER FIVE

BLAKE—OR rather Jed—was supposed to be a spatula man at the local yeast works, but he'd saved up three of his quarterly vacations to take a whole month off now. Sherry had done the same with her vacations at the fabric converter. As a result, they had time on their hands while the major part of the revolutionists were away at work; there were a number of places of entertainment, but Blake chose a newsreel theater.

He came away disgusted, and yet doubtful. All the old trappings of a dictator's propaganda bureau were there, with the usual justifications and arbitrary associations of words that had no real meaning. There was brutality enough. A revolt in Moscow against the local office of the State had been put down by Iron Guards, who moved about in complete invulnerability, using their weapons to stun the roiling crowds. There was surprisingly little bloodshed, though. But the scene where the prisoners were released mercifully back to their parents and friends was far from a happy one. All had been put through the mind-burners, and were back to the first days of infancy, mentally.

Still, there was a regular shuttle running to the Moon, and Mars was being explored. China, on the other hand, was starving; and obviously no attempt was being made to alleviate the situation. Apparently the State believed in letting local suffering go—or perhaps had insufficient resources.

He guessed that the latter was the case, particularly when a new edict of sterilization was announced for Brazil, due to unchecked birth rates. The sterilization was painless enough, and didn't impair sexuality, but such blanket use could only come from sheer necessity.

The State was loose at the seams; disease had been conquered, and while the rejuvenation process was new, secret—and obviously forbidden for general use—the progress in gerontology and geriatrics had been amazing. In making the whole world one State, the birthrate of one section had simply flooded another, leaving no natural controls. There were no wars. Progress in foods had been good, but it hadn't equaled the birth-rate; there were over ten billion inhabitants of Earth.

Perhaps the new morality had been an attempt to check the birthrate, but it had failed; public morals can be swayed—private hungers only break out more intensely. Then, apparently, had come an increasing use of sterilization against progressive feeble-mindedness, physical hereditary ills, alcoholism, sub-normal intelligence, subversive tendencies, and so on up the list until less than half the population could pass the tests. When India refused to use voluntary birth-control the first large use of the sterility process had been forced on her, leaving less than five percent of her people fertile. It hadn't helped much; China had immediately begun to flow over the borders.

And, inevitably, people suffered. Housing was bad—single-room shacks were common, except in what could be called the modern slums, thrown up to house hordes in worse conditions. Food was mostly synthetic now. The people lived poorly, even though they were on a twenty-hour week, and free to buy surprising types of luxuries at small prices.

The newsreel had referred to this as "the Period of Transition," but there was no sign of it getting anywhere.

BLAKE CAME out shaken, unable to justify the results or to condemn the ideas behind them, completely. Back in 1960, it had been a simple world, with a few minor troubles; now, he wondered. Most of the troubles here came from the relief of those simple troubles there—and it was questionable whether the dictatorship had much to do with it, beyond attempts to cure the ills so obvious then. He suspected that the brewing revolution had more connection with the bad food and inadequate housing than the more obvious high-handed State methods.

He found himself liking the people. They were what he had always dreamed of—a group devoted to liberty, willing to sacrifice themselves if necessary, with an amazing respect for each other's rights. Out of them, conceivably, a new world could come—the world he had always aimed for.

Do nothing, Blake told himself, and the plot would fail. The rebels made tests of the gun's reaction-time, measuring the period between the instant that the peephole in the weapon's shield was uncovered to the moment when firing the gun would accomplish nothing. The period was too short for most of them to pull the trigger. He, in Jed's body, had been just enough better than the others to make it possible; no automatic device would work, because they had no way of knowing where the Bigshot would be in the single room where he apparently gave himself the luxury of going without his personal shield.

Do something, and he was killing himself—and perhaps ruining what was really only the "Period of Transition" they prattled about.

He got back to the little shack where he and Sherry lived just in time to see a new development. A wail went up along the street as a great van drove up, and Blake stopped to stare at the miserable creatures that were piling out. They couldn't stand on their legs; their minds had been burned completely. And among them was Rufe.

Two fingers were missing from the gun-hands of each of them, cut off and already healing under the efficient modern surgery.

Mark met Blake and yanked him inside, where Sherry was crying. "We thought they'd got you. New orders. Not even the technicians at Sarnoff's know, but I saw a copy. All men with hairy hands are to get fifteen minute burns—enough so they'll never be more than morons, and we can't rebuild their minds. And—well, you saw the rest. Sherry, shut up! They didn't get him!"

"They will…they will…" She lay huddled for a second more. Then, as the van drove off, leaving the people to sort out their unfortunate friends, she dashed out to help. Her sobs drifted back to him, but didn't seem to hurt her usefulness in the crowd.

Blake went to the rickety cabinet where his gun lay and picked it up. Mark caught him. "That can wait. Come in here." Lather and razor were waiting, and he began shaving the back of Blake's hands deftly. "We can't do much of this—the others will have to take their chances. But we need you."

The anger wore off as the shaving was completed.

MARK STEPPED back to inspect Blake's hands. "You'll do—Sherry can take care of it the rest of the time. Jed, I still can't trust you completely, but you've got to come through. Once we get the Bigshot, we can move on down the line. All the shields have time-limits built in—that's why we never got anywhere trying to get any for our own use. In two weeks, the second group will have to recharge the trigger-battery relay; only the Bigshot has the key for that. Another ten days, and the third line drops; and it goes on down to the Guards. They have to get their shields set every day. Maybe a few of the higher group will manage to get guns from lowers they can recharge themselves—but their keys change automatically every period, so it won't help much, if we move fast. It all depends on your getting the Bigshot."

"You're going to have a busy time converting them or burning their minds," Blake guessed.

"Burning? Don't be a fool, Jed. We'll kill the bas—the sons! They've got it coming to them. And don't think we're just talking. The rebels, as they call us, outnumber the rest of the world five to one!"

Blake put the gun back on the table as if it had stung him. Killing off twenty percent of the population might help the crowding, but it wasn't his idea of a solution—particularly when a lot of the higher technicians, scientists, and coordinators necessarily belonged to the elite who owned the guns that were equipped with shields.

Anyhow, even without the shields, there were enough plain guns, and the whole State corps would have to fight back—those in secret sympathy with the rebel movement would be driven to it by self-preservation. It would be a welter of blood to make the worst war in history seem anemic.

"When?" he asked, finally. "The same date?"

Mark shook his head. "I got orders today. We move on the palace night after tomorrow—as soon as we can force through the passage we found on the maps and set up equipment to rip away the wall where you shoot. And you'd better shoot straight!"

CHAPTER SIX

THOMAS BLAKE watched them assemble, while sounds from above ground told him that operations were already in progress. They'd modeled their outward move on a slight improvement over the second revolt. It meant that a fair number of them would be killed in the crisscrossing of stun-blasts, but nobody seemed to consider that important.

It would at least keep all the local Iron Guard busy; and probably stir up their officers enough to disorganize the whole palace. There would be fighting on almost every street, and the bulk of their mob would be storming the palace itself from mined tunnels they were digging frantically. All was to be concentrated to reach its highest fury at precisely midnight.

"How do you know *he* will be there?" Blake asked.

Sherry looked at him in surprise. "He's been boasting for years that a clear conscience induces sleep, and that his puts him to bed at midnight every night. He'll never believe we have a chance until it's too late."

It sounded plausible; dictators usually showed their pride in just such stupid ways. Anyhow, Blake had to confess to himself, it was exactly the thing he'd been starting to say for the past year; he'd meant it as a joke, but such things became habits in time.

Yet he *must* know. Thomas Blake, the Bigshot, had necessarily been Thomas Blake in Jed's body forty years before. He'd heard every plan, and he should remember it.

Blake fingered the two guns he carried—one for any trouble on the street, the other for the coup they were attempting. He couldn't let these people down. The honest desperation on their faces wouldn't permit all this courage and planning to go for nothing. He couldn't kill his older self and invite such a savage massacre as only the French Reign of Terror could match.

History was becoming clearer now. Blake's fine, free colonial people had been men of courage—and men of strong hatreds. They'd slaughtered the Indians just as readily as they had marched against tyranny. And even their opposition to tyranny had been founded more on hate than on any innate love of justice. Justice, in fact, had come about as a sort of afterthought—when the men they hated had fled or were killed.

He was sweating coldly in the dank basement under the old auditorium. Some decision *had* to be made; none was possible.

The ten in the execution-party moved out at last, trying to look like non-partisans caught in the whirls of the rising rebellion, and anxiously heading homewards.

Something struck against Blake's back, and he stumbled. His hand leaped to the gun at his waist instantly, and he fired before he was sure of his target. It was a head-shot, by sheer instinct; the blow that might have only stunned, knocked the man's head back sharply, until it seemed to dangle on his neck..

SURPRISINGLY, the weapons of the others echoed his—silent in themselves, but causing loud thuds whenever the beams hit. The surprise of seeing the whole group fire into their own crowd of rebels cut short the sickness that was rising in Blake. He turned, just as one of the black-clothed Iron Guard came up.

"Good shooting," the man said. "But take it easy. That first shot was vicious and we don't want killing. Here, bunch up. So—I think I can stretch my shield enough to give us all some protection."

Sherry looked up at him with grateful awe written large on her face. "Thank you, officer. We were going home to my aunt's from a party—and then all this happened..."

The Guard nodded. "It'll get worse, from what I'm told. But right now, I guess I can escort you a ways. Where to, ma'am?"

"The subway, I guess," she answered. "We'll be safer there than on the street, anyway."

The Guard nodded, and began leading them. Some of the force from the stun blasts got through, with the shield stretched out—a trick Blake hadn't known was possible—but it helped.

Blake caught at the man's sleeve while they waited for a yelling mob to dash by. "How do you get to be a Guard?" he asked.

The man looked around in surprise. "I thought everyone knew that, citizen. We're picked when we're in school—character, intelligence, all that. Then we get twenty years training in science, sociology, and everything else you can name. It's pretty tough, but worth it—except for these riots. There the mob has all the advantage—our shields don't protect us from stones and clubs, and we can't use lethal speed on our guns without special orders. Lot of the mob gets trampled on, too."

They were at the subway, then, and Blake started down. He jerked back at a sudden gasp, to see the Guard falling, his head bloody pulp from a sap in Mark's hand.

The leader of the group put the sap away, smiling in grim satisfaction. "Darned—sorry, Sherry—dratted hypocrite. I don't mind the ones that go around beating us up on the sly or giving us tickets for standing on corners. But these mealy-mouthed polite ones! Fpha! They're too good for us! Hey, Jed, what's the matter?"

Blake held back the retching of his stomach and forced a grin to his lips. "Too much Guard," he answered, and saw an approving smile cross Sherry's lips.

He avoided looking at her then as they went down the steps. He'd heard enough to know that in general the Guards were like the one Mark had killed; they'd been conditioned into believing that to serve the State was all that mattered, but they'd also been taught manners, courtesy, and at least a normal consideration of the people under them. There was no more justice in Mark's words than in his brutal action.

The train was pulling in, and Mark waved them aboard. If the riots developed properly it might be one of the last ones to run along on its rubber-insulated monorail.

They found their mistake too late, just as the door was closing. It was a Guard train, carrying prisoners back to the palace. Apparently the Guards who had taken it over had lacked the key needed to break the automatic controls that stopped it at every station.

They were inside before the Guards at the door could stop them. Mark yelled once, and began swinging the sap. Blake skewed sideways as the train started, to pounce into the stomach of an older Guard. He kicked at a shin, jerked around the pain-doubled man, and darted for a strap. His other hand found the big clasp knife that most of the men carried, and he dragged it from his pocket. The plastic strap came loose, its heavy metal hand-hold forming a perfect close-quarters club.

THIS WAS no time to argue about the right and wrong of killing Guards. His pacifist inclinations were intellectual, and his emotions had been well conditioned in two lives: Jed had been a natural brawler, and Blake had done rather well in the usual school and high-school fracases. In a brawl of this side, the issues were simplified to the basic question of whose side you came in on.

The Guards were handicapped. They were responsible for a group of prisoners, and their normal security was useless here, since all fighting was at close quarters, with weapons too slow to be bothered by their shields. The prisoners were naturally against them—and even handcuffed, their legs were enough to upset the Guards, while some of them were able to get to the doors and prevent men from joining the police force from other cars.

Blake swung out, protecting the rest of his party on one side while they cut their own straps. Then a pattern of general mayhem began; he felt a big fist jolt against his ear and reeled, but Jed's body was rugged. He swung a backhand that dragged the handle across the Guard's teeth with a crescendo clicking. It caught one of the prisoners on the follow-through, but the man cheerfully plunged into the pleasure of breaking the Guard's ribs with his heavy shoes.

The train slowed at another station, but nobody left; the Guards were jammed in, and the citizens were too busy.

Blake's wrist was sore from the pounding when he finally switched hands. At the next station, they heaved out the unconscious Guards. Mark prepared to move back into the next car, until one of the other men caught his hand and pointed. Apparently, they'd reached their destination.

The closing doors caught Blake across the shoulders, sending him sprawling to his hands and knees. He saw that most of the party, including Sherry and Mark, were out, and then was up, dashing after them. Guards were pouring down the entrance, with a mob behind them. Mark yelled.

The group darted into the men's washroom. Sherry hesitated, but she swallowed her inculcated prudery and followed them. The door shut with a sound that indicated a lock had already been added to it. Mark knocked on a white panel, and it swung open.

"Clear sailing," he told them, breathing harshly through what remained of his teeth. One eye was swelling closed, and his lip was smashed, but he obviously didn't feel it. "Good work, Jed. I guess I was wrong about you, at that. Well, we're under the palace!"

CHAPTER SEVEN

WITH THE two who had been waiting in the tunneled passage from the washroom, there were nine of them now. Nine men to end the tightest rule any man had held on the planet and uncounted millions outside serving as a screen for their operations.

For a few minutes, all Blake's doubts had been settled, but they came back now.

"Two minutes, maybe," Mark announced. "Lew, you come with Jed and me. The rest stay back."

"I'm coming," Sherry stated. Her glance at Mark was defiant, and then surprised as the man merely shrugged.

Two minutes to make up his mind. Blake couldn't even get his ledgers out for a book-balancing in that length of time. He'd posted too many entries in the day-book, and the whole business needed a complete new audit. But now it boiled down to the simple question of whether he *could* kill himself—even if he decided he *should* do so.

He *thought* he *could*. He'd always been sure he could commit suicide for a cause he believed in, if necessary—and this was the same thing, with a forty-year lapse between pulling the trigger and dropping dead.

The passageway was crude, and they stumbled upwards slowly. They were obviously inside a wall, where tamped earth had been used to fill the space left by the masonry. It was thick with age and dirt odors, and Mark's flash barely lighted their way. They crawled up now on their hands and knees. Then a bulky piece of machinery appeared ahead, facing a blank stone wall.

Lew went to it. "All tapped. If we aimed it right, this should pull out the plug left, and there'll be a hole big enough to shoot through . Better get used to the light, Jed."

Blake focused his eyes where the flash was, while Mark brought it around until it rested on the plug that the machine was gripping. Lew touched a button, and the machine whined faintly.

For the moment, he had decided. On one side was courage and devotion; on the other side, retreat and aloofness behind thick stone walls. When in Rome…well, it was as good a rule as any now. And maybe he was only doing it to convince himself he had the courage to fire at himself.

The plug popped out and sidewise, leaving a six-inch opening. Blake got a quick view of a tremendous room, at least a hundred feet long, with a bed at the far side. On the bed, stark naked and asleep lay the older man who had been in Sarnoff's laboratory—Thomas Blake the Bigshot. Tom Blake N. He should have guessed!

The gun was already up, and swinging into position. His thoughts seemed to have swiveled off into a dimension where time was infinitely variable. It wouldn't be hard now. The man had already proven his duplicity, had tried to wipe out his own younger self. Why shouldn't that younger self eliminate him?

"He's naked!" Sherry's horrified whisper sounded beside Blake's ear, just as the trigger came back.

It was a clean miss, he had jerked at the last split second.

HELL EXPLODED inside. Gongs sounded, and Guards came pouring out of every cranny, while the old man sat up, staring quietly at the hole in the wall. His old eyes found it before the Guards did, and he pointed.

Mark let out a yell, and pushed the other three ahead of him. They went sprawling down the tunnel, just as a tremendous thwack reached their ears, what was left of Mark fell past them. Sherry was ahead, and Lew behind. Blake started to look back, but he had no need, another sound broke out, and half of Lew's head went past his ear, spattering gore.

Then they hit a curve in the tunnel. The big booming of the high-speed stasis guns went on, but they were simply cutting holes through the palace now, unable to locate their targets.

They hit the washroom, charging through those who had waited behind. The lock was stuck, and one of the men was working on it. There was no need to report the results to anyone—Sherry's face gave that away.

She was sobbing and cursing herself in the same breath. Then she met Blake's eyes hopelessly, with the expression of Judas the day after. He started toward her, but she cut him off quickly. "We'll have to split up—they saw us together, up there. I'll be at the cellar—where they brought you back—tomorrow!"

The door finally came loose, and she darted out. He could sense the feelings in her, but there was nothing he could do. He let her go, giving her time to get away, before he sped up the steps after her. The station was almost deserted, except for a dead Guard and several badly wounded citizens.

Behind him, the sound of the stasis guns came again, indicating that guards had broken down through the tunnel and were after him. He sped up the stairs, expecting to find the street, instead, he came out into a monstrous hall, crowded at the entrance by a mass of guards defending a big gate that had dropped. Blake raced up the hall, swinging off at the first stairway. He cut down another hall, and darted into a room at random. There was a fat dowager inside, stripped to ankle-length pantaloons and camisole, but she gave no trouble; she simply fainted.

On a dressing table, he spotted a gun, and picked it up. There were stasis screen controls on it, but a series of buttons along the side indicated some sort of combination lock—which explained why the citizens didn't bother to fool with them; they probably were set to explode on tampering.

He dropped it and went through the back of the suite. There windows opened on a closed court. It was a drop of no more than ten feet, and he took it. One set of windows was dark. He kicked through one of them, and banged his head against something hanging from the ceiling. By the dim light of the red and green lights on a control panel, he suddenly recognized it as the laboratory of Sarnoff.

HE KNEW the way out, now—and one which was probably less besieged than others, simply because men avoided something that was a chancre in their minds. But he halted suddenly, moving toward the control panel.

Blake was right—there was a scattering of tools in a drawer under it, and barely enough light to work by. He yanked out the two guns and opened them; they were familiar enough—mere simplifications of the complete models his brother had made.

Blake ripped the tiny coil out of one hastily, and fitted it into open space in the other. There was room enough. He found small screwdrivers and began working on the adjustments to the coils, hoping that the numbering around the slots was the same. Alpha 10 changed to Alpha 2 to give a protective sphere instead of an offensive beam; beta 5 would regulate the speed which would be denied penetration; delta 7 should be about right for energy penetration. He checked that, setting it up to 9, until the green bulbs seemed to come down to the red, and back to 7. Apparently, there had been no basic change in the little coils, and offensive and protective coils were still the same, except for setting. He found contacts within the gun for the second coil, indicating that both models were made from the same basic parts. He had to leave the defensive coil on, since he could find no way of installing a switch.

If his settings were right, he was now safe from bombs and bullets, though a club or a knife would kill him as easily as before. But the main problem was the offensive beams from other guns, and there a rough setting would cancel it out.

He shoved the gun that was now complete into its holster and headed toward the entrance.

From the side, a quiet voice reached him. "Nice work, Thomas Blake."

The lights snapped on to show Sarnoff standing expressionlessly beside the main door.

CHAPTER EIGHT

SARNOFF nodded toward the gun that had snapped out in Blake's hand. "It probably works now, just as you expect. But it wasn't that which gave you away. You might as well put it away, anyhow; naturally, I'm shielded."

Blake had already realized that, from the gun on the other's hip. He dropped his own back, trying to estimate his chances to reach the other before the man could get out the door. It seemed impossible.

Sarnoff nodded again. "You're right; you couldn't make it I've been ready for you since you tripped the alarms getting in here. I could have shot you while you were working on the gun, you see. But naturally, I didn't."

"Naturally."

"Certainly, why else do you think I faked the last half of the mind burning? I'm all in favor of your living. I'd hate to try to figure out any system of logic that would permit you to be killed without ruining most of the life I've led these last years. Anyhow, I always back the winner."

Blake let it sink in, and began breathing again. "You mean you're on the side of the rebels?"

"Hardly." A trace of a smile flickered over the other's face and vanished again. "I'm on the side of whichever one wins, though that's rather obvious, if you'll use your head. I fish you out of the past for your distinguished senior self—and I make sure that you go into the head of a man the rebel spy Mark wanted saved; he can't prove I'm on his side, but he suspects so—particularly after I showed him the rough diagram of the restorer a year ago and never noticed the parts he stole."

"Mark's dead," Blake told him.

"I know—he was a fanatic, so of course he's dead. But he wasn't the leader of the group anyhow! I have my connections, still. I'll come out on top—as a realist always will, unless he's a deliberate villain, which I'm not."

"All right," Blake conceded wearily. He had no time to talk of idealism and realism now, when his first job was to escape long enough to locate Sherry. "So what happens next?"

Sarnoff shrugged. "So you go out the door, I suppose, and into the arms of the Guards who *are* there—or down this little private stair to the subway station, where you'll never be noticed by now. And I report to your rebel leaders—whom you don't know—that you are the original Blake, complete with all plans for the James Blake statidyne gun."

Blake turned toward the little private door, and was almost surprised to find that there was a stairway there. Probably most of the so-called "public" sections of the palace had such exits.

Sarnoff's voice halted him. "Not a louse, Blake," he said quietly. "Just an opportunist, like every successful animal up the long road of evolution. And paradoxical as you may think it, I privately wish you the best of luck. I've thoroughly liked your senior self, and I would probably like you. Take care of yourself."

The laboratory was suddenly dark. Blake stumbled down the stairs, to find that the riots were nearly over, and the subways were running smoothly again. Guards were patrolling the platform, but the monotrain was already in. For the third time, Blake barely made it before the door could close.

HE GRINNED bitterly at Sarnoff's words that were still ringing in his ears. It wasn't hard to tell who'd lose, at least; Blake had forty-three cents to his name, and knew nothing about the city. The State wanted him as an attempted assassin. Now, with Sarnoff's spreading the good word, the rebels would be looking for him as a traitor to them, and the very man they most wanted to eliminate from all history. It wouldn't do to argue immutable time with them, either.

He was safe from bombs, bullets, and guns—but there was always the knife. And when she found the facts, even Sherry might be happy to use it.

He should never have been stampeded into mob action—his reason for killing the Bigshot because of the first meeting was no more valid than the Bigshot's reason for trying to destroy him in self-defense. And now that he cooled down, he could never take the secret of the guns to the rebels. There had been blood enough shed, without putting them in a position to exterminate all the other side.

He never knew exactly how he managed to get through the night. Time after time, he saw Guards or rebels patrolling, and he suspected most of them were looking for him. Probably the complete dejection and the slowness of his walk saved him, they must have been looking for a man who was skulking up dark alleys, or running from them.

He found the house where he had first come to in the cellar by sheer luck, though he knew the general location. It was locked, of course, and he realized suddenly that he did not know the secret for opening it.

But he was tired of running, and a cellar door in the shack across the street was open. He crossed to it, and went inside, leaving the door open a crack.

Daylight crept through the opening, and reached the full brightness of noon. There was no sign of Sherry. Above him, he could hear a family stirring over their noon lunch, discussing the riots. Apparently they had been involved only indirectly, but there was enough misery in their guesses as to how many of their friends would be picked up and mindburned.

At four in the afternoon, Guards came and broke into the house where the place of meeting was. They scoured it thoroughly, then posted it.

Blake knew that Sherry hadn't told on him—she should have, if she'd heard the truth about him, but he was sure somehow that she would never turn him over to the Guards. He also knew then that she'd never keep the rendezvous.

He buckled his gun on more firmly, knocked the dust off his knees where he had been kneeling, and stood up. The cellar door creaked as he went through it, but the Guards did not look up from their duty. Blake crossed the street and went up to them.

"If you're looking for a lady, she won't be here," he said, and only the deadness of his voice registered in his own ears.

The younger Guard growled impatiently. "Scram. We know what we're doing!"

"Dan!" The senior Guard glowered at the other. "That's enough of that. Citizen, the State apologizes, but I'm afraid your information is already in the papers, so we do know about it."

Blake nodded, and shuffled off down the dingy street. He found a newsstand and put down a coin for one of the papers he had managed forty years in the past. It was thinner, due to the paper scarcity, but the lack was mostly in the advertising. He had no trouble finding the story.

Sherry was dead!

She'd been found by the Guards early in the morning, with a printed label claiming she had betrayed the cause by ruining the shot. It was clearly murder.

HE MIGHT have guessed. The hatred that had flowered so long had to take root somewhere, and she had been as good a scapegoat as any other, Blake supposed. He dropped the paper into a can without bothering to read further. He'd seen that she was being kept at the palace morgue for the claiming of her body.

They'd dragged him into this crazy future to keep him from killing himself, by a tortuous logic of their own. Then they'd tossed him to the other side, to force him to kill himself. Now, the only good thing he'd found was killed, and nothing else had been accomplished. No paradox had been solved; but if the Bigshot remembered when he had been dragged here, he could have saved Sherry, at least.

Blake saw another of the Guards on the corner, and approached him quietly. "Where can I find the subway to the palace?"

"To your left three blocks," the Guard answered absently. Then he looked up; reached for his gun, and moved forward. "Your identification papers, citizen!"

"No matter," Blake told him. "I'm the assassin!"

CHAPTER NINE

BLAKE SWUNG on his heel and headed toward the subway. He didn't bother to look back at the faint sound of the gun being drawn. His shield worked or it didn't, he would have no way of knowing unless the man fired, he'd find out soon enough. Nothing happened.

Then the Guard was running up to him, white of face, with the gun shaking in his hands. The man stuttered as he grabbed for Blake's arm. "You're under arrest!"

"All right," Blake agreed. "I'm it; now you go hide."

He walked on steadily, while the Guard pawed at his arm and then desisted. Physically, he was more than a match for most of the Guards, and their superior weapons had lost all superiority. Blake could have watched the whole civilization shatter and have cared as little as he did for the shock on the other's face.

He found the subway entrance while the Guard was tardily blowing his whistle. He was beginning to think the trains ran every fifteen seconds, since one was again waiting. He climbed on, with the puffing Guard at his heels. "You'll get used to it, whatever your name is," he told the other.

"Colton," the black-clad man told him unhappily. "And why couldn't you have picked someone else? I broke a toe and got a brick over my head last night. Today—you!"

"Tough. I guess you'll just have to string along until we find some of your buddies to subdue me, Colton."

Colton nodded glumly, and they sat in silence while the quiet train moved along. Blake was emotionally numbed, and the problems that had bothered him were operating only on a semiconscious level.

No man, he supposed, could really accept predestination. The idea was something that could be agreed to on an intellectual level, but inside a man had to feel that he decided things for himself. Actually, there were no paradoxes; everything was decided, and things didn't happen because of either his actions or those of his older self—they happened only because that was the way they happened. The Bigshot was no more responsible than he was.

It wasn't hard, when you considered things carefully, to see why he'd tried to eliminate his younger self and put himself out of danger. Intellectually, he might realize nothing he did could alter the fabric of the events that must happen, but emotionally he couldn't stand by—and his logic was as much shaped by emotions as by facts.

And even explaining why he did things was a refusal to accept predestination, Blake knew. Looking for the reason behind his own or any other man's actions meant an attempt to see why something happened or didn't happen—and there was no real "why" in a universe on a fixed time-track.

He got up at the palace stop and went out with Colton at his heels. The Guard again reached for his whistle, but stopped when he saw Blake head for the door leading to the stairs that went up to Sarnoff's laboratory. The door was locked, of course, but a blast from the gun opened it.

SARNOFF was opening the upper door as Blake came to it, and he motioned the two men inside. "I heard you break the other," he explained. "I've been expecting you. Guard, there's nothing you can do—your prisoner's as untouchable as I am."

Colton shrugged, but stayed.

"Where's Sherry's body?" Blake asked woodenly.

Sarnoff moved toward the end of the room, where a couch had been brought in. He lifted the sheet silently. "She's in good hands, Tom," he said softly. "She was my daughter, though you wouldn't know that. And she hated me, long before she ran away to join your group. I used to wonder, once in a while, what happened to her. Now—I know."

Blake looked down at the still figure. Sherry still bore the look he had last seen, though her eyes were closed. Her clothing was in place, he noticed, with even her toes concealed. He was glad of that.

"She must have hated me," he said, at last.

Sarnoff shook his head. "No—she never knew; she was dead before I passed the word about you along."

His expressionless face studied her body, and then he drew the sheet up.

Blake sighed softly, and turned toward the entrance to the main palace, with Colton still at his heels. Sarnoff shook his head slightly, and moved toward another door, waiting for them until Blake shrugged and climbed into the little elevator. Then Sarnoff pressed the top button, and they moved upwards.

There was neither austerity nor over-lavishness to the private part of the palace. Blake took it for granted; he'd been brought up to have good taste, and becoming a dictator hadn't changed that.

There were a few men in the outer office, but they left at Sarnoff's motion, retreating into a second room beyond.

Here and there along the walls were niches where Guards might be stationed, but Blake could see no sign of them—they were at least well hidden.

Sarnoff picked up a phone from a desk and pressed a button. "Tell his Excellency I have the assassin," he said. Then, after a moment, he turned back to Blake. "We'll have to wait. He's taking a bath—or calling his top Guards. He's grown nervous, these last few days."

Blake dropped to the seat behind the desk. He picked up a volume there, saw that it was a leather-bound biography of himself, and started to put it down. Then he opened it and began scanning it.

There'd been war, after all. He'd had to wait two terms as Governor to become President, and then it was only a few weeks before the hydrogen bombs fell—too little time to prepare. He'd saved most of the cities with his large shields, but the terrible days had made an absolute dictatorship necessary; and through that, it hadn't been too hard to conquer the whole world, given both large supplies of bombs and a base immune to the bombs of others. Blake skimmed on, surprised to see how often Sarnoff's name cropped up. The man was obviously far more than a mere scientist.

And there was another name that meant nothing. Ainslee seemed to be almost as important as the dictator, though the people never had mentioned him.

Blake put the book back, just as the phone buzzed and a group of Guards in spotless white uniforms came out. Sarnoff motioned them aside, and they fell into step behind as Blake headed toward the door. Colton started forward, and then shrugged helplessly. He turned back slowly, probably to return to his beat.

This was it, Blake told himself. This was the point toward which the whole silly business had been driving. It seemed almost anticlimactic.

THE BIGSHOT sat at a small desk, surrounded by his Guards. He was probably shielded, but he seemed to have less faith in the shield than it deserved. His voice was nervous as he rearranged the papers before him, and some of the power seemed to have drained from his face. But he gathered himself together.

"You are charged with an attempt to assassinate your rightful ruler," he began.

Blake cut him off. "I'm here by my own will—as much as either one of us can have a will. And I'm shielded. I combined two of your citizen guns into the weapon James invented—the weapon on the papers in the secret drawer of my desk."

The older man sat stiffly for a long minute. Then he put down the papers he held. "So all my efforts go for nothing? Your brain wasn't exterminated. But there are still enough men here to overcome you physically, even if you are shielded."

"It won't work," Blake told him. "It's all happened before, from your viewpoint; and I suggest that you dismiss the Guards."

The Bigshot nodded. "Guards dismissed," he said slowly. They stared at him, but slowly withdrew, leaving only the two men who were both Thomas Blake and Sarnoff behind.

Theoretically, there was no way to end what was now a perfect stalemate—except that the Bigshot could always call back his Guards to batter Blake down with their fists; there was no way in which he could win.

But he had resolved all that before, and knew the answer. He knew that in this case, his decision to accept the facts would inevitably create those facts—so far as even the decision was his free will. Predestination seemed to be working, and that would make the decision something he had no control over, too.

"You lost," Blake told the Bigshot. "Every step shows that. If you hadn't lost—if your younger self, when you stood in my position, here—hadn't remembered that you lost, you wouldn't have gone to the trouble of getting my mind drawn here to attempt to exterminate me. I should have seen it sooner, but that doesn't matter; you have to lose."

"If I hadn't taken on Ainslee…" the Bigshot began, but his face was drawn now.

"There aren't any 'ifs,'" Blake told him remorselessly. "You lost. You're fighting with no hope at all. You can try anything you want to, but the end is already written—you lost."

He had no idea of what would happen, and yet he knew it was inevitable. Then, slowly, the answer came. He should have seen it from the beginning. No man can accept predestination within himself—yet the Bigshot knew now that there was no answer save predestination. He had to solve a completely impossible problem, and no mind could stand that.

"You lost." Blake repeated it, emotionlessly. "You lost."

And slowly, the Bigshot crumpled. He dropped his hands on his knees, and then brought his head down against them, sobbing softly.

Sarnoff stepped in quickly. "Stop it, Tom. Stop it. You don't have to solve anything now. It's all over; you don't have to solve anything."

The Bigshot looked up then, with tears streaming from his eyes, staring forlornly at the two men. "I'm lost," he said miserably. "I don't like this place. I don't like you. I want my mama!"

Blake turned to the window, while Sarnoff led the Bigshot out of the room. There, forty years from now, was the end of his own plans—the reward for all his hopes and struggles.

CHAPTER TEN

SARNOFF found Blake finally, down in the laboratory, lying on the cot where his mind had first come into the future.

"The council of the head Guards and the rebel leaders want you, Tom," he said quietly. "They've already published the plans for turning two of the citizen guns into a single complete one, in case your curiosity is still working."

Blake nodded. He'd asked for that—the only thing he could do for this tangled future; his decision was the only one he could make. Human nature couldn't be changed, and compulsory improvement was something which might or might not be good. But no society could be healthy where one group enjoyed a terrible power that the other group could not have.

There were guns enough for all to make the conversion—and that way the fanatics would find the rest of the world shielded by the time they got their own shields made and were ready to go out killing or converting others.

It was a problem that had always plagued him somewhat, since a total weapon in the hands of a crackpot could wreck incalculable damage if there were others without such a shield.

His only function, after all, had been to make sure that his original plan went through—that all men had such guns. It had been his basic motivation for going into politics, but it had only succeeded when he'd driven himself completely out of such politics.

"I suppose you'll be the next dictator," he told Sarnoff bitterly.

"Pro-tem president," the man answered. "But only pro-tem. I prefer to have Ainslee take over, if anyone has to. There's no real advantage to absolute power, and I'm still an opportunist. I'm in solid—but behind the scenes, where I'd rather be. I suspect we're in for a period of democracy, anyhow."

They'd have to be, if Silas McKinley had been right—and for a long, long spell of it—at least until something greater than the stasis gun and shield could come along.

"Then send my mind back," Blake decided. "They can get along without me."

Sarnoff began moving the machines along their tracks. And the sight of the action suddenly focused Blake's thoughts on what the return would be like—and the paradoxes his own inability to accept predestination involved.

He couldn't be such a fool as the Bigshot had been; with all he remembered, he *couldn't*.

"This body will be left a complete idiot, of course," Sarnoff said. "But your mind should snap back to your own body—and if I'm right, it will be only a few minutes in your time after you left. There's no real time-barrier for the mind—and no reason to expect the time spent here to be equaled by elapsed time in a trance back there. Maybe you can help by focusing your thoughts on when you want to return; I don't know."

Blake had wondered about that. He tried to think of his body just after his mind had left it, while Sarnoff adjusted the mind-burner. Then, without preamble or wasted farewells, the scientist depressed the switch.

For a moment, it was horrible, as it had been before. Then the full power seemed to snap his thoughts out into a roaring nothingness. Something pulled at him. Unlike the force trip into the future, the move back was almost instantaneous.

THOMAS BLAKE found his arm half-way to the light switch. He dropped it, and looked at the clock; but the faint sounds of the party still going on downstairs convinced him. He was back in his own world—and almost no time had elapsed there.

Sarnoff, Sherry, assassination…

He could feel it slipping from him. There was no machine here to intensify his thoughts, and to force them onto his brain cells and channel them into his permanent memory, as had been done by Sarnoff when his mind first touched the brain of Jed.

And the brain cells could not absorb what had happened during long days, now in these first few seconds of awakening. But now, whatever his mind-matrix was, it was slipping back into relation with those cells. It was like a dream that seems to be completely intense and to span hours, but which slips out of the mind almost as soon as that mind awakens.

Blake jumped for the wire-recorder, and began spouting the bits he still remembered into it, before they could go. But he found curiously little to dictate; he'd been in the future where he'd tried to kill himself. There'd been a girl named Sherry. And he'd had hairy hands—aside from that, he had no idea of what he'd looked like. He'd never seen a reflection of his face.

He dredged up other bits, but most of it was gone, except for the general realization that it had not been a dream. But what he had dictated was still more than he could have remembered—it was already more than he sensed he had known as his older self.

Then he glanced down to see that the recorder was still turning—but without effect. He'd forgotten to replace the spool of wire!

* * *

Gideon Pierce came into the office of Governor Blake, shaking his head. "You were right, Tom. They had a deal cooked up, just as you thought; I must be getting old."

Blake grinned at him, but he secretly agreed. Pierce should have spotted the opposition move. In time, you could get used to such business, and learn to expect the moves before they came. He'd have to watch Pierce from now on; the man had been loyal enough, but still…

Well, Blake thought, *I'm not naive any more. Idealism is a good thing, the only important thing. But a man has to be a realist, too.* Like that business of the gun James had invented. It had to be given to the people, of course—but they had to be protected from the crackpots who might seize on it first. It was a problem and one that could only be faced realistically.

"Forget it, Gideon," he said; "we all slip sometimes. Go back down there and keep them whipped into line. We've got to put that across, if I'm to get the nomination for President this time."

He watched Pierce leave, and consulted his calendar. There was only an appointment with the mathematician—a brilliant man, even if a bit too starry-eyed. Still, if his theory of cause and effect could be proved, it should make a difference. It began look as if all the predestination he'd been worrying about was as much nonsense as the argument about how many angels could dance on the head of a pin.

But that appointment could be postponed. He flipped through his book, until he came to another name. Then he reached for his intercom.

"Call up Professor Houton, Miss Brightley, and ask him if he can change that appointment to next week at the same time." he instructed. "Then get ahold of Ainslee—you have his number—and tell him it's urgent I see him this afternoon. As soon as he can make it."

Ainslee should be a good man to replace Pierce. A little cold-blooded, perhaps but he got things done…

Keepers of the House

King could remember how golden and glorious the house had seemed to men—and what the science he hated had done to his friends.

OUTWARDLY, there was nothing about that particular morning to set it apart from the thousands of other such mornings which the dog had smelled. Yet his great, gaunt body shifted nervously on the rocky shelf over the river, and his short hackles lifted slightly as the skin on his neck tautened. He raised his head, sniffing the wind that blew from the land, and his ears searched for wrongness in the sounds that reached him. Once he whined.

The feeling left from the dream was still troubling him. He had bedded down in a dry shelter back from the water. After he had scraped away the ancient, dried bones of rabbits, it had seemed like a good place. But sleep had been too busy, full of running and of tantalizing smells.

And finally, just when he was tearing at something with an almost forgotten flavor, the warm scent in his nostrils had changed to another, and a voice had snapped into his ears. He had jerked awake, shivering, with the name still ringing in his head.

"King!"

The dream memory of Doc had bothered him before, but this time even the warmth of the sun had failed to quiet it, though his nose reported no trace of a human odor now. There was something about this territory…

Abruptly, a motion in the water caught his attention. He edged forward, rising to his feet, while his eyes tracked the big fish. Overhead, a bird must have seen the same prey, since it began dropping.

King growled faintly and plunged down into the unpleasant chill of the water. Necessity and decades of near-starvation had taught him perfect form in this unnatural act. A moment later, he was heading for shore with the fish clamped between his jaws.

He found a hollowed spot of dry sand, shook the water out of his short fur, and began tearing at the fish. It was a flavorless breakfast, far inferior to the big salmon that were so easy to catch along the northwestern rivers, but it filled him well enough.

The wind was growing stronger, reminding him of the cold that was creeping down from the north as it seemed to do at regular intervals. Each year, the cold drove him south and the warmth followed to let him move back again.

Usually he took the same trail from river to river, but this time—as in a few other restless years—something had driven him to seek a new way, risking the long runs through the foodless wastelands, from river to river, looking for some end he never found.

He pawed out a stubborn bone from between his teeth and got to his feet again, the double drive overcoming the wish to rest in the warmth of the sun. Beyond the shelter of the dunes along the river, the wind was sharper and colder, tossing bits of dry sticks and rubble ahead of it.

He had no idea of why he was heading inland, except that it seemed somehow right, until the damp odors on the wind told him that the river must bend in the direction he was heading. By then, he was out of sight of the water and the plants, birds and insects that lived along it. He settled into a steady lope as he came to what had once been a raised roadway. The banked surface was comparatively free of sand, making the going easier.

The road swept past what must have once been heavily-wooded land, and King sniffed the familiar odor of rotted logs. A few trees were still standing, dead and girdled to a height above his head, but there was no life there.

The sand and dust drifted into piles and shifted before the wind, covering and uncovering the ever-present broken rabbit bones, scouring at them and the standing trunks, as if to eliminate even this final evidence that there had been life. In some sections, a few trees and plants had survived and were spreading, but the great dust-bowl area here was barren. Except for the wind and the padding of King's feet, there was no sound.

Once the road ran among the wrecks of close-packed houses, and King's hackles lifted again, his nose twitching uneasily. It had been twenty years since he had bothered to investigate a house, but this morning his mind kept prickling with strange sensations.

He hesitated at a couple of the rust-crumpled cars; the larger one held crumpled bones that almost meant something to him. Then he left the dead town behind, heading for the strengthening smell of the river.

Ten minutes later, he was staring out at a long concrete bridge that spanned the current. Beyond it lay the city.

The wind was colder now, driving along before a dull gray that threatened a storm. Below King, the water stretched out, heading toward the south and safety for the winter. He moved uncertainly away from the bridge, then dropped to his haunches, his tongue rolling out doubtfully as he stared at the bridge and the city beyond.

Something was wrong in his head. He scratched at his ear, turned to bite at the root of his tail, and still hesitated.

Finally he got to his feet and headed along the pitted surface of the bridge. A sign creaked, jerking his ears forward. It was only half a sign, without a place name, but carrying an iron engraving of its population, now smeared over with weathered paint.

King bristled toward it, smelled it cautiously, and was abruptly nosing behind it frantically. There was only the whisper of the ghost of an odor there, and it was too faint to stimulate his senses more than once. He clawed at it, whining, but the scent from his dreams refused to return.

He began running again, leaping over gaps in the paving. One newly-fallen section was impassable, and he had to search his way across twelve-inch, rusty iron beams. He slipped twice, and had to scratch and fight his way back.

At mid-point, with the limits of the small city spread out before him, he stopped to explode in a barking sound he hadn't made in thirty years. Then he was plunging on again, until the bridge was behind and he was coursing through the wide, ruined streets at a full run.

Twice he started on false trails through the shops and warehouses, but the third time something seemed to groove itself into his thoughts, like the feeling that led him back to the salmon run each year. It was weak and uncertain, as old memories fought against stronger habits, but it grew as he panted his way out of the heart of the ruined city. Glass fractured and clattered downward from one building, followed by a skull that shattered on the stones.

King avoided the shower of fragments and redoubled his speed, his big body bent in arching leaps, and his ears flattened back against his head.

He knew where he was, even before he swept through the last of the rooming house section and came to the edge of the rolling university campus. Then, for a moment, the dawning memory in his mind spun and twisted at the ruin the elements had made. But it was the lack of familiar smells that bothered him most. Even at the end, there had been the eternal odor of the chemistry laboratory, and now even that was gone.

The big gate was open. His legs had begun to bunch for the leap and scramble over it, and the tension in them died slowly. He slowed to a trot, lifting his head in a double bark that rasped the unfamiliar muscles of his throat. A huge tree had fallen across the path, but a section had been cut away with an axe. Rotted chips sounded underfoot as King passed by.

Then he was darting around one of the big red-stone buildings, heading down the path that led to the back of the campus. There most of the great tree boles still stood, with even their nakedness too thick a screen for his eyes to penetrate. He charged through the rubble of sticks and rabbit bones that filled the path there and took a sudden left turn, to come to a skidding halt.

The two-story Promethean Laboratory building still stood, and across the fence beyond, some of the familiar houses were still there. King teetered toward one of them, back toward the laboratory, and then again toward the house. He let out two high-pitched barks, and cocked his ears, listening. There was no answering sound.

A sick whine grew in his throat, until the wind suddenly shifted.

The smell was stronger this time. It was wrong—incredibly wrong—but it was beyond mistake. Doc was here! And with the instinctive identification of wind direction, he knew it had to be the laboratory.

The door was closed, but it snapped open with a groan of hinges as King hit it in full leap. He went rolling over and over across the floor of the littered hall, clawing against the stone tiles instinctively, while his mind rocked at the waves of human scent and the human voice that was beating into his ears!

The smell was so strong to his unaccustomed nostrils that he had no directional sense; at first the echoes' along the hollow corridors made it hard to locate the voice, also. He cocked his ears; studying it. It was wrong, like the smell—yet it was the voice of Doc!

"...as wrong as before. It didn't matter. It was better than starving like rabbits under the biocast. They were falling within minutes after the cable..."

King dove through the passage and into the room beyond. The voice went on without pause, coming from a box in front of him. And now the metallic quality under it and the lack of the random ultrasonic overtones of a real voice registered on him. It was only another false voice—another of the things men had, but which he had almost forgotten. Doc's voice—without Doc!

The sound dropped to the bottom of his awareness. King swung around the room. There was something in the scent that made his neck muscles tense, but he knew Doc was there. His eyes adjusted to the glaring light inside, while his nose tried to cut a trail through the thickness of the odors. Both senses located the source at the same time.

Beside the big machine with the slow-spinning rolls of tape there was a bed covered with ragged blankets. A hand lay on the edge of the tape machine, twisted into the controls, and an arm led down at the figure below on the bed.

King's tail flailed the floor, and his legs doubled for the leap that would carry him into Doc's arms. But the motion was never completed. The wrongness of the scent and the motionless figure was too great. The tail grew limp as he crouched to the floor, inching his way forward, his whine barely audible.

He raised his nose at last to the other hand that lay dropping over the side of the bed, and his tongue came out.

The hand was cool and stiff, and there was no response to welcome King's caress.

Slowly, cringing within himself, King drew himself up to look down at what lay on the bed, and to nuzzle it. It didn't look like Doc. Doc had been young and alive, clean-shaven and with dark hair. The body was too thin, and the long beard and hair were stark white. Yet the odor said unquestionably that this was Doc—and that Doc was old—and dead.

Standing with his front feet on the bed, King lifted his muzzle upwards, his mouth opening while the deep, long sound ached in his chest. But no sound came. He brought his face down to that of Doc and nuzzled again, whimpering. It did no good.

For a long time he lay there, whining and crying. The voice went on and something ticked regularly on the wall. There was the sound of the wind outside, faint here, but rising steadily. Once King heard his own name used by Doc's voice from the box, and his ears half lifted.

"...King and the other three. Probably starved by now; though; since there are no land animals left for them to feed on. King was a smart dog, but..."

His name wasn't repeated, though he listened for a while. Later, the voice stopped entirely; while the tape hummed a few more times, clicked, and began flapping a loosened end that knocked over a bottle of pills beside

Doc's frozen hand. It clicked again, and slowed to silence, leaving the ticking of the clock the only sound in the room.

Abruptly, there was a rustling noise. King shot to his feet, whirling to face the source, just as a large white rat scuttled from the shadows near the door. It went rigid at his movement, coming slowly to its hind feet, its eyes darting from King to the body of Doc. It let out a high squeak.

The dog dived for it, snarling. But a threat of familiarity was clutching at his mind, slowing his charge. The rat twisted around and through the door, quavering out a series of squeaks. It went scuttling along the hall, through the opened door, and across the steps to the wasteland beyond. By the time King reached the outside, it was heading for the great tower across the street and halfway to the rocket field.

King could smell its spoor mixed thickly with that of Doc as he leaped the fence and followed. He heard it squeal once more as it saw him, and heard its claws scrape against the rotted metal of the tower as it scurried up beyond his reach.

But he was slowing already. The tower was dead now, with the great ball of fire gone from its top, but the memory of the tingling, itching false smell that had plagued him while the fire glowed was rising in his mind to drive him back. He hated it as Doc had hated it—and there was still fear for what it had been. He stopped fifty feet beyond the massive girders, bristling as he backed around it.

The concrete hut under it was broken now, though, and the guards were gone. He saw some of the guns scattered about—or what was left of them—in the jumble of sand and human skeletons that still lay around the tower.

Some of the skeletons were further back, mixed with axes and other guns. An arm was still tangled with a shred of rope that connected to a faded metal sign. Where the great cable had been, a blackened line curved toward the tower, pitting the metal more deeply.

Somehow, King knew the tower of the tingling fire was dead. But he had waited too long. The rat had scrambled down and was heading toward the rocket field. He started after it again, halted, and reluctantly turned back toward the laboratory.

There was pleading in his whine as he found the body of Doc again, but it still bore the smell of death. Instinct told King that Doc was dead; and would never be anything but dead. Yet there was the half-remembered smell of his brother Boris, after the sweet smells and the prickings, lying on the table while Doc and the men stood around.

Boris had smelled dead—and Boris had walked again, smelling freshly alive. Before that, there had been the dead rats that would not stay dead. And the rabbits—though when the rabbits finally smelled dead, they were all dead, and no more rabbits lived.

He circled Doc uneasily, his lips lifted. He paced to the outer door, searching for any return of the rat, while his mind slowly remembered the other rats. With a quick check on Doc, King darted up the stairs, his legs making a familiar pattern of it, and into the great laboratory there.

There were no more rats. The cages were empty, and the scents he had learned here as a puppy were almost gone. Only the room itself was the same as the one that had haunted his hunger-driven dreams.

There had been the rats on the table when he was young and the tower was only a banging beyond the window. The rats that died, and the three that did not, when the men drank smelly liquid and shouted and danced all night, shaking their fists at the base of the tower. The table was still there, beyond the place where the men mixed the strange smells. The table where strange things happened to him later that he could not remember.

The tail he had owned before the last time on the table still hung there. There had been another wild night when the bandages came off, his new tail, puppy-small and weak, but growing quickly enough. This room had been a good place, and some of his later dreams had been good.

Other dreams had remembered the bad times, as they came back to his mind now. The night the tower blazed with fire, Doc swearing while King felt the tingling until it was cut off. The men arguing with Doc, not coming back—even moving toward the hated tower. The huge celebration outside when the tower blazed again, while Doc and his one friend cried. The wild frenzy of stringing wires over the Promethean lab and into a vile-smelling box. After that, there was no more tingling in his nostrils inside the lab, but things had grown worse in spite of it.

King was trembling as he finished his inspection for rats, and his legs beat a frantic tattoo down the stairs. The fear was as thick as it had been when the men came and took him and his brothers away from Doc, to jam them into planes with other dogs and dump them far away, where the rabbits were thick—and almost useless for food.

Doc had fought then, even moving outside the safety of the laboratory, but the men had taken the dogs. Yet Doc had been alive. And now he was dead.

The fear twisted in King, settling into something sick. He paced around the body, growling and whining. Once he stopped to lick the hand. It was colder now, and there was no moisture on it. The scent was growing more wrong as the body cooled.

Life had not come back while he was gone.

He licked Doc's hand again, and an answering chill went through the dog. The feeling of death began to settle deeper—a feeling inside that grew and swallowed him, a hungry feeling. He shook it away, as he would have shaken the neck of the rat, but it came back stronger than before.

There was real hunger mixed with it. Eating was never good on the trip south, and he had burned too much energy chasing about that morning. The fish had not been enough. The smell of stale food of some kind in the room tantalized him, though he could find none, and reminded him that there had been traces of the same—odors along the path the rat had taken. The saliva was rising in his mouth at the thought. It drew him out, while the death inside pressed him away.

He started off twice, to return each time for another inspection. He whimpered and tried tugging at the sleeve of the arm. The rags parted, but Doc gave no sign. The death smell was stronger. King paced about, fighting the hunger and misery until they were too much. There was the food smell, the rat—and when he came back to Doc…

A faint mist was being driven along by the wind as he reached the tower again, braving it this time without stopping. Until the rain washed it away, the spoor would be all the stronger for the moisture in the air, and he followed it easily, until it ended on the blasted area of the rocket field.

King stopped at the sight of the bent and worn take-off cradles. From the distance, the first faint roll of thunder came, and he bolted stiff-legged, snarling with fear, as if one of the monster ships he had seen the men building so frantically were blasting up again.

The excitement of the frenzied construction had drawn him to it, even when it meant sneaking away from Doc—until he had been present after the infants were all aboard, and the rocket took off. The thunder-booming roar, the gout of eye-searing flame and the smell that paralyzed his nose for hours had sent him cringing back to shiver at Doc's feet, and each new take-off had brought a fresh attack. He still wanted nothing to do with the rockets.

The cradles were empty now, however—except for something that looked like one that had crashed down and was lying on its sides, the big tubes ripped away, and the ground scorched around it. And as he looked, the distant form of the rat appeared from below it and leaped upwards through a door there.

King edged toward it, following the trail that led there, uncertain. It looked dead, but the other that had roared away, on its lightning and thunder had also seemed dead. Then lightning and thunder boomed behind him, and he forced himself to a faster trot.

The hulk seemed harmless. There were none of the chemical smells now, and the fumes of the ancient blast that had fizzled were gone. He moved gingerly toward the door, his nose twitching at the odors that came from it, just as the rat appeared.

It saw him and squeaked sharply, dashing back inside. King abandoned his caution. With a low growl, he leaped through the doorway above the ground. The edge of the metal tore at him, thin projections sticking out where it had been crudely hacked away. He snapped at it, then turned to find the rat.

There was enough light inside to see dimly. The rat had retreated into a narrow pipe that ran back. King tried to poke his nose into it, then fished with his paw. The rat drew back and snapped at him. Its teeth missed, but it was enough to teach him caution.

He drew back, crunching across a litter of dried papers, foil and junk he could not recognize. A thicker bundle twisted under his feet, and the thick, heavy smell of meat—red meat, not the weak flesh of fish—filled his nostrils. Without thinking, he snapped down.

The stuff was dry and hard, disappointing at first. But as he chewed over the salt and the odd flavorings, the almost forgotten flavor came through, sending saliva dripping from his mouth. From the odors here, he knew the rat had been eating it before he came, but it didn't matter.

He finished the package, spitting out the wax, metal, paper and plastics that surrounded it as best he could. Then his nose led him along the trail of the rat's gnawing, back to the few tons of concentrate that were left.

There was no smell to guide him from the outside of the packages, but he had learned to find food where it could be discovered. He tore into a package, gasping as a thick, fruity stuff seared at his tongue. He tried again, further away. It was food, this time. He ripped away the covering first, and settled down with the brick between his paws, working on it until it was gone.

Outside, the rain had increased to a torrent. He studied the rat and the view outside, and finally curled up against the door, blocking the rat's egress. Some rain came through, making a small puddle on the floor and wetting his coat; but he disregarded it at first, until the thirst began to grow in him. He lapped at the puddle, finding some relief.

His stomach began to feel wrong then. It was heavy, full, and miserable. He fought against it, lapping more water. The rat came out of its hole and found another brick of food. He heard it gnawing, but the effort of moving was too great.

When the sickness finally won, he felt better. But it was an hour later, while the storm raged and the lightning split the sky with waves of solid fear, before he could pull himself back to another brick. This time he ate more carefully, stopping to drink between parts of his meal. It worked better. The food stuck with him, and his hunger was finally satisfied.

He lay near the doorway of the old rocket, staring out through the darkness that was still split by lightning. The rat scurried about behind him, but he let it go. Now that it was harmless and his stomach was filled, some of the old pattern began to stir in his mind. It was one of the rats he had known so long ago, its smell grown old, but still clearly identifiable.

He had tried twice to leave the ship and force his way back to where Doc was lying, but the lightning drove him back. Now he lifted his voice in a long, mournful bark. There was no answering call from Doc. He began working himself up for another try.

Lightning crashed down in the direction of the laboratory. The building itself stood out in the glare, with every wire of its outer covering glowing white hot. There was a roll of sharp, near thunder, and then another explosion that seemed to open the laboratory up in a blossom of flame through the abating rain.

King muttered unhappily, licking his lips uneasily, while his tail curved tighter against him. But now, while the flame still smoldered around the distant building and the lightning might come back, now was no time to risk it.

He turned around several times, scraping away the litter, buried his nose in the tuft of his tail, and tried to relax. He was almost asleep when he felt the rat creep up to him. It must have recognized his smell, too, since it settled down against him as it had done when they were both together in the laboratory with Doc. He snarled faintly, then let it alone, and went to sleep. Surprisingly, there were no dreams to bother him.

The rat was gone in the morning when King awoke, and the sun was shining, though the quieter wind held a coldness that was too close to freezing to suit him. He hesitated, turning back toward the food stores. Then the sight of the rat, racing across the space near the tower, decided him. With an unhappy growl, he dropped from the hulk of the rocket and took out after it.

If the rat got there before he did, and Doc needed him…

In open running, the rat was no match for him. It drew aside, its high voice chattering, as he thundered up. He did not turn, but drove on, heading at a full run for the laboratory.

There was no laboratory! The steps were there, blackened and cracked. Some of the walls still stood. But the building he had known was gone. Beside it, the trunk of one of the big trees had been blasted apart, and now had its tattered remnants strewn over the dirt, mingling with the coals from the fire that had gutted the building.

A few were still smoking, though the rain had put out the blaze before it had completely burned out by itself. The heavy, acrid scent of damp, burned wood loaded the air, concealing everything else from his scent.

He uttered a short, anguished yelp and went dashing through the doorway. The ashes were hot, and the stones left from the floor were hotter, but he could stand them. He hardly felt them as he swung toward what had once been the room where Doc lay.

The box from which the voice had come was gone, but the twisted wreck of the tape machine was there. And beside it, charred scraps showed what had once been a bed.

King cried out as his nose touched the heat, but he was pawing frantically, disregarding the pain. He could stand it—he had to. He shoveled the refuse aside, digging for something that was his. And finally, under the charred raggedness, there were traces. There was even enough to know that it had once been Doc.

And Doc was still dead—as dead as the meat that once came from can had been dead.

King whimpered over the remains, while the rat climbed onto a section of the wall and chattered uneasily. But the dog was already backing away. He stopped beyond the hot ruins of the building to lift his head. For a second, he held the pose while the rat watched him, before his head came down and he turned slowly away.

The food in the rocket lay to his right, and the old gate through which he had first come was on his left. He licked his lips as his eyes turned to the rocket, but his legs moved unwaveringly left.

The steady walk turned into a trot, and his stride lengthened, carrying him back to the rooming house section, and on into the former business section. There had been other fires, and one had spread across several blocks. He swung around it and back to the street he had first taken.

Ahead of him, the bridge came into view, and nearer was the bank of the river on this side.

King did not waver from his course. His legs paced out onto the rotten pavement that would carry him across the stream. He moved on, slowing as he had to walk the girders again. When he was past that section, and at the mid-point of the bridge, something seemed to turn him.

The town lay behind him from here, most of it visible at the crest of the bridge. The rain and the storm had made changes, but they were too small to notice. And the university lay at the edge of King's vision, though some of the tower could be seen. He faced toward it, and then unerringly toward the place where the laboratory should have been.

Now his muzzle lifted into the air as he sank to his haunches. He seemed to brace himself, and his lungs expanded slowly. He could feel it, and the need of it. The instinct behind it was too old for remembrance, but the ritual came finally by itself, with no conscious control.

His mouth opened, and the dirge keened on the air, lifting and driving upwards toward the empty sky above.

There was only the single requiem. Then King swung back toward the distant shore, picking his way along the worn bridge.

He slipped down the crumbled bank to the thin edge of sand near the stream and turned southward, trotting on steadily with the cold wind at his back.

Somewhere, there would be a place to fish for his breakfast.

And there was Light

Volcek believed his weapon would be humane, and less destructive than the dreaded fusion bombs.

STEFANIE was still white and weak, but the worry on her face had nothing to do with her recent sickness as she rushed about the small, crudely furnished apartment, trying to appear normal. Johann Volcek studied his young wife, worrying more about her than the meeting for the moment.

If the child had only lived…

Then he smiled a bit ironically, before letting his mind come up with the old palliatives. There'd be other children for him and Stefanie—and for this half of the world. The other half would simply have to suffer painlessly through a generation, for the good of the whole world.

"But the Director, Johann…" Stefanie's voice was on the thinnest edge of hysteria. "Johann, to our place! If I'd known, I could have made curtains, at least. And can you be sure…"

"It isn't suspicion, radost moya," he assured her quickly. "I told you the Director trusts me—he has to. And he simply wants to see you. You know he's a family man himself."

But he let her work, fussing about the place, refilling his coffee, brushing an imaginary speck of dust off his coat. The doctor had told him that work was best for her—anything to get her mind off the lost child until there could be others. And the Director may have been a better distraction than any of the others, aside from the flattery of it.

Then the telephone on the wall rang sharply, and he answered it, smiling back at her, "Volcek."

"Good, Johann." It was the Director's Secretary of Science, Jean Petrecci and Volcek's sponsor. "We shall be there soon—and it's a beautiful day for the test, not so?"

Johann agreed quickly, though he had not yet had time to look through the windows even, with Stefanie's worry over the visit of the Director. But as he looked out now, he saw that it was a good day, clear, with only thin wisps of cloud in the sky.

Then, in the street below, there was a stirring, first of big cars, and then the shouts of the people. It was silenced, and the creaking elevator began to thump upwards, Stefanie made a last frantic dash into the bedroom, brushing nervously at her hair, and came out just as the knock sounded.

Johann had been right—the Director must have trusted him, since the big man had come up with only three of his guards, and now came thrusting his broad shoulders in, his greyed head not even darting about the room, his eyes leading him toward the Volceks.

Quick admiration filled his eyes at the sight of Stefanie, and his gruff voice was soft, the voice the radio brought them when he was the Father of the State, or when he was telling them of the new plans for more food and better living.

"Sit—I'm only one of you, you know. Ah, Johann, this is the little Stefanie. I've wanted to meet you, to see the one Johann has spoken of so often." His language was perfect, but with the queer stilted effect it always had when he was not reading a prepared speech.

Watching Stefanie stammer over the honor of the Director's presence, and then relax gradually as the spell of the man took over, Johann began to smile more naturally. The Director was talking of his own beginnings—in much less than this—and the moving they would soon be doing, into a newer apartment, a fine new suburb. And surprisingly, he was talking of his own wife and children, and Stefanie was answering.

REMEMBERING STORIES of the Director, Johann found it hard to recognize this as reality. The man had come up from the lowest ranks, an iron hand leading him up the ladder of Centralia's autocratic bureaucracy. But now the hand was sheathed, and even Stefanie began to smile.

Then it was over, and the Director was rising. Johann kissed his wife quickly, embarrassed slightly at the Director's approving smile, and they were out in the elevator, heading toward the big, waiting cars.

"Now I trust you, Johann Volcek," the Director told him. "Now I can go with you to this test. With such a wife waiting for you, there can be no trickery against the State. No—don't say it! It is not you I could distrust—it is everyone I must distrust. But not now. What does the doctor say?"

"Another year." For a time they had been afraid that Stefanie could never have children again, but the new treatments had apparently been effective. Centralia's progress in all phases of gynecology had been spectacular.

The Director nodded. "Good. The State needs such children as you will have. And a man has need of little ones. But tell me—you still feel sure of this test?"

Then the talk became technical.

Johann was sure. There had been smaller tests, during the two years the project had been going on, and all of them had been effective.

Then cold fingers ran over him, tingling at the ends of his nerves, as he realized the trick semantics was playing on him.

Test? It had been the name they had given it, and in time it had come to be no more than that in his mind—a test of his theories. But this was not just a test. This was the feat itself, the step that would bring an end to half the world, the culmination of the hopes of Centralia, and the final, positive proof of the ideas of Volcek.

He had been almost unaware of the power that had grown from his idea, but now it hit him. It wasn't easy to do that to half a world, even in these days. But it had to be done.

Thirty years before, there had been a sprawling group of small nations and several large powers. But with the beginning of the atomic age, that had shaken itself down until now there were actually only the two hemispheres. Centralia had most of the world's population, but the West had achieved equality by its head start in the sciences and in industry. For thirty, years, little nation had accreted to big nation, until now there were the two of them. Nominally, the little nations still existed; but it was a polite fiction, like the fiction of bland softness the Director had adopted before Stefanie.

And this was not a world where two powers could exist. They had somehow achieved it, while the accretion of control over the neighboring states went on. There had been fracas piled onto struggle, but never outright war. Now, though, things had reached a stage where each side knew that sooner or later the hydrogen-bombs must fall, and where those bombs were of a size and efficiency that might even end the world. There were even rumors of solar-phoenix bombs which could turn the world into a flaming, lesser sun.

Volcek sighed. This was better than that. Better that half the world should slow down and come to a gradual halt than that the rain of hell should descend from the heavens, perhaps igniting the world itself.

THEY WERE AT THE laboratories, now, and Volcek got out of the car behind the Director, vaguely conscious that taking second place was a mark of honor. Inside the building, one of the rooms had been cleared, leaving a few seats, a stand, and a single board of levers against the wall. Already, the seats were taken, and men were rising to salute the Director.

Ki Fong, Tsamatsu, Bhandaputra, Simonolov, Schwartzkopf, Jordssen—all of the big names of government and science were there. Some were scowling intently as they tried to digest the printed formulae on the big blackboard which gave part of the theory behind Volcek's work; others were smiling, assured only that this was the day when Centralia would come into its own. And some, as always, were estimating Volcek, wondering how his importance would conflict with their own.

The Director smiled thinly, dropping an arm over Volcek's shoulder. "After this day, Johann, you'll need bodyguards. I have seen to that. And Petrecci…well, we shall see…"

Johann caught himself before he could wince. He'd liked Petrecci, had no desire to replace him. But if the implication of the Director's words was what he thought…still, it would be good for Stefanie. She had had too much trouble, and it was time life smiled on her a little. It would be good for their children, too, to grow up with comfort, even a little luxury, tutored perhaps with the children of the Director, himself. As Secretary of Science, Johann Volcek could give his family a great deal. He caught Petrecci's eyes on him, and turned his head quickly back to the other men.

At the Director's nod, he began outlining the facts to them. Some already knew of what was being done here, but all were listening as if the Director himself were speaking.

He could only give the barest facts. He'd been experimenting with a means of controlling fission for some power application, working on the problem of getting hydrogen to fission at temperatures below the millions of degrees where it normally began, and in tiny amounts. And by sheer accident, he had stumbled on a process where nitrogen fissioned, instead—two atoms of nitrogen combining into one, straining the nucleus that now held fourteen protons and fourteen neutrons, distorting it until some of the binding force of the nucleus released energy, and it broke up into simpler atoms again—as if both fission and fusion were going on.

It had not been successful, from a commercial angle, but it had produced an unexpected result. The mice which had been kept to test out danger of radiation had not been killed—but they had been sterile, as events proved, from then on. The release of radiation was not quite normal gamma rays; it was subtler than that—some queerly polarized radiation that struck at the fertility of animals and ended it.

"But you were not sterilized," Ki Fong interrupted him.

"I was lucky—I had been using a shield that was heavy enough to turn aside the radiation—the four-foot walls of the oven where the experiment was conducted. It only leaked out through the panel we later found had a crack in it—but that was toward the mice."

Three years had been spent in testing it on mice, before the reports had found Petrecci, and brought him to the little laboratory of Johann Volcek. By then, Volcek had developed a complete control of the process, and had learned to fuse and fission oxygen as well as nitrogen, but without the production of sterilizing radiation this time.

After that, there had been no more mice. Volcek shuddered, trying to conceal it, as he remembered the prisoners who had stood before the portal of the oven, and gone away, sterile. And there had been tests in the big, deserted wastes near the Gobi, where balls of fire had leaped from his tiny little devices, and cracked themselves into flaming energy that grew and spread before vanishing. More sterility had followed.

"It requires very little apparatus," Volcek said, finally. He pulled a small tube from a drawer near the wall, and held it out to them. "This is the source. A small battery, these coils, tubes, this little crucible—nothing more. Once we knew why it started the fusion, it was easy to simplify."

And it was simple. A man could carry one of the devices with him in a small bag, and it was meaningless in appearance. It could be built into a radio, as if it were part of the tuning device. It could slip past customs, harmless in its looks, and be spread wherever wanted.

And now…

THE DIRECTOR TOOK over, then, telling them what had already been done. In every city and hamlet, from coast to coast and from polar cap to polar cap, the West was covered with these tiny little devices, each equipped with a little crystal delicately attuned to one here, so that they would all function at once.

There would be no war. Centralia had labored to avoid war in spite of the hatred and lusts of the West. Now, they would be even more agreeable, even more meek. They would take the insults; they would not fight. Because, once the nitrogen of the air had done its job, there would be only a generation of patience, while no more children were born to the West. And some day, there would be only one Power—Centralia.

Schwartzkopf asked the question that was bothering the others, though he already knew the answer. "But these balls of fissioning or fusioning nitrogen—when they go off over the West, they are too much like atomic bombs. Won't the West feel it is attacked and retaliate with their genuine bombs?"

"We, too, shall be attacked!" It was Volcek's other process, of course. Simultaneously, there would be released similar "bombs" over all of the territory of Centralia. The heat and power would do a minor amount of damage, of course—but this process produced no sterilizing radiation. "Only New Zealand will be free."

New Zealand had somehow held out of the two coalitions, by its hardest efforts and with the help of its location. It was weakly allied to the West, but too remote.

The Director smiled again, the tight smile that was reserved for private meetings. "We shall, of course, accuse the West—but within the hour, when word of their trouble comes, we shall ask for a truce to find the culprit. Simple, is it not?"

The clock on the wall indicated five minutes before zero hour, and Volcek wiped his hands surreptitiously against his coat. It was simple enough, this use to which they had put his discoveries. And, he told himself again, it was better than any rain of real atomics. The West would not be hurt seriously—it would simply die out slowly, as no more children were born. It was really the most merciful solution to the politics of this world.

He could picture some of the panic, of course, when the little tubes did their work. First a tiny spark would form in the tube, with a spitting and hissing. Then it would grow, breaking out of the tube and through walls or anything in its way, growing and rising, spreading erratically horizontally, moving with a strange random motion, as it climbed upwards and grew larger and larger. It would reach the size of a normal atomic bomb, in a few minutes. And some would be killed by its heat, as some buildings would catch fire from it.

But mostly, there would be the terror as the people in the cities saw it spread its visible radiation and heard the familiar crackling thunder of its detonation. The terror would kill some of them, in their panic-flight, even while the thing itself drifted upwards until it found a layer of air too thin for it to go on and it came to an automatic end.

But they would mostly escape, except for bad cases of "sunburn" and the results of their own panic. Dry material flamed quickly before its peculiar radiation, but men were not made of dry material, and it was almost harmless. They would simply have no children. And that was better than most of them could expect in a day when each morning marked the beginning of a new fear of hydrogen bombs or worse.

One more minute.

Volcek had expected the Director to move to the panel where the big switch would cut on the surprisingly small oscillator that would trigger the little crystals in the tube projectors. But the Director was stepping back, motioning him forward. "You, Johann—it is an honor I have reserved for you."

THERE WAS SILENCE IN the laboratory room as Volcek moved slowly toward the board. He straightened, his eyes going down to his coat, where a bit of lint clung to it. Stefanie would have spotted it at once and rushed to brush it off, Stefanie who knew nothing of what his great work was, but who was awed by having a husband who could receive a visit from the Director. Stefanie who could have other children, after all, in this world that would have ultimate peace in spite of all the war threats, because of the work her husband was now about to do.

Suddenly, he wondered how many Stefanies there might be in the West. How many women would wait for the children they wanted, and never find them? How many would curse him, when they finally realized the truth, without ever knowing that he was the man they were cursing?

He cut off the thought, savagely. There would be others in the long centuries to come, who would know his name and would then bless him, as their children grew up without the threat of war and extinction. His children would be proud of him—his and Stefanie's.

He touched the switch that was to set off the harmless, fake "bombs" over their own world first. The Director was at his side, his face no longer smiling, but narrowed to that of a wolf.

Then the Director chuckled, and the edge of his lips curled up. "Let there be light," he quoted, and his eyes showed that he knew the original usage of the term in the Book he was quoting.

And there was light, as Johann's finger hit the switch. A tiny, spitting, hissing thing lifted from the nearby city, going up and forward in weird, erratic movements, growing larger, and spreading out, now beginning the muttered, staccato thunder that was not unlike a plutonium bomb.

The Director reached over and pressed the other switch that would send the sterilizing bombs up over the West—but he did not depress it fully. He stopped, and nodded to Volcek, and again Johann's hand went out, pushing the lever of the switch.

He should have brought Stefanie—if only she could have known nothing of the results. She would have been proud of him then, as the Director solemnly shook the hand that had done its work, and the other men began to cluster around him.

Then they moved toward the windows, hesitantly at first, not quite sure that this fire in the heavens over the city beyond was really the safe kind. But the Director led them, together with Volcek, and they stood gazing out.

It was a huge ball of blazing fire in the sky now, partially softened by the filters that had sprung shut over the windows automatically, and the mutter of its detonation reached them as they stood there.

There was some damage, of course, even here. Some of the older wooden buildings near where it had first appeared were bursting into flames, and the distant figures of people had gone into a panic—they had to believe it was real, just as the West must believe for a time that both powers had received the same treatment.

Stefanie? But Volcek had taken care of that, with a drug in her coffee. She would be asleep, unaware of the tumult, and not one of the mob trying frantically to escape what could never harm them.

NOW THE BALL OF FIRE was rising upwards more steadily, its own heat driving it up as a blast of hot air is carried up over a fire. The brightness began to fade as they watched, moving up and turning smaller, shrinking, and finally going away.

Volcek sighed, and the Director echoed it, a satisfied sigh, and a somewhat regretful one. "It is hard to see even a few of my people hurting themselves," the Director said slowly. "But it is best. And—it is done."

He turned to Volcek, and Johann straightened, reminding himself that whatever the Director said must be remembered. He would have to tell Stefanie—and someday, he could tell his children, and his grandchildren. He must remember it.

But the Director's words were never spoken. There was a shout from the windows, and they swung back, to see another tiny flame leaping up, this time nearer, growing and spitting.

There was something wrong with it. The other had grown more slowly. This raged out, savagely growing more sure of itself as it leaped toward them, then darted sidewise.

Volcek turned suddenly to the instruments packed in the drawers. The spectrovisor and the diffractograph came out in his shaking hands, and he slapped them down onto the wooden sill of the window, already beginning to smoke faintly.

Then his hands steadied as he adjusted the instruments.

One look was enough. This was the nitrogen-fusion, not the harmless oxygen reaction.

His eyes met the Director's, and he nodded, but the nod was unnecessary. The Director had already guessed.

They moved toward him, a harsh mob sound coming from them, but the Director was before them.

"No! Stop!" The voice that had been trained to command a power greater than men had ever held before stopped them. "No, if the West has scientists too, that is no fault of Johann Volcek. Johann, you did not fail; you will not suffer."

Volcek heard him, and saw them fall back. He thought again of the lint on his coat, and looked down at it. He picked it off, while the others drew back, and the Director was assuring him that all would be well with him.

Stefanie would have no children now. There would be no grandchildren to hear the Director's senseless words, telling him he would not suffer.

You don't suffer when you've killed a race.

The Last Lunacy

Whoever held the moon, ruled Earth. And the rulers found a way to bring the moon monstrously close to Earth, without a break-up. But if the moon could be moved one way, it could be moved another…

LARA SHIVERED in the breeze that was stirring, and the scant covering she wore barely moved in it, a few bits of gauze stirring with the moving air. She stared at them, trying to realize that here on the surface of the earth the breeze was normal, not a sign of something passing nearby. It was cold, after the uniform Lunar shelter, but she had been warned of that.

Now she crouched down, peering over the rubble that clogged what had once been a great street. There were only the buildings, and no signs of movement. Seen from a distance, as when she landed her tiny flitter, the buildings had seemed unharmed; from this spot, the pits and cracks showed all too plainly. She wondered how the Blues could live here in the shadow of the Great Builders and think no more of the buildings than possible shelters.

But above her, the gigantic sphere of the moon shown down, reminding her that she had work to do. She shivered again, took a last quick look down the street, and dashed rapidly into the shadow of a building.

It wasn't so bad there, though she missed the brightness of the fluorescents on Luna. For a moment, she paused with her eyes closed, to let her near-eidetic memory paint the ancient map for her. The subway—whatever *it* was—had run underground here, and reports had indicated it was still open.

She had trouble finding the entrance, but the map had been right; it was easier going there, with cautious uses of her infra-red night-scanner. She could almost welcome the smell of mold and decay that permeated the tunnel.

Half an hour slow travelling led her near where the Attractor lay. She breathed easier, scanning carefully for the hidden entrance. She wasn't sure at first; then her eyes made out the cracks, and she moved forward, unconsciously shaking the hair back from a face she knew to be completely beautiful in a regal way as she prepared to fulfill her mission.

The heavy hands that caught her throat were noiseless—and stronger than human muscles could be. A grunt sounded, and the grip on her neck tightened, until her breath was completely cut off.

Then her attacker paused, running hard hands over her body. She struggled again and the shock of the sensations lent fresh fury to her efforts. But the hands had loosened.

"I'll be damned!" The voice was deep, firm, and as shocked as her own mind. Sudden yellow light sprang on, and she saw a blue hand going down from a helmet of some sort, while a yellow nimbus surrounded the blue body. He shook his head, staring at her, and his muscular hands swung her around, while his eyes made a careful study of every feature, until the scraps of clothing seemed to vanish before them. "A woman! A Lunatic!"

She tried to make her voice commanding, cutting off the fear, and succeeded. "A Master, Blue! You've pawed and you've stared, but I excuse that as ignorance of what you did. Don't provoke me further!"

He laughed. His eyes dropped—but only as far as her bosom. "I've seen Lunatic women from a distance—I ferried supplies up from here for a year. But I always thought the old accounts exaggerated. I used to dream about catching a real woman, sometime. Come here—maybe the books didn't exaggerate the rest of it, either..."

"Filth!" The little electrogun came out with a whipping motion, but he was quicker. He plucked it out of her hand, examined it, and pocketed it quietly. Lara jerked forward, and her teeth were raging for his neck.

He caught her, lifted her against all her fury. Then, before she could realize his intentions, her face was yanked around and his came down, forcing his lips against hers. And again, the shocking sensations sucked the energy from her body, until she could only stand frozen and white-faced until it was over.

HIS BLUE-SKINNED face crinkled into a grin. "Pleasant enough, but the ancient books exaggerated. Stand still! And this time, cooperate, or I'll squeeze your throat until your head pops off like a pit from a plum. You know how—you've books enough. At least, you've all you could find, leaving none for your blue slaves, as you thought. But things change in two centuries; cooperate, damn you!"

Lara shivered with rage, but the Blue obviously wasn't exaggerating—and she would do no good as a dead Master. Somehow, she caught control of her mind. His words gave her some clue—there'd been times when she had had her own romantic dreams of what the past had been like. And she'd had a few scraps of film. Now she summoned what skill she could, trying to relax and be soft against him, until his guard dropped.

But the sheer savage force he put into it was more than she had expected. She was gasping, uncertain, when he released her.

"It improves. But it can wait. What were you doing here?" He saw her gesture, and shook his head. "I'm not a slave, Lunatic. I'm one of the dead, according to your records. That's why I hide myself and my laboratories here—along with the books. I'm not in awe of you, but I know enough not to let you escape. I'm trading you a little life for common sense. Why were you going into my laboratories? As a spy?"

He had thrown the door the crack was supposed to conceal back now, and was dragging her after him, into a huge cavern, filled with the wrecks of great generators and a surprising collection of the tools of physics. Her eyes leaped unconsciously toward the camouflaged controls of the Attractor, spotted them, and went back to the laboratory. A Blue who did not respect the Masters! One who had read and studied—and now one who was doing science, the great forbidden act for the Blues!

"Then the rumors—" She couldn't finish it; it was starkly incredible. The Blues couldn't revolt. They were born to be slaves, reared as such, and knew no other fate. Besides, they had no weapons—or should have had none. This laboratory and the yellow nimbus about him left her less certain.

"War," he admitted calmly. "We have a debt to settle. Tomorrow night, we take the first steps. We've labored down here too long in want, to maintain a few of you in luxury on the moon. Now it's over. By the way, my name is Brucc; and since you're my woman by ancient right of conquest, what's yours?"

She told him, recognizing that there was no resisting his strength. "I could give you freedom, luxury—a woman Blue—as many as you want!"

He grimaced. "I've seen them. Fat, soft breeding animals you keep on the moon to maintain your stock. I revolted because I was to be a male breeder! After the mutation your war bred in my people, you had a hard time keeping it pure, didn't you? And it's only transmitted through the female. Too bad those females were unable fully to calcify their bones, and were imbeciles without exception. But don't expect me to increase your slaves! I...come here!"

"What—what—?" Anything to change the subject, to sway his mind, to give her time to think... "And didn't my people suffer? You had breeding females saved for you by our kindness—while we almost lost our last men."

"Yeah, I've seen those, too. You should have put them to work instead of letting them turn into such fragile little things. The histories of a place called France had 'dandies' in them that made your men look like lisping weaklings. Now be still; I've got to get out and direct things in another hour."

He reached for her again, and she shrank back. "What do you intend—want—?"

He told her, and his reason for the advisability of cooperation left no room for argument. And finally, as she met his eyes, she could feel tears on her own. Surprisingly, his own look softened, and the arms that drew her to him were strangely gentle. But he shook his head.

"You can't really believe what a slave thinks—I don't believe it myself. Do you think I want a stupid war of vengeance? I'm not a fool. But if I take you out there, they'll do things you couldn't imagine. I can't let you go back to report to the Lunatics. And somehow, you might get free if I leave you—unless I know you'll never dare go back. This way, you won't. They'd hear—I'd see to that—

and you'd wish our rebels had done their worst. Patrician pride in purity!"

He hesitated, and finally laughed again, grimly. "Tyrants on the moon, pig-men turning to blood-crazed jackals on earth. I wanted to be a student once, like those of old. Maybe you had dreams. But now we're what our worlds have made us. Cry if you want to."

SHE DIDN'T cry, then; but when he finally left, fastening the door behind him, she was crying. There was no rage in her now, nor even the drive to escape. There was no place to escape. In that, he'd been only too correct; she wasn't of the Moon now, and she could never be a Blue. She tried to whip her body into fury, but it was as limp as her mind.

From a small shaft above, the cries and rallying sounds of a mob came down, and she realized it must comprise all the Blues on earth. But the war against her pitifully few people seemed eons away. It wouldn't matter, anyhow. The moon was safe; it had always been inviolate, impregnable. Who owned the moon owned earth.

It had been that way when the first spaceship crawled up to it and established a base. It had proven so when a rival nation had struck at it, and the radioactives from the moon had wiped out most of the earth and brought the mutation of Blueness. Did it matter if nearly all the men on Luna had died as well, so that the women had to take over?

They had done well enough in two centuries, too; they'd found the shield against gravity, and learned to use it to create gravity. Moon surface now was at normal earth gravity, while a few miles up, the encircling shield cut off all gravity from earth, to enable them to approach within a distance easy for space-ferrying. In the early days the moon would have broken up from gravitational pulls at five times that distance: now, held by the bare thread of the Attractor field that was artificially maintained between the two bodies, it circled slowly in a small orbit, still ruling the earth below it. The moon would always rule.

In the darkness, something small and furry scurried along the wall, and she shrieked, drawing back into a corner. The strength came back to her legs, and she made the laboratory table in a great leap, curling up against the wall, and into a cubbyhole of sorts that was there. The animal had gone. She waited for another, but it did not seem there were more, since none appeared. The one had been as frightened as she was.

Then the lethargy that had replaced all her other emotions began to assert itself. The cries of the Blues above faded away and the thin shaft of light dimmed. She huddled back into the cubbyhole and let the sleep she had never expected wash over her.

It was a scurry of little feet that awakened her. The animal had come back—with all its friends. Something sharp dashed its clawy feet across her legs!

From somewhere, a hand fell over her mouth, and an arm lifted her quivering, leaping body back against the wall. "Shut up, you fool! If any of the men hear you… They're only rats, scared by my coming back. *Hush.* Do you have to behave as the old books said women did? You're safe."

He started to shake free, but she clung to him, digging her face into his shoulder, trying to cover all of her body with his. He shook her free, grinning again, and pointed to food he'd brought. "Eat it. If you knew the risk I'm running in sneaking back here when the men are getting the ships ready, you'd know it isn't to be wasted."

"Ships?"

"Of course. For every ship that was ruined between here and Luna, two were faked. We've been accumulating them for three generations. And we've finally found the shield we wanted against your radiation weapons—this yellow glow you see. My father began it, I finished it. Here, eat the rest of it."

IT SHOOK her. But there was still the great anti-gravity outer shield. It could be hardened down until nothing could get through, except the Attractor field. And there was another thing that could be done.

He swept the crumbs into the cloth and stuck it into a pouch at his side. "You can climb the shaft, if you want, up to a little opening. You can see the despised Blues taking off after your precious Lunatics. And since it's too late for you to warn Luna—if you were fool enough to try—I won't lock you in."

The door was barely closing behind him when the scurrying came again. He leaped back, slamming it shut and grabbing for her, to cut off her cry. But the scream died as she buried her head against his breast. "They—they—Bruce, stay here!"

"Because of a few rats, half-tame ones?" He pulled her face up, started to turn away, and then swung back. The grin was crooked on his face, and his arms were tautening slowly. "Well, why not? For a time."

She broke free long enough to use a word she hadn't known she knew. He made no answer, but his face twisted, and she knew suddenly that he hated himself as thoroughly as she could hate him—or herself—hated the wrongness with all this outward fulfillment of his boyhood dreams of what might have been long ago. For a moment she clung tighter to him, shaking her head, sharing the hatred. There was a rat in a shaft of light, watching her. It no longer mattered. Behind Bruce, her hand found a crumbled bit of rock, and threw it. The rat scampered away, and she found his lips again.

There was no shock now in the caress. She was no longer of Luna, and whatever happened here on this subject world to give her even a moment's forgetfullness was welcome.

But memories came back, after he had gone, along with the too-long neglected job she had come to do. She found the Attractor, and culled the needed facts from her mental pictures, setting back the force of it in its false-front of generator controls. They had sent her down to correct a sudden, unexplainable shift of the moon two percent closer to earth. Now let them wonder why the planet moved out to twice its former distance—out where the salvaged ships of the Blues could never reach it, with the size of their fuel tanks. It was her last gesture toward the world that had been ripped from her with a grin and a savage hand.

Then she climbed slowly up the shaft, still vague in her movements and without purpose in her mind. Sometime, she promised herself, she'd find a knife to use on his back; but he was still too watchful. Then she could kill herself. But she'd think of that some other time. She worked her way up, to find a tiny ledge just under the small opening. Beyond, she could see three ships being moved out into a cleared space, while another took off. But the moon was invisible, hidden by part of the building. A bit of the sky showed, however, totally wrong.

"Halloo!" The call came from below, and she looked down, upsetting a bit of rubble. "Halloo, Bruce. Time to—Hey! Hey! Men! A Lunatic—a White!"

The man began climbing up the shaft, but Lara wasted no time. The broken rock around the opening to the outside crumbled in her fingers, and went spinning down against the climber. She shoved her shoulders through the opening, found it wide enough, and was out—squarely in front of a heavy, muscular Blue.

Chaos broke out then. She was darting, running, leaping in and out, barely missing hands that kept coming closer. And the cry rose higher behind her. Suddenly, her arm was grabbed in a crushing fist, and she went spinning around, to be thrown over a yellow-glowing Blue's shoulder.

"Shut up! Lie still!" Bruce's voice hit her ears, jerking her head down to see it was he who had caught her. "You fool. Maybe they'll think I've captured you for a second."

But they were already breaking away from the others. Then the cry came up from behind, the man who'd first seen her calling his news to the others. Bruce added a bit more to his speed, but her weight told against him.

His breathing was heavy, but he gasped out a few words. "Book about ape-man when kids—used to play—hang on, if timber's still there. Hang on!"

THEY WERE falling through emptiness, down a huge, deep shaft as the words came out. She screamed, and heard his own voice echo it, just as his arms caught something, threatening to tear her from his shoulders by the shock. He groaned, then wiggled onto his stomach, and wormed rapidly under an overhang. Above, voices called down, and a light flashed on, showing muddy water at the bottom.

"Safe," he finally told her. "They think we're down there, dead. Safe, at least until we have to show ourselves to get tools, or the war kills us all. We can crawl through here, into another tunnel, follow that about three miles, and be outside the old city. I used to have a cave on a hill there, when I was eight, before they put me on full-time work to satisfy your people. Damn the Lunatics. They could have come down after the war and bred with us; there could have been a start toward a new race—we have some rather nice inherited abilities, such as triple reaction time. Instead, they had to play Ruler and Slave, and breed both true. Ouch, watch that place—broken glass."

"Why'd you save me?" she asked, later. "You're an outcast now, too—aren't you?"

"Instinct. Not because I wanted to. Pure instinct to save a mate, whatever you think of her. Same drive that's half responsible for the Blue's hatred of Luna, and the Lunatics' cold-blooded fanaticism today. Repressed instincts. Men don't breed like cattle. Less than five hundred Blues here. How many on Luna?"

"Blues—thirty-five women. Maybe two hundred of—of the others. Bruce, how much further?"

"Fifteen yards, and we can walk."

They went on silently then. And finally they came out to a broken road among trees that wandered up a hill. They were in a clearing near the top, and Bruce went into a tiny cave, coming out with an old velviplast robe and air mattress that he threw on a rock. She had slumped against it, and he had to lift her up and turn her head to the sky. She was tired, emotionally spent, and she sank back against him almost gratefully.

The sky was red.

She studied it, making no sense of it. The moon was glowing with a brilliant red that seemed to set the whole sky afire—and it was nearer—nearer than it had ever been. It should have been further away.

"Heterodyned," he said. "They found your gravity-shield frequency, and they've set up a counter force. It's heating up, it seems. I knew they had it, but didn't know it would work."

"But—" Then she understood. They must have been trying it out for weeks. It couldn't cut through the gravity shield until it broke it completely, of course. But it was wasting some of its energy in Attractor force, channeling itself to a frequency that stepped up the little force applied, and bringing the moon in closer.

SOMETHING nagged at her, but she shook it off. She was an outcast—what difference did it make? And the change was still unreal, after the fixed orbits of her whole life. She bent her head up toward the sky, and he kissed her. She made no attempt to draw away, even tried responding. It was pleasant, in a way, if she didn't think about it.

"All the men from here are up there—we're all there's left on earth," he told her. "Be quite a spectacle when the shield cracks. The moon will get down within two hundred miles of earth, at her velocity. And then the Blues will have their fill of blood and revenge, I suppose!"

The nagging thought hit her. "Roche's limit!"

"Huh?"

"Roche's limit. At that range, it's going to crack up, like Saturn's rings—even if it doesn't draw nearer, it's within less than a fifth of the distance it would have to be to stand. Bruce! Bruce, we've got to go back."

He shook his head. "Let it crack. All the moon ever brought was lunacy. It used to be in every superstition as the source of insanity. And it turned out to be the biggest insanity of all. To hell with it!"

"It'll take us with it, Bruce, it can be stopped. That's what I came for—to change the real attraction that holds us; it isn't gravity any more—the shield is perfect, as long as it stands. Your people, the others, Earth itself…"

"Does it matter?" he asked, and his grin was back, twisted more than ever. "Maybe it does. Maybe earth does, at least. It wasn't her fault we went wrong. All right, lead on; we can make it in an hour, if we hurry."

The moon was sinking lower as they went, and her legs were leaden. Somewhere, he found a horse, and put her on it, leading the animal, but they made slow time. He dashed into another building at the edge of the tall buildings and came back with dark bread and thick molasses dripping from it, handing it to her while he swallowed what she left. He was right—they needed nourishment badly.

But at last they reached the laboratory, and he shoved back the half-opened door. The moon was brighter now, so lurid that no light was needed as she found her way by the illumination from the shaft, and began playing with the difficult dials of the deceptive panel.

She dragged him out, up the ladders that led through various levels. And finally he looked up, and his grunt was the first really surprised sound she had heard.

The moon was moving outward, picking up speed as it went at a seemingly impossible rate, and shrinking almost visibly. Its color had dropped a fraction, also.

"The Attractor can also repulse, if reversed—and it has full power now—plus the waste energy from the shield, which will take form in negative Attraction as well as positive. I'm a field expert—or was. Maybe they'll be able to get a ship down and anchor on Mars, since it's heading for that orbit. Mars will have three moons and we'll have none, then."

He nodded. "Unless they kill each other off. If they don't, let them learn to breed like humans—and feed themselves on their hydroponics. Well, there goes the next to the last lunacy."

She looked at him, trying to make sense of his final words, but he only grinned at her. His arms came out, picking her up and setting her on the horse. "We'll go back near the cave—there's an old house there, still sturdy. We can sleep in the cave tonight, start rebuilding tomorrow. Or you can take the horse and go where you like. But you'll probably starve to death without me to show you how to live. That's the last lunacy, Lara—the two of us, this whole business between us. It's over, too."

But he kept his hand on the horse's neck, guiding it.

She studied the hand, blue in color, but strong and lithe, sure of itself, sometimes cruel in its mockery, but equally gentle when it should be. The color, along with defects in the females, was passed on by the female Blues only. Their children would be the old color of men before the mutation. But they'd need hands like that in the world which was left for them to repopulate.

"Let's hurry back to the cave, beloved," she said. The last word came hard, from the rusty files of history. But time would remedy that.

He reached up, lifted her down onto his shoulder, and then into his arms. His legs were steady and unfaltering as he marched forward with her toward the cave.

Neither looked up for the receding moon.

Let 'Em Breathe Space!

Eighteen men and two women in the closed world of a space ship for five months can only spell tension and trouble—but in this case, the atmosphere was *literally poisoned.*

Five months out from Earth, we were halfway to Saturn and three-quarters of the way to murder. At least, I was. I was sick of the feuding, the worries and the pettiness of the other nineteen aboard. My stomach heaved at the bad food; the eternal smell of people, and the constant sound of nagging and complaints. For ten lead pennies, I'd have gotten out into space and tried walking back to Earth. Sometimes I thought about doing it without the pennies.

But I knew I wasn't that tough, in spite of what I looked. I'd been built to play fullback, and my questionable brunet beauty had been roughed up by the explosion years before as thoroughly as dock fighting on all the planets could have done. But sometimes I figured all that meant was that there was more of me to hurt, and that I'd had more experience screaming when the anodyne ran out.

Anyhow, whole-wheat pancakes made with sourdough for the ninth "morning" running was too damned much! I felt my stomach heave over again, took one whiff of the imitation maple syrup, and shoved the mess back fast while I got up faster.

It was a mistake. Phil Riggs, our scrawny, half-pint meteorologist, grinned nastily and reached for the plate. "'Smatter, Paul? Don't you like your breakfast? It's good for you—whole wheat contains bran. The staff of life. Man, after that diet of bleached paste..."

There's one guy like that in every bunch. The cook was mad at us for griping about his coffee, so our group of scientists on this cockeyed Saturn Expedition were getting whole wheat flour as punishment, while Captain Muller probably sat in his cabin chuckling about it. In our agreement, there was a clause that we could go over Muller's head on such things with a unanimous petition—but Riggs had spiked that. The idiot liked bran in his flour, even for pancakes!

Or else he was putting on a good act for the fun of watching the rest of us suffer.

"You can take your damned whole wheat and staff it—" I started. Then I shrugged and dropped it. There were enough feuds going on aboard the cranky old *Wahoo!* "Seen Jenny this morning, Phil?"

He studied me insolently. "She told Doc Napier she had some stuff growing in hydroponics she wanted to look at. You're wasting your time on that babe, boy!"

"Thanks for nothing," I muttered at him, and got out before I really decided on murder. Jenny Sanderson was our expedition biologist. A natural golden blonde, just chin-high on me, and cute enough to earn her way through a Ph. D. doing modeling. She had a laugh that would melt a brass statue, which she used too much on Doc Napier, on our chief, and even on grumpy old Captain Muller—but sometimes she used it on me, when she wanted something. And I never did have much use for a girl who was the strong independent type where there was a man to do the dirty work, so that was okay.

I suppose it was natural, with only two women among eighteen men for month after month, but right then I probably liked Doc Napier less than the captain, even. I pulled myself away from the corridor to hydroponics, started for observation, and then went on into the cubbyhole they gave me for a cabin. On the *Wahoo*, all a man could do was sleep or sit around and think about murder.

Well, I had nobody to blame but myself. I'd asked for the job when I first heard Dr. Pietro had collected funds and priorities for a trip to study Saturn's rings at close hand. And because I'd done some technical work for him on the Moon, he figured he might as well take me as any other good all-around mechanic and technician. He hadn't asked me, though—that had been my own stupid idea.

Paul Tremaine, self-cure expert! I'd picked up a nice phobia against space when the superliner *Lauri Ellu* cracked up with four hundred passengers on my first watch as second engineer. I'd gotten free and into a suit, but after they rescued me, it had taken two years on the Moon before I could get up nerve for the shuttle back to Earth. And after eight years home, I should have let well enough alone. If I'd known anything about Pietro's expedition, I'd have wrapped myself in my phobia and loved it.

But I didn't know then that he'd done well with priorities and only fair with funds. The best he could afford was the rental of the old Earth-Mars-Venus triangle freighter. Naturally, when the *Wahoo's* crew heard they were slated for what would be at least three years off Earth without fancy bonus rates, they quit. Since nobody else would sign on, Pietro had used his priorities to get an injunction that forced them back aboard. He'd stuffed extra oxygen, water, food and fertilizer on top of her regular supplies, then, filled her holds with some top level fuel he'd gotten from a government assist, and set out. And by the time I found out about it, my own contract was iron-bound, and I was stuck.

As an astrophysicist, Pietro was probably tops. As a man to run the Lunar Observatory, he was a fine executive. But as a man to head up an expedition into deep space...somebody should have given him back his teething ring.

Not that the *Wahoo* couldn't make the trip with the new fuel; she'd been one of the early survey ships' before they turned her into a freighter. But she was meant for a crew of maybe six, on trips of a couple of months. There were no game rooms, no lounges, no bar or library—nothing but what had to be. The only thing left for most of us aboard was to develop our hatreds of the petty faults of the others. Even with a homogeneous and willing crew, it was a perfect set-up for cabin fever, and we were as heterogeneous as they came.

Naturally the crew hated the science boys after being impressed into duty, and also took it out on the officers. The officers felt the same about both other groups. And the scientists hated the officers and crew for all the inconveniences of the old *Wahoo*. Me? I was in no-man's land—technically in the science group, but without a pure science degree; I had an officer's feelings left over from graduating as an engineer on the ships; and I looked like a crewman.

It cured my phobia, all right. After the first month out, I was too disgusted to go into a fear funk. But I found out it didn't help a bit to like space again and know I'd stay washed up as a spaceman.

We'd been jinxed from the start. Two months out, the whole crew of scientists came down with something Doc Napier finally diagnosed as food poisoning; maybe he was right, since our group ate in our own mess hall, and the crew and officers who didn't eat with us didn't get it. Our astronomer, Bill Sanderson, almost died. I'd been lucky, but then I never did react to things much. There were a lot of other small troubles, but the next major trick had been fumes from the nuclear generators getting up into our quarters—it was always our group that had the trouble. If Eve Nolan hadn't been puttering with some of her trick films at the time—she and Walt Harris had the so-called night shift—and seen them blacken, we'd have been dead before they discovered it. And it took us two weeks of bunking with the sullen crew and decontamination before we could pick up life again. Engineer Wilcox had been decent about helping with it, blaming himself. But it had been a mess.

Naturally, there were dark hints that someone was trying to get us; but I couldn't see any crewman wiping us out just to return to Earth, where our contract, with its completion clause, would mean he wouldn't have a dime coming to him. Anyhow, the way things were going, we'd all go berserk before we reached Saturn.

The lunch gong sounded, but I let it ring. Bullard would be serving us whole wheat biscuits and soup made out of beans he'd let soak until they turned sour. I couldn't take any more of that junk, the way I felt then. I heard some of the men going down the corridor, followed by a confused rumble of voices. Then somebody let out a yell. "Hey, *rooob!*"

That meant something. The old yell spacemen had picked up from carney people to rally their kind around against the foe. And I had a good idea of who was the foe. I heard the yell bounce down the passage again, and the slam of answering feet.

Then the gravity field went off. Or rather, was cut off. We may have missed the boat in getting anti-gravity, if there is such a thing, but our artificial gravity is darned near fool-proof.

It was ten years since I'd moved in free fall, but Space Tech had done a good job of training good habits. I got out of my bunk, hit the corridor with a hand out, bounced, kicked, and dove toward the mess hall without a falter. The crewmen weren't doing so well—but they were coming up the corridor fast enough.

I could have wrung Muller's neck. Normally, in case of trouble, cutting gravity is smart. But not here, where the crew already wanted a chance to commit mayhem, and had more experience than the scientists.

Yet, surprisingly, when I hit the mess hall ten feet ahead of the deckhands, most of the scientists were doing all right. Hell, I should have known Pietro, Sanderson and a couple others would be used to no-grav; in astronomical work, you cut your eye teeth on that. They were braced around the cook, who huddled back in a corner, while our purser-steward, Sam, was still singing for help.

The fat face of the cook was dead white. Bill Sanderson, looking like a slim, blond ballet dancer and muscled like an apache expert, had him in one hand and was stuffing the latest batch of whole wheat biscuits down his throat. Bill's sister, Jenny, was giggling excitedly and holding more biscuits.

The deckhands and Grundy, the mate, were almost at the door, and I had just time enough to slam it shut and lock it in their faces. I meant to enjoy seeing the cook taken down without any interruption.

Sam let out a final yell, and Bullard broke free, making a mess of it without weight. He was sputtering out bits of the biscuit. Hal Lomax reached out a big hand, stained with the chemicals that had been his life's work, and pushed the cook back.

And suddenly fat little Bullard switched from quaking fear to a blind rage. The last of the biscuit sailed from his mouth and he spat at Hal. "You damned hi-faluting black devil. You—*you* sneering at my cooking. I'm a white man, I am—I don't have to work for no black ni…"

I reached him first, though even Sam started for him then. You can deliver a good blow in free-fall, if you know how. His teeth against my knuckles stopped my leap, and the back of his head bounced off the wall. He was unconscious as he drifted by us, moving upwards. My knuckles stung, but it had been worth it. Anyhow, Jenny's look more than paid for the trouble.

The door shattered then, and the big hulk of Mate Grundy tumbled in, with the two deckhands and the pair from the engine room behind him. Sam let out a yell that sounded like protest, and they headed for us—just as gravity came on.

I pulled myself off the floor and out from under Bullard to see the stout, oldish figure of Captain Muller standing in the doorway, with Engineer Wilcox slouched easily beside him, looking like the typical natty space officer you see on television. Both held gas guns.

"All right, break it up!" Muller ordered. "You men get back to your work. And you, Dr. Pietro—my contract calls for me to deliver you to Saturn's moon, but it doesn't forbid me to haul you the rest of the way in irons. I won't have this aboard my ship!"

Pietro nodded, his little gray goatee bobbing, his lean body coming upright smoothly. "Quite right, Captain. Nor does it forbid me to let you and your men spend the sixteen months on the moon—where *I* command—in irons. Why don't you ask Sam what happened before you make a complete fool of yourself, Captain Muller?"

Sam gulped and looked at the crew, but apparently Pietro was right; the little guy had been completely disgusted by Bullard. He shrugged apologetically. "Bullard insulted Dr. Lomax, sir. I yelled for someone to help me get him out of here, and I guess everybody got all mixed up when gravity went off, and Bullard cracked his head on the floor. Just a misunderstanding, sir,"

Muller stood there, glowering at the cut on my knuckles, and I could feel him aching for a good excuse to make his threat a reality. But finally, he grunted and swung on his heel, ordering the crew with him. Grundy threw us a final grimace and skulked off behind him. Finally there was only Wilcox, who grinned, shrugged, and shut the door quietly behind him. And we were left with the mess freefall had made of the place.

I spotted Jenny heading across the room, carefully not seeing the fatuous glances Pietro was throwing her way, and I swung in behind. She nodded back at me, but headed straight for Lomax, with an odd look on her face. When she reached him, her voice was low and businesslike.

"Hal, what did those samples of Hendrix's show up?"

Hendrix was the Farmer, in charge of the hydroponics that turned the carbon dioxide we breathed out back to oxygen, and also gave us a bit of fresh vegetables now and then. Technically, he was a crewman, just as I was a scientist; but actually, he felt more like one of us.

Lomax looked surprised. "What samples, Jenny? I haven't see Hendrix for two weeks."

"You—" She stopped, bit her lip, and frowned. She swung on me. "Paul, have you seen him?"

I shook my head. "Not since last night. He was asking Eve and Walt to wake him up early, then."

"That's funny. He was worried about the plants yesterday and wanted Hal to test the water and chemical fertilizer. I looked for him this morning, but when he didn't show up I thought he was with you, Hal. And—the plants are dying!"

"All of them?" The half smile wiped off Hal's face, and I could feel my stomach hit my insteps. When anything happens to the plants in a ship, it isn't funny.

She shook her head again. "No about a quarter of them. I was coming for help when the fight started. They're all bleached out. And it looks like—like chromazone!"

That really hit me. They developed the stuff to fight off fungus on Venus, where one part in a billion did the trick. But it was tricky stuff; one part in ten-million would destroy the chlorophyll in plants in about twenty hours, or the hemoglobin in blood in about fifteen minutes. It was practically a universal poison.

Hal started for the door, then stopped. He glanced around the room, turned back to me, and suddenly let out a healthy bellow of seeming amusement. Jenny's laugh was right in harmony. I caught the drift, and tried to look as if we were up to some monkey business as we slipped out of the room. Nobody seemed suspicious.

Then we made a dash for hydroponics, toward the rear of the ship. We scrambled into the big chamber together, and stopped. Everything looked normal among the rows of plant-filled tanks, pipes and equipment. Jenny led us down one of the rows and around a bend.

The plants in the rear quarter weren't sick—they were dead. They were bleached to a pale yellow, liked boiled grass, and limp. Nothing would save them now.

"I'm a biologist, not a botanist—" Jenny began.

Hal grunted sickly. "Yeah. And I'm not a life hormone expert. But there's one test we can try."

He picked up a pair of rubber gloves from a rack, and pulled off some wilted stalks. From one of the healthy tanks, he took green leaves. He mashed the two kinds together on the edge of a bench and watched. "If it's chromazone, they've developed an enzyme by now that should eat the color out of those others."

In about ten seconds, I noticed the change. The green began to bleach before my eyes.

Jenny made a sick sound in her throat and stared at the rows of healthy plants. "I checked the valves, and this sick section is isolated. But—if chromazone got into the chemicals... Better get your spectroanalyzer out, Hal, while I get Captain Muller. Paul, be a dear and find and Hendrix, will you?"

I shook my head, and went further down the rows. "No need, Jenny," I called back. I pointed to the shoe I'd seen sticking out from the edge of one of the tanks. There was a leg attached.

I reached for it, but Lomax shoved me back. "Don't—the enzymes in the corpse are worse than the poison, Paul. Hands off." He reached down with the gloves and heaved. It was Hendrix, all right—a corpse with a face and hands as white as human flesh could ever get. Even the lips were bleached out.

Jenny moaned. "The fool! The stupid fool. He *knew* it was dangerous without gloves; he suspected chromazone, even though none's supposed to be on board. And I warned him..."

"Not against this, you didn't," I told her. I dropped to my knees and took another pair of gloves. Hendrix's head rolled under my grasp. The skull was smashed over the left eye, as if someone had taken a sideswipe at Hendrix with a hammer. No fall had produced that. "You should have warned him about his friends. Must have been killed, then dumped in there."

"Murder!" Hal bit the word out in disgust. "You're right, Paul. Not too stupid a way to dispose of the body, either—in another couple of hours, he'd have started dissolving in that stuff, and we'd never have guessed it was murder. That means this poisoning of the plants wasn't an accident. Somebody poisoned the water, then got worried when there wasn't a report on the plants; must have been someone who thought it worked faster on plants than it does. So he came to investigate, and Hendrix caught him fooling around. So he got killed."

"But who?" Jenny asked.

I shrugged sickly. "Somebody crazy enough—or desperate enough to turn back that he'll risk our air and commit murder. You'd better go after the captain while Hal gets his test equipment. I'll keep watch here."

It didn't feel good in hydroponics after they left. I looked at those dead plants, trying to figure whether there were enough left to keep us going. I studied Hendrix's body, trying to tell myself the murderer had no reason to come back and try to get me.

I reached for a cigarette, and then put the pack back. The air felt almost as close as the back of my neck felt tense and unprotected. And telling myself it was all imagination didn't help—not with what was in that chamber to keep me company.

CHAPTER TWO

Muller's face was like an iceberg when he came down—but only after he saw Hendrix. Before then I'd caught the fat moon-calf expression on his face, and I'd heard Jenny giggling. Damn it, they'd taken enough time. Hal was already back, fussing over things with the hunk of tin and lenses he treated like a newborn baby.

Doc Napier came in behind them, but separately. I saw him glance at them and look sick. Then both Muller and Napier began concentrating on business. Napier bent his nervous, bony figure over the corpse, and stood up almost at once. "Murder all right."

"So I guessed, Dr. Napier," Muller growled heavily at him. "Wrap him up and put him between hulls to freeze. We'll bury him when we land. Tremaine, give a hand with it, will you?"

"I'm not a laborer, Captain Muller!" Napier protested. I started to tell him where he could get off, too.

But Jenny shook her head at us. "Please. Can't you see Captain Muller is trying to keep too many from knowing about this? I should think you'd be glad to help. Please?"

Put that way, I guess it made sense. We found some rubber sheeting in one of the lockers and began wrapping Hendrix in it; it wasn't pleasant, since he was beginning to soften up from the enzymes he'd absorbed. "How about going ahead to make sure no one sees us?" I suggested to Jenny.

Muller opened his mouth, but Jenny gave one of her quick little laughs and opened the door for us. Doc looked relieved. I guessed he was trying to kid himself. Personally, I wasn't a fool—I was just hooked; I knew perfectly well she was busy playing us off against one another, and probably having a good time balancing the books. But hell, that's the way life runs.

"Get Pietro up here!" Muller fired after us. She laughed again, and nodded. She went with us until we got to the 'tween-hulls lock, then went off after the chief. She was back with him just as we finished stuffing Hendrix through and sealing up again.

Muller grunted at us when we got back, then turned to Lomax again. The big chemist didn't look happy. He spread his hands toward us, and hunched his shoulders. "A fifty-times overdose of chromazone in those tanks—fortunately none in the others. And I can't find a trace of it in the fertilizer chemicals or anywhere else. Somebody deliberately put it in those tanks."

"Why?" Pietro asked. We'd filled him in with the rough details, but it still made no sense to him.

"Suppose you tell me, Dr. Pietro," Muller suggested. "Chromazone is a poison most people never heard of. One of the new *scientific* nuisances."

Pietro straightened, and his goatee bristled. "If you're hinting…"

"I am *not* hinting, Dr. Pietro. I'm telling you that I'm confining your group to their quarters until we can clean up this mess, distil the water that's contaminated, and replant. After that, if an investigation shows nothing, I *may* take your personal bond for the conduct of your people. Right now I'm protecting my ship."

"But captain—" Jenny began.

Muller managed a smile at her. "Oh, not you, of course, Jenny. I'll need you here. With Hendrix gone, you're the closest thing we have to a Farmer now."

"Captain Muller," Pietro said sharply. "Captain, in the words of the historical novelists—drop dead! Dr. Sanderson, I forbid you to leave your quarters so long as anyone else is confined to his. I have ample authority for that."

"Under emergency powers—" Muller spluttered over it, and Pietro jumped in again before he could finish.

"Precisely, Captain. Under emergency situations, when passengers aboard a commercial vessel find indications of total irresponsibility or incipient insanity on the part of a ship's officer, they are considered correct in assuming command for the time needed to protect their lives. We were poisoned by food prepared in your kitchen, and were nearly killed by radioactivity through a leak in the engine room—and no investigation was made. We are now confronted with another situation aimed against our welfare—as the others were wholly aimed at us—and you choose to conduct an investigation against our group only. My only conclusion is that you wish to confine us to quarters so we cannot find your motives for this last outrage. Paul, will you kindly relieve the captain of his position?"

They were both half right, and mostly wrong. Until it was proved that our group was guilty, Muller couldn't issue an order that was obviously discriminatory and against our personal safety in case there was an attack directed on us. He'd be mustered out of space and into the Lunar Cells for that. But on the other hand, the "safety for passengers" clause Pietro was citing applied only in the case of overt, direct and physical danger by an officer to normal passengers. He might be able to weasel it through a court, or he might be found guilty of mutiny. It left me in a pretty position.

Jenny fluttered around. "Now, now—" she began.

I cut her off. "Shut up, Jenny. And you two damned fools cool down. Damn it, we've got an emergency here all right—we may not have air plants enough to live on. Pietro, we can't run the ship—and neither can Muller get through what's obviously a mess that may call for all our help by confining us. Why don't you two go off and fight it out in person?"

Surprisingly, Pietro laughed. "I'm afraid I'd put up a poor showing against the captain, Paul. My apologies, Captain Muller."

Muller hesitated, but finally took Pietro's hand, and dropped the issue.

"We've got enough plants," he said, changing the subject. "We'll have to cut out all smoking and other waste of air. And I'll need Jenny to work the hydroponics, with any help she requires. We've got to get more seeds planted, and fast. Better keep word of this to ourselves. We—"

A shriek came from Jenny then. She'd been busy at one of the lockers in the chamber. Now she began ripping others open and pawing through things inside rubber-gloves. "Captain Muller! The seeds! The seeds!"

Hal took one look, and his face turned gray.

"Chromazone," he reported. "Every bag of seed has been filled with a solution of chromazone! They're worthless!"

"How long before the plants here will seed?" Muller asked sharply.

"Three months," Jenny answered. "Captain Muller, what are we going to do?"

The dour face settled into grim determination. "The only sensible thing. Take care of these plants, conserve the air, and squeeze by until we can reseed. And, Dr. Pietro, with your permission, we'll turn about for Earth at once. We can't go on like this. To proceed would be to endanger the life of every man aboard."

"Please, Danton." Jenny put her hand on Pietro's arm. "I know what this all means to you, but—"

Pietro shook her off. "It means the captain's trying to get out of the expedition, again. It's five months back to Earth—more, by the time we kill velocity. It's the same to Saturn. And either way, in five months we've got this fixed up, or we're helpless. Permission to return refused, Captain Muller."

"Then if you'll be so good as to return to your own quarters," Muller said, holding himself back with an effort that turned his face red, "we'll start clearing this up. And not a word of this."

Napier, Lomax, Pietro and I went back to the scientists' quarters, leaving Muller and Jenny conferring busily. That was at fifteen o'clock. At sixteen o'clock, Pietro issued orders against smoking.

Dinner was at eighteen o'clock. We sat down in silence. I reached for my plate without looking. And suddenly little Phil Riggs was on his feet, raving. "Whole wheat! Nothing but whole wheat bread! I'm sick of it—sick! I won't—"

"Sit down!" I told him. I'd bitten into one of the rolls on the table. It was white bread, and it was the best the cook had managed so far. There was corn instead of baked beans, and he'd done a fair job of making meat loaf. "Stop making a fool of yourself, Phil."

He slumped back, staring at the white bun into which he'd bitten. "Sorry. Sorry. It's this air—so stuffy. I can't breathe. I can't see right—"

Pietro and I exchanged glances, but I guess we weren't surprised. Among intelligent people on a ship of that size, secrets wouldn't keep. They'd all put bits together and got part of the answer. Pietro shrugged, and half stood up to make an announcement.

"Beg pardon, sirs." We jerked our heads around to see Bullard standing in the doorway.

He was scared stiff, and his words got stuck in his throat. Then he found his voice again. "I heard as how Hendrix went crazy and poisoned the plants and went and killed himself and we'll all die if we don't find some trick, and what I want to know, please, sirs, is are what they're saying right and you know all kinds of tricks and can you save us because I can't go on like this not knowing and hearing them talking outside the galley and none of them telling me—"

Lomax cut into his flood of words. "You'll live, Bullard. Farmer Hendrix did get killed in an accident to some of the plants, but we've still got air enough. Captain Muller has asked the help of a few of us, but it's only a temporary emergency."

Bullard stared at him, and slowly some of the fear left his face—though not all of it. He turned and left with a curt bow of his head, while Pietro added a few details that weren't exactly lies to Lomax's hasty cover-up, along with a grateful glance at the chemist. It seemed to work, for the time being—at least enough for Riggs to begin making nasty remarks about cooked paste.

Then the tension began to build again. I don't think any of the crew talked to any of our group. And yet, there seemed to be a chain of rumor that exchanged bits of information. Only the crew could have seen the dead plants being carried down to our refuse breakdown plant; and the fact it was chromazone poisoning must have been deduced from a description by some of our group. At any rate, both groups knew all about it—and a little bit more, as was usual with rumors—by the second day.

Muller should have made the news official, but he only issued an announcement that the danger was over. When Peters, our radioman-navigator, found Sam and Phil Riggs smoking and dressed them down, it didn't make Muller's words seem too convincing. I guessed that Muller had other things on his mind; at least he wasn't in his cabin much, and I didn't see Jenny for two whole days.

My nerves were as jumpy as those of the rest. It isn't too bad cutting out smoking; a man can stand imagining the air is getting stale; but when every unconscious gesture toward cigarettes that aren't there reminds him of the air, and when every imagined stale stench makes him want a cigarette to relax, it gets a little rough.

Maybe that's why I was in a completely rotten mood when I finally did spot Jenny going down the passage; with the tight coveralls she was wearing emphasizing every motion of her hips. I grabbed her and swung her around. "Hi, stranger. Got time for a word?"

She sort of brushed my hand off her arm, but didn't seem to mind it. "Why, I guess so, Paul. A little time. Captain Muller's watching the 'ponics."

"Good," I said, trying to forget Muller. "Let's make it a little more private than this, though. Come on in."

She lifted an eyebrow at the open door of my cabin, made with a little giggle, and stepped inside. I followed her, and kicked the door shut. She reached for it, but I had my back against it.

"Paul!" She tried to get around me, but I wasn't having any. I pushed her back onto the only seat in the room, which was the bunk. She got up like a spring uncoiling. "Paul Tremaine, you open that door. You know better than that. Paul, please!"

"What makes me any different than the others? You spend plenty of time in Muller's cabin—and you've been in Pietro's often enough. Probably Doc Napier's, too."

Her eyes hardened, but she decided to try the patient and reason-with-the-child line. "That is different. Captain Muller and I have a great deal of business to work out."

"Sure. And he looks great in lipstick!"

It was a shot in the dark, but it went home. I wished I'd kept my darned mouth shut; before I'd been suspecting it—now I knew. She turned pink and tried to slap me, which won't work when the girl is sitting on a bunk and I'm on my feet. "You mind your own business!"

"I'm doing that. Generations should stick together, and he's old enough to be your father!"

She leaned back and studied me. Then she smiled slowly, and something about it made me sick inside. "I like older men, Paul. They make people my own age seem so callow, so unfinished. It's so comforting to have mature people around. I always did have an Electra complex."

"The Greeks had plenty of names for it, kid," I told her. "Don't get me wrong. If you want to be a slut, that's your own business. But when you pull the innocent act on me, and then fall back to sophomore psychology—"

This time she stood up before she slapped. Before her hand stung my face, I was beginning to regret what I'd said. Afterwards, I didn't give a damn. I picked her up off the floor, slapped her soundly on the rump, pulled her tight against me, and kissed her. She tried scratching my face, then went passive and wound up with one arm around my neck and the other in the hair at the back of my head. When I finally put her down she sank back onto the bunk, breathing heavily.

"Why, Paul!" And she reached out her arms as I came down to meet them. For a second, the world looked pretty good.

Then a man's hoarse scream cut through it all, with the sound of heavy steps in panic flight. I jerked up. Jenny hung on. "Paul…Paul…" But there was the smell of death in the air, suddenly. I broke free and was out into the corridor. The noise seemed to come from the shaft that led to the engine room, and I jumped for it, while I heard doors slam.

This time, there was a commotion, like a wet sack being tossed around in a pentagonal steel barrel, and another hoarse scream that cut off in the middle to a gargling sound.

I reached the shaft and started down the center rail, not bothering with the hand-grips. I could hear something rustle below, followed by silence, but I couldn't see a thing; the lights had been cut.

I could feel things poking into my back before I landed; I always get the creeps when there's death around, and that last sound had been just that—somebody's last sound. I *knew* somebody was going to kill me before I could find the switch. Then I stumbled over something, and my hair stood on end. I guess my own yell was pretty horrible. It scared me worse than I was already. But my fingers found the switch somehow, and the light flashed on.

Sam lay on the floor, with blood still running from a wide gash across his throat. A big kitchen knife was still stuck in one end of the horrible wound. And one of his fingers was half sliced off where the blade of a switch-blade shiv had failed on him and snapped back.

Something sounded above me, and I jerked back. But it was Captain Muller, coming down the rail. The man had obviously taken it all in on the way down. He jerked the switch-blade out of Sam's dead grasp and looked at the point of the knife. There was blood further back from the cut finger; but none on the point.

"Damn!" Muller tossed it down in disgust. "If he'd scratched the other man, we'd have had a chance to find who it was. Tremaine, have you got an alibi?"

"I was with Jenny," I told him, and watched his eyes begin to hate me. But he nodded. We picked Sam up together and lugged his body up to the top of the shaft, where the crowd had collected. Pietro, Peters, the cook, Grundy and Lomax were there. Beyond them, the dark-haired, almost masculine head of Eve Nolan showed, her eyes studying the body of Sam as if it were a negative in her darkroom; as usual, Bill Sanderson was as close to her as he could get. But there was no sign now of Jenny. I glanced up the corridor, but saw only Wilcox and Phil Riggs, with Walt Harris trailing them, rubbing the sleep out of his eyes.

Muller moved directly to Pietro. "Six left in my crew now, Dr. Pietro. First Hendrix, now Sam. Can you still say that the attack is on *your* crew when mine keep being killed? This time, sir, I demand…"

"Give 'em hell, Captain," ape-man Grundy broke in. "Cut the fancy stuff, and let's get the damned murdering rats!"

Muller's eyes quartered him, spitted his carcass, and began turning him slowly over a bed of coals. "Mister Grundy, I am master of the *Wahoo*. I fail to remember asking for' your piratical advice. Dr. Pietro, I trust you will have no objections if I ask Mr. Peters to investigate your section and group thoroughly?"

"None at all, Captain Muller," Pietro answered. "I trust Peters. And I feel sure you'll permit me to delegate Mr. Tremaine to inspect the remainder of the ship."

Muller nodded curtly. "Certainly. Until the madman is found, we're all in danger. And unless he is found, I insist I must protect my crew and my ship by turning back to Earth."

"I cannot permit that, sir."

"Your permission for that was not requested, Dr. Pietro. Yes, Bullard?"

The cook had been squirming and muttering to himself for minutes. Now he darted out toward Grundy, and his finger pointed to Lomax. "He done it! I seen him. Killed the only friend I had, he did. They went by my galley—and—and he grabbed my big knife, that one there. And he killed Sam."

"You're sure it was Lomax?" Muller asked sharply.

"Sure I'm sure. Sam, he was acting queer lately. He was worried. Told me he saw something, and he was going to know for sure. He borrowed my switch-blade knife that my wife gave me. And he went out looking for something. Then I heard him a-running, and I looked up, and there was this guy, chasing him. Sure, I seen him with my own eyes."

Eve Nolan chuckled throatily, throwing her mannish-cut hair back from her face. She was almost pretty with an expression on her countenance, even if it was amused disgust. "Captain Muller, that's a nice story. But Dr. Lomax was with me in my darkroom, working on some spectroanalysis slides. Bill Sanderson and Phil Riggs were waiting outside for us. And Mr. Peters saw us come out together when we all ran down here."

Peters nodded. Muller stared at us for a second, and the hunting lust died out of his eyes, leaving them blank and cold. He turned to Bullard. "Bullard, an explanation might make me reduce your punishment. If you have anything to say, say it now!"

The cook was gibbering and actually drooling with fear. He shook, and sweat popped out all over him. "My knife—I hadda say something. They stole my knife. They wanted it to look like I done it. God, Captain, you'da done the same. Can't punish a man for trying to save his life. I'm a good man, I am. Can't whip a good man! Can't—"

"Give him twenty-five lashes with the wire, Mr. Grundy," Muller said flatly.

Pietro let out a shriek on top of the cook's. He started forward, but I caught him. "Captain Muller's right," I told him. "On a spaceship, the full crew is needed. The brig is useless, so the space-enabling charter recognizes flogging. Something is needed to maintain discipline."

Pietro dropped back reluctantly, but Lomax faced the captain. "The man is a coward, hardly responsible, Captain Muller. I'm the wounded party in this case, but it seems to me that hysteria isn't the same thing as maliciousness. Suppose I ask for clemency?"

"Thank you, Dr. Lomax," Muller said, and actually looked relieved. "Make it ten lashes, Mr. Grundy. Apparently no real harm has been done, and he will not testify in the future."

Grundy began dragging Bullard out, muttering about damn fool ground lubbers always sticking their noses in. The cook caught at Lomax's hand on the way, literally slobbering over it. Lomax rubbed his palm across his thigh, looking embarrassed.

Muller turned back to us. "Very well. Mr. Peters will begin investigating the expedition staff and quarters; Mr. Tremaine will have free run over the rest of the ship. And if the murderer is not turned up in forty-eight hours, we head back to Earth."

Pietro started to protest again, but another scream ripped down the corridor, jerking us all around. It was Jenny, running toward us. She was breathing hoarsely as she nearly crashed into Dr. Pietro.

Her face was white and sick, and she had to try twice before she could speak.

"The plants!" she gasped out. "Poison! They're dying!"

CHAPTER THREE

It was chromazone again. Muller had kept most of the gang from coming back to hydroponics, but he, Jenny, Pietro, Wilcox and myself were enough to fill the room with the smell of sick fear. Now less than half of the original space was filled with healthy plants. Some of the tanks held plants already dead, and others were dying as we watched; once beyond a certain stage, the stuff acted almost instantly—for hours there was only a slight indication of something wrong, and then suddenly there were the dead, bleached plants.

Wilcox was the first to speak. He still looked like some nattily dressed hero of a space serial, but his first words were ones that could never have gone out on a public broadcast. Then he shrugged. "They must have been poisoned while we were all huddled over Sam's body. Who wasn't with us?"

"Nonsense," Pietro denied. "This was done at least eighteen hours ago, maybe more. We'd have to find who was around then."

"Twenty hours, or as little as twelve," Jenny amended. "It depends on the amount of the dosage, to some extent. And…" She almost managed to blush. "Well, there have been a lot of people around. I can't even remember. Mr. Grundy and one of the men. Mr. Wilcox, Dr. Napier—oh, I don't know!"

Muller shook his head in heavy agreement. "Naturally. We had a lot of work to do here. After word got around about Hendrix, we didn't try to conceal much. It might have happened when someone else was watching, too. The important thing, gentlemen, is that now we don't have reserve enough to carry us to Saturn. The plants remaining can't handle the air for all of us. And while we ship some reserve oxygen..."

He let it die in a distasteful shrug. "At least this settles one thing. We have no choice now but to return to Earth!"

"Captain Muller," Pietro bristled quickly, "that's getting to be a monomania with you. I agree we are in grave danger. I don't relish the prospect of dying any more than you do—perhaps less, in view of certain peculiarities! But it's now further back to Earth than it is to Saturn. And before we can reach either, we'll have new plants—or we'll be dead!"

"Some of us will be dead, Dr. Pietro," Wilcox amended it. "There are enough plants left to keep some of us breathing indefinitely."

Pietro nodded. "And I suppose, in our captain's mind that means the personnel of the ship can survive. Captain Muller, I must regard your constant attempt to return to Earth as highly suspicious in view of this recurrent sabotage of the expedition. Someone here is apparently either a complete madman or so determined to get back that he'll resort to anything to accomplish his end. And you have been harping on returning over and over again."

Muller bristled, and his heavy fist tightened. Then he drew himself up to his full dumpy height. "Dr. Pietro," he said stiffly, "I am as responsible to my duties as any man here—and my duties involve protecting the life of every man and woman on board; if you wish to return, I shall be *most* happy to submit this to a formal board of inquiry."

"Just a minute," I told them. "You two are forgetting that we've got a problem here. Damn it, I'm sick of this fighting among ourselves. We're a bunch of men in a jam, not two camps at war now. I can't see any reason why Captain Muller would want to return that badly."

Muller nodded slightly. "Thank you, Mr. Tremaine. However, for the record, and to save you trouble investigating there is a good reason. My company is now building a superliner; if I were to return within the next six months, they'd promote me to captain of that ship—a considerable promotion, too."

For a moment, his honesty seemed to soften Pietro. The scientist mumbled some sort of apology, and turned to the plants. But it bothered me; if Muller had pulled something, the smartest thing he could have done would be to have said just what he did.

Besides, knowing that Pietro's injunction had robbed him of a chance like that was enough to rankle in any man's guts and make him work up something pretty close to insanity. I marked it down in my mental files for the investigation I was supposed to make, but let it go for the moment.

Muller stood for a minute longer, thinking darkly about the whole situation. Then he moved toward the entrance to hydroponics and pulled out the ship speaker mike. "All hands and passengers will assemble in hydroponics within five minutes," he announced. He swung toward Pietro. "With your permission, Doctor," he said caustically.

The company assembled later looked as sick as the plants. This time, Muller was hiding nothing. He outlined the situation fully; maybe he shaded it a bit to throw suspicion on our group, but in no way we could pin down. Finally he stated flatly that the situation meant almost certain death for at least some of those aboard.

"From now on, there'll be a watch kept. This is closed to everyone except myself, Dr. Pietro, Mr. Peters, and Dr. Jenny Sanderson. At least one of us will be here at all times, equipped with gas guns. Anyone else is to be killed on setting foot inside this door!" He swung his eyes over the group. "Any objections?"

Grundy stirred uncomfortably. "I don't go for them science guys up here. Takes a crazy man to do a thing like this, and everybody knows..."

Eve Nolan laughed roughly. "Everybody knows you've been swearing you won't go the whole way, Grundy. These jungle tactics should be right up your alley."

"That's enough," Muller cut through the beginnings of the hassle. "I trust those I appointed—at least more than I do the rest of you. The question now is whether to return to Earth at once or to go on to Saturn. We can't radio for help for months yet. We're not equipped with sharp beams, we're low powered, and we're off the lanes where Earth's pick-ups hunt. Dr. Pietro wants to go on, since we can't get back within our period of safety; I favor returning, since there is no proof that this danger will end with this outrage. We've agreed to let the result of a vote determine it."

Wilcox stuck up a casual hand, and Muller nodded to him. He grinned amiably at all of us. "There's a third possibility, Captain. We can reach Jupiter in about three months, if we turn now. It's offside, but closer than anything else. From there, on a fast liner, we can be back on Earth in another ten days."

Muller calculated, while Peters came up to discuss it. Then he nodded. "Saturn or Jupiter, then. I'm not voting, of course. Bullard is disqualified to vote by previous acts." He drew a low moan from the sick figure of Bullard for that, but no protest. Then he nodded. "All those in favor of Jupiter, your right hands please."

I counted them, wondering why my own hand was still down. It made some sort of sense to turn aside now. But none of our group was voting—and all the others had their hands up, except for Dr. Napier. "Seven," Muller announced. "Those in favor of Saturn."

Again, Napier didn't vote. I hesitated, then put my hand up. It was crazy, and Pietro was a fool to insist. But I knew that he'd never get another chance if this failed, and...

"Eight," Muller counted. He sighed, then straightened. "Very well, we go on. Dr. Pietro, you will have my full support from now on. In return, I'll expect every bit of help in meeting this emergency. Mr. Tremaine was correct; we cannot remain camps at war."

Pietro's goatee bobbed quickly, and his hand went out. But while most of the scientists were nodding with him, I caught the dark scowl of Grundy, and heard the mutters from the deckhands and the engine men. If Muller could get them to cooperate, he was a genius.

Pietro faced us, and his face was serious again. "We can hasten the seeding of the plants a little, I think, by temperature and light-and-dark cycle manipulations. Unfortunately, these aren't sea-algae plants, or we'd be in comparatively little trouble. That was my fault in not converting. We can, however, step up their efficiency a bit. And I'm sure we can find some way to remove the carbon dioxide from the air."

"How about oxygen to breathe?" Peters asked.

"That's the problem," Pietro admitted. "I was wondering about electrolyzing water."

Wilcox bobbed up quickly. "Can you do it on AC current?"

Lomax shook his head. "It takes DC."

"Then that's out. We run on 220 AC. And while I can rectify a few watts, it wouldn't be enough to help. No welders except monatomic hydrogen torches, even."

Pietro looked sicker than before. He'd obviously been counting on that. But he turned to Bullard. "How about seeds? We had a crop of tomatoes a month ago—and from the few I had, they're all seed. Are any left?"

Bullard rocked from side to side, moaning. "Dead. We're all gonna be dead. I told him, I said, you take me out there, I'll never get back. I'm a good man, I am. I wasn't never meant to die way out here. I—I—"

He gulped and suddenly screamed. He went through the door at an awkward shuffle, heading for his galley. Muller shook his head, and turned toward me. "Check up, will you, Mr. Tremaine? And I suggest that you and Mr. Peters start your investigation at once. I understand that chromazone would require so little hiding space that there's no use searching for it. But if you can find any evidence, report it at once."

Peters and I left. I found the galley empty. Apparently Bullard had gone to lie on his stomach in his bunk and nurse his terror. I found the freezer compartments, though—and the tomatoes. There must have been a bushel of them, but Bullard had followed his own peculiar tastes. From the food he served, he couldn't stand fresh vegetables; and he'd cooked the tomatoes down thoroughly and run them through the dehydrator before packing them away.

It was a cheerful supper, that one! Bullard had half-recovered and his fear was driving him to try to be nice to us. The selection was good, beyond the inevitable baked beans; but he wasn't exactly a chef at best, and his best was far behind him. Muller had brought Wilcox, Napier and Peters down to our mess with himself, to consolidate forces, and it seemed that he was serious about cooperating. But it was a little late for that.

Overhead, the fans had been stepped up to counteract the effect of staleness our minds supplied. But the whine of the motors kept reminding us our days were counted. Only Jenny was normal; she sat between Muller and Pietro, where she could watch my face and that of Napier. And even her giggles had a forced sound.

There were all kinds of things we could do—in theory. But we didn't have that kind of equipment. The plain fact was that the plants were going to lose the battle against our lungs. The carbon dioxide would increase, speeding up our breathing, and making us all seem to suffocate. The oxygen would grow thinner and thinner, once our supplies of bottled gas ran out. And eventually, the air wouldn't support life.

"It's sticky and hot," Jenny complained, suddenly.

"I stepped up the humidity and temperature controls," I told her. She nodded in quick comprehension, but I went on for Muller's benefit. "Trying to give the plants the best growing atmosphere. We'll feel just as hot and sticky when the carbon dioxide goes up, anyhow."

"It must already be up," Wilcox said. "My two canaries are breathing faster."

"Canaries," Muller said. He frowned, though he must have known of them. It was traditional to keep them in the engine room, though the reason behind it had long since been lost. "Better kill them, Mr. Wilcox."

Wilcox jerked, and his face paled a bit. Then he nodded. "Yes, sir."

That was when I got scared. The idea that two birds breathing could hurt our chances put things on a little too vivid a basis. Only Lomax seemed unaffected. He shoved back now, and stood up.

"Some tests I have to make, Captain. I have an idea that might turn up the killer among us."

I had an idea he was bluffing, but I kept my mouth shut. A bluff was as good as anything else, it seemed.

At least, it was better than anything I seemed able to do. I prowled over the ship, sometimes meeting Peters doing the same, but I couldn't find a bit of evidence. The crewmen sat watching with hating eyes. And probably the rest aboard hated and feared us just as much. It wasn't hard to imagine the man who was behind it all deciding to wipe one of us out. My neck got a permanent crimp from keeping one eye behind me. But there wasn't a shred of evidence I could find.

In two more days, we began to notice the stuffiness more. My breathing went up enough to notice. Somehow, I couldn't get a full breath. And the third night, I woke up in the middle of my sleep with the feeling something was sitting on my chest; but since I'd taken to sleeping with the light on, I saw that it was just the stuffiness that was bothering me. Maybe most of it had been psychological up until then. But that was the real thing.

The nice part of it was that it wouldn't be sudden—we'd have days to get closer and closer to death; and days for each one to realize a little more that every man who wasn't breathing would make it that much easier for the rest of us. I caught myself thinking of it when I saw Bullard or Grundy.

Then trouble struck again. I was late getting to the scene this time, down by the engine room. Muller and Bill Sanderson were ahead of me, trying to separate Hal Lomax and Grundy, and not doing so well. Lomax brought up a haymaker as I arrived, and started to shout something. But Grundy was out of Muller's grasp, and up, swinging a wrench. It connected with a dull thud, and Lomax hit the floor, unconscious.

I picked Grundy up by the collar of his jacket, heaved him around and against a wall, where I could get my hand against his esophagus and start squeezing. His eyeballs popped, and the wrench dropped from his hands. When I get mad enough to act that way, I usually know I'll regret it later. This time it felt good, all the way. But Muller pushed me aside, waiting until Grundy could breathe again.

"All right," Muller said. "I hope you've got a good explanation, before I decide what to do with you."

Grundy's eyes were slitted, as if he'd been taking some of the Venus drugs. But after one long, hungry look at me, he faced the captain. "Yes, sir. This guy came down here ahead of me. Didn't think nothing of it, sir. But when he started fiddling with the panel there, I got suspicious." He pointed to the external control panel for the engine room, to be used in case of accidents. "With all that's been going on, how'd I know but maybe he was gonna dump the fuel? And then I seen he had keys. I didn't wait, sir. I jumped him. And then you come up."

Wilcox came from the background and dropped beside the still figure of Lomax. He opened the man's left hand and pulled out a bunch of keys, examining them. "Engine keys, Captain Muller. Hey—it's my set! He must have lifted them from my pocket. It looks as if Grundy's found our killer!"

"Or Lomax found him!" I pointed out. "Anybody else see this start, or know that Lomax didn't get those keys away from Grundy when he started trouble?"

"Why, you—" Grundy began, but Wilcox cut off his run. It was a shame. I still felt like pushing the man's Adam's apple through his medulla oblongata.

"Lock them both up, until Dr. Lomax comes to," Muller ordered. "And send Dr. Napier to take care of him. I'm not jumping to any conclusions." But the look he was giving Lomax indicated that he'd already pretty well made up his mind. And the crew was positive. They drew back sullenly, staring at us like animals studying a human hunter, and they didn't like it when Peters took Grundy to lock him into his room. Muller finally chased them out, and left Wilcox and me alone.

Wilcox shrugged wryly, brushing dirt off his too-clean uniform. "While you're here, Tremaine, why not look my section over? You've been neglecting me."

I'd borrowed Muller's keys and inspected the engine room from top to bottom the night before, but I didn't mention that. I hesitated now; to a man who grew up to be an engineer and who'd now gotten over his psychosis against space too late to start over, the engines were things better left alone. Then I remembered that I hadn't seen Wilcox's quarters, since he had the only key to them.

I nodded and went inside. The engines were old, and the gravity generator was one of the first models. But Wilcox knew his business. The place was slick enough, and there was the good clean smell of metal working right. I could feel the controls in my hands, and my nerves itched as I went about making a perfunctory token examination. I even opened the fuel lockers and glanced in. The two crewmen watched with hard eyes, slitted as tight as Grundy's, but they didn't bother me. Then I shrugged, and went back with Wilcox to his tiny cabin.

I was hit by the place before I got inside. Tiny, yes, but fixed up like the dream of every engineer. Clean, neat, filled with books and luxuries. He even had a tape player I'd seen on sale for a trifle over three thousand dollars. He turned it on, letting the opening bars of Haydn's Oxford Symphony come out. It was a binaural, ultra-fidelity job, and I could close my eyes and feel the orchestra in front of me.

This time I was thorough, right down the line, from the cabinets that held luxury food and wine to the little drawer where he kept his dress-suit studs; they might have been rutiles, but I had a hunch they were genuine cat'seyes.

He laughed when I finished, and handed me a glass of the first decent wine I'd tasted in months. "Even a small ozonator to make the air seem more breathable, and a dehumidifier, Tremaine. I like to live decently. I started saving my money once with the idea of getting a ship of my own—" There was a real dream in his eyes for a second. Then he shrugged. "But ships got bigger and more expensive. So I decided to live. At forty, I've got maybe twenty years ahead here, and I mean to enjoy it. And—well, there are ways of making a bit extra..."

I nodded. So it's officially smuggling to carry a four ounce Martian fur to Earth where it's worth a fortune, considering the legal duty. But most officers did it now and then. He put on Sibelius' Fourth while I finished the wine. "If this mess is ever over, Paul, or you get a chance, drop down," he said. "I like a man who knows good things—and I liked your reaction when you spotted that Haydn for Hohmann's recording. Muller pretends to know music, but he likes the flashiness of Möhlwehr."

Hell, I'd cut my eye teeth on that stuff; my father had been first violinist in an orchestra, and had considered me a traitor when I was born without perfect pitch. We talked about Sibelius for awhile, before I left to go out into the stinking rest of the ship. Grundy was sitting before the engines, staring at them. Wilcox had said the big ape liked to watch them move...but he was supposed to be locked up.

I stopped by Lomax's door; the shutter was open, and I could see the big man writhing about, but he was apparently unconscious. Napier came back from somewhere, and nodded quickly.

"Concussion," he said. "He's still out, but it shouldn't be too serious.

"Grundy's loose." I'd expected surprise, but there was none. "Why?"

He shrugged. "Muller claimed he needed his mate free to handle the crew, and that there was no place the man could go. I think it was because the men are afraid they'll be outnumbered by your group." His mouth smiled, but it was suddenly bitter. "Jenny talked Pietro into agreeing with Muller."

Mess was on when I reached the group. I wasn't hungry. The wine had cut the edge from my appetite, and the slow increase of poison in the air was getting me, as it was the others. Sure, carbon dioxide isn't a real poison—but no organism can live in its own waste, all the same. I had a rotten headache. I sat there playing a little game I'd invented—trying to figure which ones I'd eliminate if some had to die. Jenny laughed up at Muller, and I added him to the list. Then I changed it, and put her in his place. I was getting sick of the little witch, though I knew it would be different if she'd been laughing up at me. And then, because of the sick-calf look on Bill Sanderson's face as he stared at Eve, I added him, though I'd always liked the guy. Eve, surprisingly, had as many guys after her as Jenny; but she didn't seem interested. Or maybe she did—she'd pulled her hair back and put on a dress that made her figure look good. Either flattery was working, or she was entering into the last-days feeling most of us had.

Napier came in and touched my shoulder. "Lomax is conscious, and he's asking for you," he said, too low for the others to hear.

I found the chemist conscious, all right, but sick—and scared. His face winced, under all the bandages, as I opened the door. Then he saw who it was, and relaxed. "Paul—what happened to me? The last I remember is going up to see that second batch of plants poisoned. But—well, this is something I must have got later…"

I told him, as best I could. "But don't you remember anything?"

"Not a thing about that. It's the same as Napier told me, and I've been trying to remember. Paul, you don't think—?"

I put a hand on his shoulder and pushed him back gently. "Don't be a damned fool, Hal. I know you're no killer."

"But somebody is, Paul. Somebody tried to kill me while I was unconscious!"

He must have seen my reaction. "They did, Paul. I don't know how I know—maybe I almost came to—but somebody tried to poke a stick through the door with a knife on it. They want to kill me."

I tried to calm him down until Napier came and gave him a sedative. The doctor seemed as sick about Hal's inability to remember as I was, though he indicated it was normal enough in concussion cases. "So is the hallucination," he added. "He'll be all right tomorrow."

In that, Napier was wrong. When the doctor looked in on him the next time, the big chemist lay behind a door that had been pried open, with a long galley knife through his heart. On the bloody sheet, his finger had traced something in his own blood.

"*It was…*" But the last "s" was blurred, and there was nothing more.

CHAPTER FOUR

I don't know how many were shocked at Hal's death, or how many looked around and counted one less pair of lungs. He'd never been one of the men I'd envied the air he used, though, and I think most felt the same. For awhile, we didn't even notice that the air was even thicker.

Phil Riggs broke the silence following our inspection of Lomax's cabin. "That damned Bullard! I'll get him. I'll get him as sure as he got Hal!"

There was a rustle among the others, and a suddenly crystallized hate on their faces. But Muller's hoarse shout cut through the babble that began, and rose over even the anguished shrieking of the cook. "Shut up, the lot of you! Bullard couldn't have committed the other crimes. Anyone of you is a better suspect. Stop sniveling, Bullard, this isn't a lynching mob, and it isn't going to be one!"

"What about Grundy?" Walt Harris yelled.

Wilcox pushed forward. "Grundy couldn't have done it. He's the logical suspect, but he was playing rummy with my men."

The two engine men nodded agreement, and we began filing back to the mess hall, with the exception of Bullard, who shoved back into a niche trying to avoid us. Then, when we were almost out of his sight, he let out a shriek and came blubbering after us.

I watched them put Hal Lomax's body through the 'tween hulls lock, and turned toward the engine room. I could use some of that wine, just as the ship could have used a trained detective. But the idea of watching helplessly while the engines purred along to remind me I was just a handyman for the rest of my life got mixed up with the difficulty of breathing the stale air, and I started to turn back. My head was throbbing, and for two cents I'd have gone out between the hulls beside Lomax and the others and let the foul air spread out there and freeze…

The idea was slow coming. Then I was running back toward the engines. I caught up with Wilcox just before he went into his own quarters. "Wilcox!"

He swung around casually, saw it was me, and motioned inside. "How about some Bartok, Paul? Or would you rather soothe your nerves with some first-rate Buxtehude organ…"

"Damn the music," I told him. "I've got a wild idea to get rid of this carbon dioxide, and I want to know if we can get it working with what we've got."

He snapped to attention at that. Half-way through my account he fished around and found a bottle of Armagnac. "I get it. If we pipe our air through the passages between the hulls on the shadow side, it will lose its heat in a hurry. And we can regulate its final temperature by how fast we pipe it through—just keep it moving enough to reach the level where carbon dioxide freezes out, but the oxygen stays a gas. Then pass it around the engines—we'll have to cut out the normal cooling set-up, but that's okay—warm it up… Sure, I've got equipment enough for that. We can set it up in a day. Of course, it won't give us any more oxygen, but we'll be able to breathe what we have. To success, Paul!"

I guess it was good brandy, but I swallowed mine while calling Muller down, and never got to taste it.

It's surprising how much easier the air got to breathe after we'd double-checked the idea. In about fifteen minutes, we were all milling around in the engine room, while Wilcox checked through equipment. But there was no question about it. It was even easier than we'd thought. We could simply bypass the cooling unit, letting the engine housings stay open to the between-hulls section; then it was simply a matter of cutting a small opening into that section at the other end of the ship and installing a sliding section to regulate the amount of air flowing in. The exhaust from the engine heat pumps was reversed, and run out through a hole hastily knocked in the side of the wall.

Naturally, we let it flow too fast at first. Space is a vacuum, which means it's a good insulator. We had to cut the air down to a trickle. Then Wilcox ran into trouble because his engines wouldn't cool with that amount of air. He went back to supervise a patched-up job of splitting the coolers into sections, which took time. But after that, we had it.

I went through the hatch with Muller and Pietro. With air there there was no need to wear space suits, but it was so cold that we could take it for only a minute or so. That was long enough to see a faint, fine mist of dry ice snow falling. It was also long enough to catch a sight of the three bodies there. I didn't enjoy that, and Pietro gasped. Muller grimaced. When we came back, he sent Grundy in to move the bodies to a hull-section where our breathing air wouldn't pass over them. It wasn't necessary, of course. But somehow, it seemed important.

By lunch, the air seemed normal. We shipped only pure oxygen at about three pounds pressure, instead of loading it with a lot of useless nitrogen. With the carbon dioxide cut back to normal levels, it was as good as ever. The only difference was that the fans had to be set to blow in a different pattern. We celebrated, and even Bullard seemed to have perked up. He dug out pork chops and almost succeeded in making us cornbread out of some coarse flour I saw him pouring out of the food chopper. He had perked up enough to bewail the fact that all he had was canned spinach instead of turnip greens.

But by night, the temper had changed—and the food indicated it again. Bullard's cooking was turning into a barometer of the psychic pressure. We'd had time to realize that we weren't getting something for nothing. Every molecule of carbon-dioxide that crystallized out took two atoms of oxygen with it, completely out of circulation.

We were also losing water vapor, we found; normally, any one of our group knew enough science to know that the water would fall out before the carbon dioxide, but we hadn't thought of it. We took care of that, however, by having Wilcox weld in a baffle and keep the section where the water condensed separate from the carbon dioxide snowfall. We could always shovel out the real ice, and meantime the ship's controls restored the moisture to the air easily enough.

But there was nothing we could do about the oxygen. When that was gone, it stayed gone. The plants still took care of about two-thirds of our waste—but the other third was locked out there between the hulls. Given plants enough, we could have thawed it and let them reconvert it; a nice idea, except that we had to wait three months to take care of it, if we lived that long.

Bullard's cooking began to get worse. Then suddenly, we got one good meal. Eve Nolan came down the passage to announce that Bullard was making cake, with frosting, canned huckleberry pie, and all the works. We headed for the mess hall, fast.

It was the cook's masterpiece. Muller came down late, though, and regarded it doubtfully. "There's something funny," he said as he settled down beside me. Jenny had been surrounded by Napier and Pietro. "Bullard came up babbling a few minutes ago. I don't like it. Something about eating hearty, because he'd saved us all, forever and ever. He told me the angels were on our side, because a beautiful angel with two halos came to him in his sleep and told him how to save us. I chased him back to the galley, but I don't like it."

Most of them had already eaten at least half of the food, but I saw Muller wasn't touching his. The rest stopped now, as the words sank in, and Napier looked shocked. "No!" he said, but his tone wasn't positive. "He's a weakling, but I don't think he's insane—not enough to poison us."

"There was that food poisoning before," Pietro said suddenly. "Paul, come along. And don't eat anything until we come back."

We broke the record getting to the galley. There Bullard sat, beaming happily, eating from a huge plate piled with the food he had cooked. I checked on it quickly—and there wasn't anything he'd left out. He looked up, and his grin widened foolishly.

"Hi, docs," he said. "Yes, sir, I knowed you'd be coming. It all came to me in a dream. Looked just like my wife twenty years ago, she did, with green and yellow halos. And she told it to me. Told me I'd been a good man, and nothing was going to happen to me. Not to good old Emery Bullard. Had it all figgered out."

He speared a big forkful of food and crammed it into his mouth, munching noisily. "Had it all figgered. Pop-corn. Best damned pop-corn you ever saw, kind they raise not fifty miles from where I was born. You know, I didn't useta like you guys. But now I love everybody. When we get to Saturn, I'm gonna make up for all the times I didn't give you pop-corn. We'll pop and we'll pop. And beans, too. I useta hate beans. Always beans on a ship. But now we're saved, and I love beans!"

He stared after us, half coming out of his seat. "Hey, docs, ain't you gonna let me tell you about it?"

"Later, Bullard," Pietro called back. "Something just came up. We want to hear all about it."

Inside the mess hall, he shrugged. "He's eating the food himself. If he's crazy, he's in a happy stage of it. I'm sure he isn't trying to poison us." He sat down and began eating, without any hesitation.

I didn't feel as sure, and suspected he didn't. But it was too late to back out. Together, we summarized what he'd told us, while Napier puzzled over it. Finally the doctor shrugged. "Visions. Euphoria. Disconnection with reality. Apparently something of a delusion that he's to save the world. I'm not a psychiatrist, but it sounds like insanity to me. Probably not dangerous. At least, while he wants to save us, we won't have to worry about the food. Still…"

Wilcox mulled it over, and re_atic_ the eating he had neglected before.

"Grundy claimed he'd been down near the engine room, trying to get permission to pop something in the big pile. I thought Grundy was just getting his stories mixed up. But—pop-corn!"

"I'll have him locked in his cabin," Muller decided. He picked up the nearest handset, saw that it was to the galley, and switched quickly. "Grundy, lock Bullard up. And no rough stuff this time." Then he turned to Napier. "Dr. Napier, you'll have to see him and find out what you can."

I guess there's a primitive fear of insanity in most of us. We felt sick, beyond the nagging worry about the food. Napier got up at once. "I'll give him a sedative. Maybe it's' just nerves, and he'll snap out of it after a good sleep. Anyhow, your mate can stand watching."

"Who can cook?" Muller asked. His eyes swung down the table toward Jenny.

I wondered how she'd get out of that. Apparently she'd never told Muller about the scars she still had from spilled grease, and how she'd never forgiven her mother, or been able to go near a kitchen since. But I should have guessed.

She could remember my stories, too. Her eyes swung up toward mine pleadingly.

Eve Nolan stood up suddenly. "I'm not only a good cook, but I enjoy it," she stated flatly, and there was disgust in the look she threw at Jenny. She swung toward me. "How about it, Paul, can you wrestle the big pots around for me?"

"I used to be a short order cook when I was finishing school," I told her. But she'd ruined the line. The grateful look and laugh from Jenny weren't needed now. And curiously, I felt grateful to Eve for it. I got up and went after Napier.

I found him in Bullard's little cubbyhole of a cabin. He must have chased Grundy off, and now he was just drawing a hypo out of the cook's arm. "It'll take the pain away," he was saying softly. "And I'll see that he doesn't hit you again. You'll be all right, now. And in the morning, I'll come and listen to you. Just go to sleep. Maybe she'll come back and tell you more."

He must have heard me, since he signaled me out with his hand, and backed out quietly himself still talking. He shut the door and clicked the lock.

Bullard heard it, though. He jerked to a sitting position, and screamed. "*No!* No! He'll kill me! I'm a good man…"

He hunched up on the bed, forcing the sheet into his mouth. When he looked up a second later, his face was frozen in fear, but it was a desperate, calm kind of fear. He turned to face us, and his voice raised to a full shout, with every word as clear as he could make it.

"All right. Now I'll never tell you the secret. Now you can all die without air. I promise I'll never tell you what I know!"

He fell back, beating at the sheet with his hand and sobbing hysterically. Napier watched him. "Poor devil," the doctor said at last. "Well, in another minute the shot will take effect. Maybe he's lucky. He won't be worrying for awhile. And maybe he'll be rational tomorrow."

"All the same, I'm going to stand guard until Muller gets someone else here," I decided. I kept remembering Lomax.

Napier nodded, and half an hour later Bill Sanderson came to take over the watch. Bullard was sleeping soundly.

The next day, though, he woke up to start moaning and writhing again. But he was keeping his word. He refused to answer any questions. Napier looked worried as he reported he'd given the cook another shot of sedative. There was nothing else he could do.

Cooking was a relief, in a way. By the time Eve and I had scrubbed all the pots into what she considered proper order, located some of the food lockers, and prepared and served a couple of meals, we'd evolved a smooth system that settled into a routine with just enough work to help keep our minds off the dwindling air in the tanks. In anything like a kitchen, she lost most of her mannish pose and turned into a live, efficient woman. And she could cook.

"First thing I learned," she told me. "I grew up in a kitchen. I guess I'd never have turned to photography if my kid brother hadn't been using our sink for his darkroom."

Wilcox brought her a bottle of his wine to celebrate her first dinner. He seemed to want to stick around, but she chased him off after the first drink. We saved half the bottle to make a sauce the next day.

It never got made. Muller called a council of war, and his face was pinched and old. He was leaning on Jenny as Eve and I came into the mess hall; oddly, she seemed to be trying to buck him up. He got down to the facts as soon as all of us were together.

"Our oxygen tanks are empty," he announced. "They shouldn't be—but they are. Someone must have sabotaged them before the plants were poisoned—and done it so the dials don't show it. I just found it out when the automatic switch to a new tank failed to work. We now have the air in the ship, and no more. Dr. Napier and I have figured that this will keep us all alive with the help of the plants for no more than fifteen days. I am open to any suggestions."

There was silence after that, while it soaked in. Then it was broken by a thin scream from Phil Riggs. He slumped into a seat and buried his head in his hands. Pietro put a hand on the man's thin shoulders. "Captain Muller—"

"Kill 'em!" It was Grundy's voice, bellowing sharply. "Let 'em breathe space! They got us into it! We can make out with the plants left! It's our ship!"

Muller had walked forward. Now his fist lashed out, and Grundy crumpled. He lay still for a second, then got to his feet unsteadily. Jenny screamed, but Muller moved steadily back to his former place without looking at the mate. Grundy hesitated, fumbled in his pocket for something, and swallowed it.

"Captain, sir!" His voice was lower this time.

"Yes, Mr. Grundy?'

"How many of us can live off the plants?"

"Ten—perhaps eleven."

"Then—then give us a lottery!"

Pietro managed to break in over the yells of the rest of the crew. "I was about to suggest calling for volunteers, Captain Muller. I still have enough faith in humanity to believe…"

"You're a fool, Dr. Pietro," Muller said flatly. "Do you think Grundy would volunteer? Or Bullard? But thanks for clearing the air, and admitting your group has nothing more to offer. A lottery seems to be the only fair system."

He sat down heavily. "We have tradition on this; in an emergency such as this, death lotteries have been held, and have been considered legal afterwards. Are there any protests?"

I could feel my tongue thicken in my mouth. I could see the others stare about, hoping someone would object, wondering if this could be happening. But nobody answered, and Muller nodded reluctantly. "A working force must be left. Some men are indispensable. We must have an engineer, a navigator, and a doctor. One man skilled with engine room practice and one with deck work must remain."

"And the cook goes," Grundy yelled. His eyes were intent and slitted again.

Some of both groups nodded, but Muller brought his fist down on the table. "This will be a legal lottery, Mr. Grundy. Dr. Napier will draw for him."

"And for myself," Napier said. "It's obvious that ten men aren't going on to Saturn—you'll have to turn back, or head for Jupiter. Jupiter, in fact, is the only sensible answer. And a ship can get along without a doctor that long when it has to. I demand my right to the draw."

Muller only shrugged and laid down the rules. They were simple enough. He would cut drinking straws to various lengths, and each would draw one. The two deck hands would compare theirs, and the longer would be automatically safe. The same for the pair from the engine room. Wilcox was safe. "Mr. Peters and I will also have one of us eliminated," he added quietly. "In an emergency, our abilities are sufficiently alike."

The remaining group would have their straws measured, and the seven shortest ones would be chosen to remove themselves into a vacant section between hulls without air within three hours, or be forcibly placed there. The remaining ten would head for Jupiter if no miracle removed the danger in those three hours.

Peters got the straws, and Muller cut them and shuffled them. There was a sick silence that let us hear the sounds of the scissors with each snip. Muller arranged them so the visible ends were even. "Ladies first," he said. There was no expression on his face or in his voice.

Jenny didn't giggle, but neither did she balk. She picked a straw, and then shrieked faintly. It was obviously a long one. Eve reached for hers—

And Wilcox yelled suddenly. "Captain Muller, protest! Protest! You're using all long straws for the women!" He had jumped forward, and now struck down Muller's hand, proving his point.

"You're quite right, Mr. Wilcox," Muller said woodenly. He dropped his hand toward his lap and came up with a group of the straws that had been cut, placed there somehow without our seeing it. He'd done a smooth job of it, but not smooth enough. "I felt some of you would notice it, but I also felt that gentlemen would prefer to see ladies given the usual courtesies."

He reshuffled the assorted straws, and then paused. "Mr. Tremaine, there was a luxury liner named the *Lauri Ellu* with an assistant engineer by your name; and I believe you've shown a surprising familiarity with certain customs of space. A few days ago, Jenny mentioned something that jogged my memory. Can you still perform the duties of an engineer?"

Wilcox had started to protest at the delay. Now shock ran through him. He stared unbelievingly from Muller to me and back, while his face blanched. I could guess what it must have felt like to see certain safety cut to a fifty percent chance, and I didn't like the way Muller was willing to forget until he wanted to take a crack at Wilcox for punishment. But…

"I can," I answered. And then, because I was sick inside myself for cutting under Wilcox, I managed to add, "But I—I waive my chance at immunity."

"Not accepted," Muller decided. "Jenny, will you draw?"

It was pretty horrible. It was worse when the pairs compared straws. The animal feelings were out in the open then. Finally, Muller, Wilcox, and two crewmen dropped out. The rest of us went up to measure our straws.

It took no more than a minute. I stood staring down at the ruler, trying to stretch the tiny thing I'd drawn. I could smell the sweat rising from my body. But I knew the answer. I had three hours left!

"Riggs, Oliver, Nolan, Harris, Tremaine, Napier and Grundy," Muller announced.

A yell came from Grundy. He stood up, with the engine man named Oliver, and there was a gun in his hand. "No damned big brain's kicking me off my ship," he yelled. "You guys know me. Hey, *roooob!*"

Oliver was with him, and the other three of the crew sprang into the group. I saw Muller duck a shot from Grundy's gun, and leap out of the room. Then I was in it, heading for Grundy. Beside me, Peters was trying to get a chair broken into pieces. I felt something hit my shoulder, and the shock knocked me downward, just as a shot whistled over my head.

Gravity cut off!

Someone bounced off me. I got a piece of the chair that floated by, found the end cracked and sharp, and tried to spin towards Grundy, but I couldn't see him. I heard Eve's voice yell over the other shouts. I spotted the plate coming for me, but I was still in midair. It came on steadily, edge on, and I felt it break against my forehead. Then I blacked out.

CHAPTER FIVE

I had the granddaddy of all headaches when I came to. Doc Napier's face was over me, and Jenny and Muller were working on Bill Sanderson. There was a surprisingly small and painful lump on my head. Pietro and Napier helped me up, and I found I could stand after a minute.

There were four bodies covered with sheets on the floor. "Grundy, Phil Riggs, Peters and a deckhand named Storm," Napier said. "Muller gave us a whiff of gas and not quite in time."

"Is the time up?" I asked. It was the only thing I could think of.

Pietro shook his head sickly. "Lottery is off. Muller says we'll have to hold another, since Storm and Peters were supposed to be safe. But not until tomorrow."

Eve came in then, lugging coffee. Her eyes found me, and she managed a brief smile. "I gave the others coffee," she reported to Muller. "They're pretty subdued now."

"Mutiny!" Muller helped Jenny's brother to his feet and began helping him toward the door. "Mutiny! And I have to swallow that!"

Pietro watched him go, and handed Eve back his cup. "And there's no way of knowing who was on which side. Dr. Napier, could you do something..."

He held out his hands that were shaking, and Napier nodded. "I can use a sedative myself. Come on back with me."

Eve and I wandered back to the kitchen. I was just getting my senses back. The damned stupidity of it all. And now it would have to be done over. Three of us still had to have our lives snuffed out so the others could live—and we all had to go through hell again to find out which.

Eve must have been thinking the same. She sank down on a little stool, and her hand came out to find mine. "For what? Paul, whoever poisoned the plants knew it would go this far! He had to! What's to be gained? Particularly when he'd have to go through all this, too! He must have been crazy!"

"Bullard couldn't have done it," I said slowly.

"Why should it be Bullard? How do we know he was insane? Maybe when he was shouting that he wouldn't tell, he was trying to make a bribe to save his own life. Maybe he's as scared as we are. Maybe he was making sense all along, if we'd only listened to him. He—"

She stood up and started back toward the lockers, but I caught her hand. "Eve, he wouldn't have done it—the killer—if he'd had to go through the lottery! He knew he was safe! That's the one thing we've been overlooking. The man to suspect is the only man who could be sure he would get back! My God, we saw him juggle those straws to save Jenny! He knew he'd con_atic the lottery."

She frowned. "But…Paul, he practically suggested the lottery! Grundy brought it up, but he was all ready for it." The frown vanished, then returned. "But I still can't believe it."

"He's the one who wanted to go back all the time. He kept insisting on it, but he had to get back without violating his contract." I grabbed her hand and started toward the nose of the ship, justifying it to her as I went. "The only man with a known motive for returning, the only one completely safe—and we didn't even think of it!"

She was still frowning, but I wasn't wasting time. We came up the corridor to the control room. Ahead the door was slightly open, and I could hear a mutter of Jenny's voice. Then there was the tired rumble of Muller.

"I'll find a way, baby. I don't care how close they watch, we'll make it work. Pick the straw with the crimp in the end—I can do that, even if I can't push one out further again. I tell you, nothing's going to happen to you."

"But Bill—" she began.

I hit the door, slamming it open. Muller sat on a narrow couch with Jenny on his lap. I took off for him, not wasting a good chance when he was handicapped. But I hadn't counted on Jenny. She was up, and her head banged into my stomach before I knew she was coming. I felt the wind knocked out, but I got her out of my way—to look up into the muzzle of a gun in Muller's hands.

"You'll explain this, Mr. Tremaine," he said coldly. "In ten seconds, I'll have an explanation or a corpse."

"Go ahead," I told him. "Shoot, damn you! You'll get away with this, too, I suppose. Mutiny, or something. And down in that rotten soul of yours, I suppose you'll be gloating at how you made fools of us. The only man on board who was safe even from a lottery, and we couldn't see it Jenny. I hope you'll be happy with this butcher. Very happy!"

He never blinked. "Say that about the only safe man aboard again," he suggested.

I repeated it, with details. But he didn't like my account. He turned to Eve, and motioned for her to take it up. She was frowning harder, and her voice was uncertain, but she summed up our reasons quickly enough.

And suddenly Muller was on his feet. "Mr. Tremaine, for a damned idiot, you have a good brain. You found the key to the problem, even if you couldn't find the lock. Do you know what happens to a captain who permits a death lottery, even what I called a legal one? He doesn't captain a liner—he shoots himself after he delivers his ship, if he's wise! Come on, we'll find the one indispensable man. You stay here, Jenny—you too, Eve!"

Jenny whimpered, but stayed. Eve followed, and he made no comment. And then it hit me. The man who had *thought* he was indispensable, and hence safe—the man I'd naturally known in the back of my head could be replaced, though no one else had known it until a little while ago.

"He must have been sick when you ran me in as a ringer," I said, as we walked down toward the engine hatch. "But why?"

"I've just had a wild guess as to part of it," Muller said.

Wilcox was listening to the Buxtehude when we shoved the door of his room open, and he had his head back and eyes closed. He snapped to attention, and reached out with one hand toward a drawer beside him. Then he dropped his arm and stood up, to cut off the tape player.

"Mr. Wilcox," Muller said quietly, holding the gun firmly on the engineer. "Mr. Wilcox, I've detected evidence of some of the Venus drugs on your two assistants for some time. It's rather hard to miss the signs in their eyes. I've also known that Mr. Grundy was an addict. I assumed that they were getting it from him naturally. And as long as they performed their duties, I couldn't be choosy—an old ship like this. But for an officer to furnish such drugs—and to smuggle them from Venus for sale to other planets—is something I cannot tolerate. It will make things much simpler if you will surrender those drugs to me. I presume you keep them in those bottles of wine you bring aboard?"

Wilcox shook his head slowly, settling back against the tape machine. Then he shrugged and bowed faintly. "The chianti, sir."

I turned my head toward the bottles, and Eve started forward. Then I yelled as Wilcox shoved his hand down toward the tape machine. The gun came out on a spring as he touched it.

Muller shot once, and the gun missed Wilcox's fingers as the engineer's hand went to his hip where blood was flowing.

He collapsed into the chair behind him, staring at the spot stupidly. "I cut my teeth on *tough* ships, Mr. Wilcox," Muller said savagely.

The man's face was white, but he nodded slowly, and a weak grin came onto his lips. "Maybe' you didn't exaggerate those stories at that," he conceded slowly. "I take it I drew a short straw."

"Very short. It wasn't worth it. No profit from the piddling sale of drugs is worth it."

"There's a group of strings inside the number one fuel locker," Wilcox said between his teeth. The numbness was wearing off, and the shattered bones in his hip were beginning to eat at him. "Paul, pull up one of the packages and bring it here, will you?"

I found it without much trouble—along with a whole row of others, fine cords cemented to the side of the locker. The package I drew up weighed about ten pounds. Wilcox opened it and scooped out a thimbleful of greenish powder. He washed it down and wine.

"Fatal?" Muller asked.

The man nodded. "In that dosage, after a couple of hours. But it cuts out the pain—ah, better already. I won't feel it. Captain, I was never piddling. Your ship has been the sole source of this drug to Mars since a year or so after I first shipped on her. There are about seven hundred pounds of pure stuff out there. Grundy and the others would commit public murder daily rather than lose the few ounces a year I gave them. Imagine what would happen when Pietro conscripted the *Wahoo* and no drugs arrived. The addicts find out no more is coming—they look for the peddlers—and *they* start looking for their suppliers..."

He shrugged. "There might have been time and ways, if I could have gotten the ship back to Earth or Jupiter. It might have been re-commissioned into the Earth-Mars-Venus run, even. Pietro's injunction caught me before I could transship, but with another chance, I might have gotten the stuff to Mars in time. Well, it was a chance I took. Satisfied?"

Eve stared at him with horrified eyes. Maybe I was looking the same. It was plain enough now. He'd planned to poison the plants and drive us back. Murder of Hendrix had been a blunder when he'd thought it wasn't working properly. "What about Sam?" I asked.

"Blackmail. He was too smart. He'd been sure Grundy was smuggling the stuff, and raking off from him. He didn't care who killed Hendrix as much as how much Grundy would pay to keep his mouth shut—with murder around, he figured Grundy'd get rattled. The fool did, and Sam smelled bigger stakes. Grundy was bait to get him down near here. I killed him."

"And Lomax?"

"I don't know. Maybe he was bluffing. But he kept going from room to room with a pocketful of chemicals, making some kind of tests. I couldn't take a chance on his being able to spot chromazone. So I had Grundy give him my keys and tell him to go ahead—then jump him."

And after that, when he wasn't quite killed, they'd been forced to finish the job. Wilcox shrugged again. "I guess it got out of hand. I'll make a tape of the whole story for you, Captain. But I'd appreciate it if you'd get Napier down here. This is getting pretty messy."

"He's on the way," Eve said. We hadn't seen her call, but the doctor arrived almost immediately afterwards.

He sniffed the drug, and questioned us about the dose Wilcox had taken. Then he nodded slowly. "About two hours, I'd say. No chance at all to save him. The stuff is absorbed almost at once and begins changing to something else in the blood. I'll be responsible, if you want."

Muller shrugged. "I suppose so. I'd rather deliver him in irons to a jury, but… Well, we still have a lottery to hold!"

It jerked us back to reality sharply. Somehow, I'd been fighting off the facts, figuring that finding the cause would end the results. But even with Wilcox out of the picture, there were twelve of us left—and air for only ten!

Wilcox laughed abruptly. "A favor for a favor. I can give you a better answer than a lottery."

"Popcorn! Bullard!" Eve slapped her head with her palm. "Captain, give me the master key." She snatched it out of his hand and was gone at a run.

Wilcox looked disappointed, and then grinned. "Popcorn and beans. I overlooked them myself. We're a bunch of city hicks. But when Bullard forgot his fears in his sleep, he remembered the answer—and got it so messed up with his dream and his new place as a hero that my complaint tipped the balance. Grundy put the fear of his God into him then. And you didn't get it. Captain, you don't dehydrate beans and popcorn—they come that way naturally. You don't can them, either, if you're saving weight. They're seeds—put them in tanks and they grow!"

He leaned back, trying to laugh at us, as Napier finished dressing his wound. "Bullard knows where the lockers are. And corn grows pretty fast. It'll carry you through. Do I get that favor? It's simple enough—just to have Beethoven's Ninth on the machine and for the whole damned lot of you to get out of my cabin and let me die in my own way…"

Muller shrugged, but Napier found the tape and put it on. I wanted to see the louse punished for every second of worry, for Lomax, for Hendrix—even for Grundy. But there wasn't much use in vengeance at this point.

"You're to get all this, Paul," Wilcox said as we got ready to leave. "Captain Muller, everything here goes to Tremaine.

I'll make a tape on that, too. But I want it to go to a man who can appreciate Hohmann's conducting."

Muller closed the door. "I guess it's yours," he admitted. "Now that you're head engineer here, Mr. Tremaine, the cabin is automatically yours. Take over. And get that junk in the fuel locker cleaned out—except enough to keep your helpers going. They'll need it, and we'll need their work."

"I'll clean out his stuff at the same time," I said. "I don't want any part of it."

He smiled then, just as Eve came down with Bullard and Pietro. The fat cook was sobered, but already beginning to fill with his own importance. I caught snatches as they began to discuss Bullard's knowledge of growing things. It was enough to know that we'd all live, though it might be tough for a while.

Then Muller gestured upwards. "You've got a reduced staff, Dr. Pietro. Do you intend going on to Saturn?"

"We'll go on," Pietro decided. And Muller nodded. They turned and headed upwards.

I stood staring at my engines. One of them was a touch out of phase and I went over and corrected it. They'd be mine for over two years—and after that, I'd be back on the lists.

Eve came over beside me, and studied them with me. Finally she sighed softly. "I guess I can see why you feel that way about them, Paul," she said. "And I'll be coming down to look at them. But right now, Bullard's too busy to cook, and everyone's going to be hungry when they find we're saved."

I chuckled, and felt the relief wash over me finally. I dropped my hand from the control and caught hers—a nice, friendly hand.

But at the entrance I stopped and looked back toward the cabin where Wilcox lay. I could just make out the second movement of the Ninth beginning.

I never could stand the cheap blatancy of Hohmann's conducting.

Shadows of Empire

The Fifth Army was being recalled from Mars, and Earth's far-flung empire was beginning to fade...

WE SLIPPED out of the post while Mars' sky was still harsh and black, and the morning was bitter with cold. Under us was the swish of the treads slapping the worn old sands, and from the lorries came the muttered grumbling of the men, still nursing their hangovers. The post was lost in the greyness behind us, and the town was just beginning to stir with life as we left it. But it was better that way; the Fifth had its orders back to Earth after ten generations outside, and the General wanted no civilian fuss over our going.

It had been enough, just hearing the click at the gate, and seeing the few pinched-faced, scared people along the streets as we passed. Most of us had been there well over ten years, and you can't keep men segregated from the townspeople in the outposts. Well, they'd had their leave the night before, and now we were on our way; the less time spent thinking about going, the less chance for thoughts of desertion to ripen.

At that, two of the men had sneaked off into the wastelands with a sand-tractor and lorry. I'd have liked to find them; after twenty years with the Service, things like that get under your skin. But we couldn't wait for a week hunting them, when the Emperor had his seal on our orders.

Now a twist in the road showed the town in the dim dawn-light, with the mayor running up tardily and tripping over a scrap of a flag. And old Jake, the tavern-keeper, still stood among the empty boxes from which he'd tossed cartons of cigarettes to us as he went by. Lord knows how much we still owed him, but he'd been Service once himself, and I don't think that was on his mind. Yeah, it was a good town, and we'd never forget it; but I was glad when the road twisted back and the rolling dunes cut it off from view. I'm just plain people, myself, not one of your steel-and-ice nobility like the General.

And that was why I was still only a Sergeant-Major, even though I had to take second command nowadays. In the old times, of course, they'd have sent out young nobles to take over, with proper titles, but I guess they liked it better back on Earth now. For that matter, we'd had few enough replacements in my time, except those we'd recruited ourselves from the town and country around. But what the hell—we managed. The Fifth lacked a few men and some fancy brass, but I never heard a marauding Torrakh laugh over it, even after bad fuel grounded our last helicopter.

Now the little red sun came up to a point where we could turn the heaters off our aspirators. We were passing through a pleasant enough country, little farms and canal-berry orchards. The farm folks must have figured we were out on a raid again, because they only waved at us, and went on with their work; the thick-wooled sheep went on blatting at themselves with no interest in us. Behind me, someone struck up a half-hearted marching song on an old lectrozith, and the men picked it up.

That was better. I sighed to myself, found one of my legs had gone to sleep, and nursed the prickles out of it while the miles slipped behind, and the hamlets and farms began to thin out. In a little while we were reaching the outskirts of the northern desert, and the caterpillar tracks settled down to a steady sifting slap that's music to a man's ears. We ate lunch out of our packs while the red dunes rolled on endlessly in front of us.

IT WAS a couple hours later when the General's tractor dropped abreast of me and his so-called adjutant vaulted to my seat, his usually saturnine face pinched into a wry grin. Then the radio buzzed and he lifted it to my ear with a finger over his lips.

The General's precise voice clipped out, "Close up ranks, Sergeant; we've spotted a band of Torrakhi moving in the direction of the town. Probably heard we're leaving, and they're already moving up; but they'd be happy to stop for a straggler, so keep together."

"Right, sir," I answered out of habit, and added the words on the slip of paper Stanislaus was shaking under my nose. "But couldn't we take a swipe at them first?"

"No time. This looks like the rear guard, and the main body is probably already infiltering through the wastelands. The town will have to shift for itself."

"Right, sir," I said again, and the radio clicked off, while the Slav went on grinning to himself. There wasn't a Torrakh within miles, and I knew it, but the General usually knew what he was doing. I wasn't so dumb I couldn't guess at it.

Stanislaus stretched his lank frame on the seat and nodded slowly. "Yeah, he's crazy, too—which is why he's a good General, 'Major. A few like him in higher places, and we'd be on Mars for another generation or so. Though it wouldn't make much difference in the long run... *Vanitas, vanitatum! There is no remembrance of former generations, neither shall there be any remembrance of the latter generations that are to come, among those that shall come after!*...That's Ecclesiastes, and worth more than the whole Book of Revelations."

"Or a dozen gloomy Slavs! There was talk of replacing the Fifth back when I was still a buck private. You should have been a preacher!"

"And in a way, I was, 'Major...*lest evil days come and the years draw nigh when thou shalt say, I have no pleasure in them.* But a prophet's without honor, and as you say, I'm a gloomy Slav, even though they usually send replacements before they withdraw the Service. Well, lay on, MacDuff, for the greater glory of the Empire!"

I wasn't going to admit he had, me, but I couldn't think of anything to say to that, so I shut up. The gloom-birds probably were around before that stuff was written, but civilization was still going on, though there were rumors about things back on Earth. But somehow, he always managed to make me start smelling old attics piled high with rubbish and beginning to mould. I turned and looked sideways, just as the first outskirts of an old canal swung into view.

They still call them canals, at least, though even the old time astronomers knew they weren't, before Mars was ever reached. But they must have been quite something, ten or fifteen thousand years ago, when the V'nothi built the big earthenware pipe-lines thousands of miles across the planet to section it and break up the sand-shifts that were ruining it. The big osmotic pumps were still working after a fashion, and there was a trickle of moisture flowing even yet, leaking out into the bleeder lines and keeping the degenerate scrub trees going in fifty mile swaths around them.

THE V'NOTHI had disappeared before the Pyramids were put up, leaving only pictures of themselves in the ruins, looking like big, good-natured Vikings, complete to brawn and winged helmets. Their women folk must have been really something, even with fur all over them. Archeologists were still swearing every time they looked at those pictures and wondered what men on horseback were doing on Mars, and why no bones had ever been found! Some of them were even guessing that the V'nothi were Earthmen, maybe from an early peak of civilization we remembered in the Atlantis myths. But even if they were, there was a lot about them to drive a man nuts without worrying about their origin. If you ask me, they were just plain domesticated animals for some other race. Still, whoever the real boss was, it must have been quite a world in their time.

Even the canal-trees weren't natural; no other plants on Mars had bellows growing out of them to supercharge themselves with air, ozone, and traces of water vapor. Even over the drone of the tractor motors, I could hear the dull mutter of their breathing. And at sundown, when they all got together in one long, wild groan…well, when I first heard that, I began to have dreams about what the master race was, though I'm not exactly imaginative. Now I'm older, and just don't know, nor much care.

But the air was drier and thinner here, where they desiccated it and Stanislaus was breathing it with a sort of moral rectitude about him, and nodding as if he liked it. "Dust of Babylon, eh, 'Major? They went up a long way once, further in some ways than we've climbed yet. In a thousand years or less, they pulled themselves up to our sciences, dropped them, and began working on what we'd call sheer magic. Sometimes, just thinking of what the records hint at scares me. They built themselves up to heaven, before the curse of bigness struck them down; and being extremists, it wasn't just a retreat, but a final rout."

"Meaning we're due for the same, 'Laus?" I always did like the way he pronounced his name, to rhyme with house.

"No, 'Major; we're not the same—we retreat. Ninevah, Troy, Rome—they've gone, but the periphery always stays to hibernate and come out into another springtime. An empire decays, but it takes a long time dying, and so far there's always been a certain amount passed on to the next surge of youthfulness. We've developed a racial phoenix-complex. But of course you don't believe the grumblings of a gloomy Slav who's just bitter that his old empire is one of the later dust heaps?"

"No," I told him. "I don't."

He got up, knocking ashes off his parka with long, flickering fingers, and his voice held an irritating chuckle. "Stout fella, pride of the Empire, and all that! I congratulate you, 'Major, and damn it, I envy you!" And he was over the treads and running toward where the General's tractor had stopped, like a long, drawn-out cat. If he hadn't had the grace of a devil, his tongue would have gotten him spitted on a rapier years before.

I didn't dwell on even such pleasant thoughts. The men had stopped singing, and the first reaction of forced cheer was over. They were good joes, all in all, but after the long years at the post among the townspeople, they couldn't help being human. So I dropped back to the end of the line and kept my eyes peeled for any that might suddenly decide to develop engine trouble and lag behind. It's always the first day arid night that are the hardest.

THEIR grumbling sounded normal enough when we pulled off the trail away from the tree-mutterings well after sundown, and I felt better; it's when they stop grousing that you have to watch them. All the same, I made them dig in a lot deeper than we needed, though it gets cold enough to freeze a man solid at night. They were sweating and stepping up the power in their aspirators before I was satisfied, and the berylite tent tops barely stuck up over the sand.

That would give them something trivial to beef about, and work their muscles down to good condition for sleeping. A good meal and a double ration of grog would finish the trick nicely, and I'd already given orders for that—which left me nothing to do but go in where Stanislaus was sprawled out on a cot, dabbling with his food and nodding in time to the tent aspirator's whine.

"Nice gadget, that—efficient," he commented, and the pinched grin was on his face. "Of course, the air's thick enough to breathe when a man's not working, but it's still a nice thing to have."

I knew what he meant, of course. The old timers had done a lot of foolish things, like baking out enough oxygen to keep the air pressure up almost to Earth normal. But it wasn't economical, and we were modern enough to get along without such nonsense. While I ate, I told him so, along with some good advice about how to get along with Emperors. Besides, it was a damn sight better aspirator than they'd had in the pioneer days.

I might as well have saved my breath. He waited until I ran down, and nodded amiably. "Absolutely, absolutely. And very well put, 'Major. As the Romans said when Theodoric's Gauls gave them orders, we're modern and up to date. Being of the present time, we're automatically modern. As for the Emperor, I wouldn't think of blaming him for what's inevitable, though I'd like a chance to argue the point with him, if I didn't have a certain fondness for my neck. Meantime, Mars rebuilds the seals in its houses and puts in little wind machines. And behold, all was vanity and a striving after wind! You really should read Ecclesiastes. Well, sleep tight, 'Major!"

He ducked under a blanket and was snoring in less than five minutes. I never could sleep well under a tin tent with a man who snores; and it was worse this time, somehow, though I finally did drop off.

We were dug out and ready to march in the morning when the General's scheme bore fruit; our deserters showed up over the dunes, hotfooting it down on us. They must have spotted my tractor, because they didn't waste any time in coming up to me. The damned fools! Naturally, they had to bring the two women along with them, instead of dumping them near town. They must have been stinko drunk when they started, though the all-night drive had sobered them up—the drive plus half freezing to death and imagining Torrakhi behind every bush.

I'd never seen those two brig birds salute with quite such gusto, though, as they hopped down, and Stanislaus' amused snort echoed my sentiments. But the big guy started the ball rolling, with only a dirty look at the Slav. "Sir! We couldn't help being AWOL, we..."

"Were caught by Torrakhi, of course," the General's smooth voice filled in behind me, and I stepped out of the picture on the double. "Very clever of you to escape, tractor and all. Unfortunately, there were no Torrakhi; the message your set was fitted to unscramble was a trap, based on the assumption that you'd rather take your chances with us than with a marauding band of nomads infiltrating around you. I suppose I could have you shot; and if I hear one sniveling word from you, I will! Or I could take you back to Earth in chains."

His lips pressed out into a thin, white line and his eyes flicked over to Stanislaus for a bare second. "You wouldn't like that. There's a new Emperor, not the soft one we had before. I served under him once...and I rather suspect he'd reward me for bringing you back with us, after the proper modern Imperial fashion of gratitude. However, for the good of the Fifth, you're already listed as fatalities. Sergeant, do you know these women?"

"Their names are on our books, sir."

"Quite so. And they knew what they were mixed up in. Very well, leave them their side arms, but fill the tractor and lorry they returned with some of your men, and prepare to break camp. You've already forgotten all this; and that goes for the men, as well!" He swung on his heel and mounted his tractor without another look at the deserters, who were just beginning to realize what he'd meant.

STANISLAUS elected to ride with me as we swung back toward the canal road, watching the four until the dunes swallowed them. Then he shrugged and lit his cigarette. "Not orthodox, 'Major, but effective; you can stop worrying about desertions. And take it from me, it was the right thing to do; I happen to know—rather well in fact—why our precise and correct leader thought it wise to fake the books. But I won't bore you with it. As to those four—well, some of the pioneers were up against worse odds, but *de mortuis nil nisi bonum.* Nice morning, don't you think?"

It was, as a matter of fact, and we were making good time. The trail swung out, heading due south now, and away from the canal, and the sands were no longer cluttered with the queer pits always found around the canal-trees. By noon, we'd put a hundred more miles behind us, and the men were hardening into the swing of things, though they still weren't doing the singing I like to hear on the march—the good, clean filth that's somehow the backbone of Service morale. I sent a couple of tractors out to scout, just to break the monotony, though there wouldn't be anything to see so near the end of the desert.

Surprisingly, however, they hadn't been gone ten minutes when the report came back: Torrakhi to the left flank! A moment later, we were snapping into a tight phalanx and hitting up a rise where we could see; but by then we knew that there was no danger. They were just a small band, half a mile away, jolting along on their lama-mounts at an easy lope. Then they spotted us and beat back behind the dunes and out of sight. A small marauding band, turning back north from sacking some fool outlier's farm, probably.

But it was unusual to see them so far south. We'd never been able to eliminate them entirely, any more than the V'nothi before us had but we'd kept the wild quasi-human barbarians in line, pretty much. And now we were swinging back to the trail again, leaving them unchecked to grow bold in raiding; there wasn't anything else we could do, since they hadn't attacked and we were under Imperial seal. Well, maybe the Second Command would get them for us some time. I hoped so.

Stanislaus might say what he would, but he was still Service, and it had hit him, too. "Notice the long rifle they pulled? What make would you say?"

"Renegade pirates on Callisto, it looked like, at a guess. But the exiles couldn't get past the Out Fleet to trade with Torrakhi."

He flipped his cigarette away and turned to face me, dead serious and quiet about it. "The Out Fleet's just a propaganda myth, 'Major. They pulled it back before I...uh, left Earth..."

He couldn't know that, and I had no business believing him; yet somehow, I was sure he did know, and whatever else he was, he was not a liar. But that would mean that the Earth-Mars trade...

"Exactly," he said, as if he'd read the thought. "And now we're going back to help put down a minor little uprising in the Empire, so I hear. Write your own ticket."

But even if it were true, it didn't prove anything. Sure, it looked bad, but I've learned you can't judge from half-knowledge. A lot of times when I've gone out swearing at the orders, I've come back alive because they weren't the kind I'd have given. Heck, even if the mesotron rifle was Callistan, there was no telling how old it was; maybe they'd pulled the Out Fleet back for the second reason that it wasn't needed. But it did look odd, their keeping up the pretense.

WE CAMPED that night at an old abandoned fort dating back to pioneer days, and then shoved on in the morning through little hamlets and the beginning of settled land. The people looked fairly hard and efficient, but it was pleasant, after the desert, and the men seemed more cheerful. Here the road was kept surfaced, and the engines went all out. A little later, we took the grousers off, and by the time another night had passed, we were in well-settled country. From then on, it was all soft going and the miles dropped off as regular as clockwork, though I missed the swish of the sand under the treads.

As we went on, the land and the people got softer, with that comfortable look I'd missed up where Torrakhi are more than things to scare children with. And the farms were bigger and better kept. For that matter, I couldn't see a man working with a rifle beside him. The Service had done that. When we first hit Mars, in the pioneer days, there hadn't been a spot on its face where a man could close both eyes. Now even the kids went running along the road alone. Oh, sure, there were some abandoned villas, here and there, but I don't think the nobles were too much missed.

And that was civilization and progress, whatever Stanislaus thought about it. Let them pull the Out Fleet back and call in the Fifth. As long as Mars had spots on it like this, it didn't look too bad for the Empire. I wanted to throw it in the Slav's face, but I knew it wouldn't do any good. He'd have some kind of answer. Better let sleeping dogs lie.

And besides, he was riding with the General again, and even at night he was busy writing in some big book and not paying attention to anything else. In a way, it was all to the good. Still, I dunno. At least, when he was spouting out his dogma, I had a chance to figure up some kind of answer to myself. There wasn't much I could do about the look on his face.

But I noticed that we always seemed to make camp about the time we were well away from the cities, and it was something to think over, along with the guff that had begun among the men. It looked as if the General meant to keep us away from any rumors going, around, and that was odd; ordinarily civilian scuttlebutt means nothing to the Service.

And now that the novelty had worn off, there was something wrong about the number of farms we'd pass that were abandoned and that had been for a long time. There were little boarded-up stores in some of the villages, and once we went by a massive atomic by-products plant, dead and forgotten. And the softness on the people's faces began to look less pretty; one good-sized band of Torrakhi could raise hob with a whole county, even without mesotron rifles from Callisto.

THE ONE time I did speak to a native, I had no business doing it. We'd been rolling along, with me at the rear for the moment, and there was this fine-looking boy of about twelve walking along the road. What got me was the song he was singing and the way he came to a Service salute at the sight of me. Well, the General wasn't in sight, and the kid took my slowing up as a hint to hop onto the lug rail.

"Fifth, isn't it, sir?"

"Right. But where the deuce did you learn that ditty and the proper way to address a non-com?"

He grinned the way healthy kids know how, before they grow old enough to forget. "Gramps was in the Fifth when they raised the siege of Bharene, sir, and he told me all about it before he died. Gee, it must have been great when he was young!"

"And now?"

"Aw, now they say you're going back to Earth, and Gramps wouldn't have liked that. He was a Martian, like me… Look, I live up there, so I gotta go. Thanks for the lift, Sergeant!"

So even the kids knew we were going back, and now we were just another Service Command, instead of the backbone of Mars. Strange, I hadn't thought of what it would mean, going back where people had never heard of us before. But I could see where the General was right in not letting us mix with people here. Damn it, we were still the Fifth, and nothing could change that, Mars or Earth, Emperor or Torrakh!

We didn't spend too much time looking at the country after that, though it grew even prettier as we went on. The tractors' were beginning to carbon up under the fuel we had to requisition, and we were busy nursing them along and watching for trouble. At the post, we'd had our own purifying plant to get the gum out of the plant fuels, but here we had to take pot luck. And it was a lot worse than I'd expected. But then, a man tends to gloss over his childhood and think things were better then, I dunno. Maybe it had always been that bad.

Anyhow, we made it, in spite of a few breakdowns. It was dusk when the lights of Marsport showed up, and we went limping through the outskirts. When we hit the main drag, a motor cop ran ahead of us with his siren open, though there wasn't any need. I couldn't help wondering where the cars were, and how they managed to dig up so many bicycles. We must have looked like the devil, since we'd pushed too fast to bother much with shining up, but there were some cheers from the crowds that assembled, and a few women's faces with the look of not having seen uniforms in years. The men woke up at that, yelling the usual things, but I could feel their disappointment in the city.

Then we halted, and Stanislaus came back, while a fat and stuffy little man in noble's regalia strode up to the

General's tractor, fairly sniffing the dirt on our gear as he came. Well, he could have used a better shave himself, and a little less hootch would have improved his dignity. The Slav chuckled. "Methinks this should be good, unless the O.M. has lost his touch. Flip the switch, 'Major; I left the radio turned on."

But no sound came out of it except a surprised grunt from the official as he looked at the odd-patterned ring on the General's finger. I never knew what it stood for, but all the air went out of the big-shot's sails, and he couldn't hand over the official message fast enough after that. He was mopping sweat from his face when the crowd swallowed him. I've seen a busted sergeant act that way when he suddenly remembered he was pulling rank he no longer had.

"Don't bother cutting off yet, Sergeant," the radio said quietly, and it was my turn to grin. Stanislaus should have known better than to try putting anything over. "Umm. I'm going to be tied up with official business at the Governor's, so you'll go ahead. Know where the auxiliary port is? Good. Bivouac there, and put the men to policing themselves and the hangars. No passes. That's all."

HE SWITCHED to a waiting car, leaving the tractor to his driver, and we went on again, out through the outskirts and past the main spaceport that was dark and I couldn't tell much about it, but I remembered the mess of the old auxiliary field. They'd built it thirty miles out in barren land to handle the overflow during the old colonizing period, and it had been deserted and weed-grown for years, with hangars falling apart. It was worse than I'd remembered, though there were some lights on and a group of Blue Guards to let us in and direct us to the left side of the field.

Some clearing had been done, but there was work enough to keep us all busy as beavers, and there would be for days, if we stayed that long. At least it gave me a good excuse for announcing confinement to grounds, though they took it easier than I'd expected; it seemed they already knew in some way. And at last I was finished with giving orders and had a chance to join the Slav in inspecting the ships I'd already noticed down at the end of the field.

I'd seen the like of the double turret cruiser before, but the two big ones were different, even in the dim lights of the field. They were something out of the history books, and no book could give any idea of their size. The rocket crews about them, busy with their own affairs, were like ants running around a skyscraper by comparison. Either could have held the whole Command and left room for cargo besides.

"So we're waiting for the Second Command, 'Laus?"

He jerked his head back from a reverent inspection of the big hulks and nodded at me slowly. "You improve, 'Major, though you forgot to comment on the need of a cruiser between Mars and Earth... Two hundred years! And they're still sounder than the hunk of junk sent out to protect them. There was a time when men knew how to build ships—and how to use them. Now there are only four left out of all that were built. Any idea where the other two are?"

"Yeah." I'd failed to recognize them because of their size, but it hadn't been quite dark enough to conceal them completely. "Back at the other port, picking up the South Commands. Damn it, 'Laus, did you have to infect me with your pessimism?"

"You're going back to Earth, 'Major,'" he answered, as if that were explanation enough. "The optimist sees the doughnut, the pessimist, the hole. And you get a better view of things through a hole than through a hunk of sweetened dough. And as Havelock Ellis put it, the place where optimism most flourished is the lunatic asylum. Come on back and I'll lend you Ecclesiastes while I finish my book."

And I was just dumb enough to read it. But I might have had the same nightmares anyway. I'd gotten a good look at the faces of the rocket gang.

In the morning, I was too busy bossing the stowing of our gear to do much thinking, though. Even with maps of the corridors, I'd have been lost in the ship without the help of one of the pilots, a bitter-faced young man who seemed glad to fill his time, but who refused to talk beyond the bare necessities. When the General came back at noon, the men were all quartered inside, except for those who were detailed to help load the collection of boxes that began to come from Marsport.

He nodded curt approval and went to the radio in his cabin. And about an hour later, I looked up to see the Second Command come in and go straight to the second ship, a mile away. They could have saved themselves the trouble, as far as I was concerned; I had no desire to compare notes with the other group. But I guess it was better for the men, and it was a lot easier than posting guards overnight to see they didn't mix. A hell of a way to run the Service, I thought; but of course, it wasn't the Service anymore—just the Second and Fifth Commands, soon to be spread around on Earth!

IT WAS after taps when they brought the civilians aboard; but I was still enjoying the freedom of second in command, and I was close enough to get a good look at them and the collection of special tools they were bringing along with the rest of their luggage. I'd always figured the technical crafts came out from automatic Earth to the outlands where their skills were still needed. But that seemed to be just another sign that the old order was changing. I turned to make talk with the pilot who was beside me, and then thought better of it.

But for once, he was willing to break his silence, though he never took his eyes off the little group that was filing in. "They're needed, Sergeant! Atomic technicians are in demand again, along with plutonium. That's what the rear trucks are carrying, and they'll be loading it between hulls tonight—all that can be arranged safely. Of course, I'm not supposed to tell you. But I was born here, and it's not like the last job we had, ferrying out the Venus Commands. Care to join me in getting drunk?"

It was an idea. Plutonium is valuable in particular only for bombs, for which it's still the best material. And atom bombs are the messiest, lousiest, and most inefficient weapons any fighting man ever swore at. They're only good for ruining the land until you can't finish a decent mopping-up, and poisoning the atmosphere until your own people begin dying. Not a single one had been dropped in the five centuries since we came up with the superior energy weapons. So now we were carrying the stuff back to Earth, where they already had the accumulated waste from all their piles.

But I caught a signal from the car the General was using as I turned, and I changed my mind, I was in the mood for Stanislaus now, and whiskey's a pretty poor mental cathartic, anyway. This time I could see that the information I poured out at him wasn't something he already knew.

"So. *Even so are the sons of men snared in an evil time, when it falleth suddenly upon them.*" He let it sink in slowly, then shrugged. "Well, maybe it'll be faster, that way. But it won't matter to me. I'm due in Marsport to attend my funeral—a lovely casket, I understand, though it's a pity we're so pressed for time I can't have military honors. Only the simple dignity of civilian rites. Thought you might like to bid me fond adieu, for old times' sake."

"Yeah, sure. And bring me back a bottle of the same."

He shook his head gently, and the darned fool's voice was serious. "I wish I could, 'Major. I'd like nothing better than having you along to listen to my theories of our racial phoenix-complex. But I've done the next best thing in leaving the book that's my labor of love in your cabin. All right, I was ribbing you, and I'm being transferred out to the Governor's service by special orders. Does that make sense to you?"

It did, put that way. It meant that after all the years of wishing he'd clam up, I was going to miss him plenty, now that I'd been converted, and probably sit alone biting my tongue to keep from spouting the same brand of pessimism. But I wasn't much good at saying it, and he cut me off in the middle.

"Then bite it. That stuff won't go, back there, though you're better off for having found out in advance. Trust the General to see you through. He made a mistake once, but he's wiser now. Forget Ecclesiastes and remember a jingle of Kipling's instead: *Now these are the Laws of the Jungle, and many and mighty are they; but the head and the hoof of the Law, and the haunch and the hump is—Obey!* Betray rhymes as well, but it takes a lot more background and practice. Now beat it, before I really start preaching!"

I DIDN'T need to hunt up the pilot; I had a bottle of Martian canal juice of my own in the cabin. But I'd consumed more of the book than the bottle when morning came and a knock sounded outside.

The General came in when I grunted, his face pinched with fatigue, and his eyes red with lack of sleep. He nodded at the book, dropped onto the cot, and poured himself a generous slug before he looked at me.

"A remarkable book, Bill, by a remarkable man. But you know that by now. Dynamite, of course, but something we'll have to smuggle in to save for a possible posterity. And stop looking so damned surprised. Any man Stanislaus trusted with that is my equal or my better, as far as I'm concerned. After we land I have ways of seeing you get knighthood and a Colonel's title, so you're practically an officer, anyhow. And I'm neither General nor Duke—just a messenger boy for the late deceased Stanislaus Korzynski. He died of canal fever day before yesterday, you know."

It was coming too thick and fast, and I didn't answer that. I reached for the bottle and poured a shot down my throat without bothering with a glass. The General held out his, watched me fill it, and downed the shot before going on again. "Not much of a Serviceman, am I, Bill? But it has to be that way. Nobody knows the name he used, but there are plenty on Earth who remember his face. Or haven't you figured out yet who he was from the book?"

"I've had my suspicions," I admitted. "Only I dunno whether I'm crazy or he was." "Neither. You're right, he's the supposedly assassinated Prince Stellius Asiaticus, rightful ruler of the Empire! Here's a note he sent you."

There wasn't much to it: *Friend 'Major—it was over the hill for me, after all. If you have children, as I intend to, pass on my new name to them, and someday our offspring may get together and discuss the phoenix bird. Elmer C. Clesiastes.*

"The phoenix," the General muttered over my shoulder while he reached for the bottle. "Now what the deuce did he mean by that?'

"What is it, anyway?"

"A legendary bird of Grecian mythology—the only one of its kind. It lived for a few hundred years, then built itself a funeral pyre and sat fanning the flames with its wings until it was consumed. After that, a new bird hatched out of the ashes and started all over again. That's why they used it for the symbol of immortality."

Below us, the rockets rumbled tentatively and then bellowed out, while the force of the jets crushed us back against the wall. Beyond the porthole, Mars dropped away from us, as the Empire turned back to its nest. But I wasn't thinking much of that, impressive though it was.

Somehow, I was going to have the children Stanislaus had mentioned, and I'd live long enough to see that they remembered the name he'd chosen, atom bombs or no bombs. Because I knew him at last, and the pessimist was a prince, all right—the Prince of Optimists.

The General and I sat toasting him and discussing the phoenix legend and civilization's ups and downs while Mars changed from a world to a round ball in the background of space. It wasn't military or proper, but we felt much better by the time we found and confiscated the second bottle.

Battleground

We know that the human race must struggle to survive—and that on the outcome may hang disaster. But just how wide is Armageddon?

BEYOND THE observation port of the hypercruiser *Clarion* lay the utter blackness of nothing. The ship was effectively cutting across space without going through it, spanning parsecs for every subjective day of travel.

There were neither stars, space nor time around them, and only the great detectors built into the ship could keep them from being hopelessly lost. These followed a trail of energy laid down on the way out from Earth years before, leading them homeward, solar system by solar system.

Acting Captain Lenk stood with his back to the other three, studying their sullen reflections in the port. It was better than facing them directly, somehow, even though it showed his own bald scalp, tautly hollow face and slump-shouldered body.

"All right," he said at last. "So we vote again. I'll have to remind you we're under orders to investigate all habitable planets on a line back to Earth. I vote we follow orders. Jeremy?"

The xenologist shrugged faintly. His ash-blond coloring, general slimness and refinement of features gave him a look of weakness, but his voice was a heavy, determined bass. "I stand pat. We didn't explore the last planet enough. I vote we go back and make a thorough job of it."

"Home—at once!" The roar came from the squat, black bearded mineralogist, Graves. "God never meant man to leave the world on which He put him! Take us back, I say, where…"

"Aimes?" Lenk cut in quickly.

They'd heard Graves' violently fundamentalist arguments endlessly, until the sound of his voice was enough to revive every antagonism and hatred they had ever felt. Graves had been converted to the newest and most rapidly expanding of the extreme evangelical faiths just before they had left. And unfortunately for the others, he had maintained that his covenant to go on the exploration could not be broken, even though venturing into space was a cardinal sin.

Aimes glowered at the others from under grizzled eyebrows. Of them all, the linguodynamicist took part in the fewest arguments and apparently detested the others most. He turned his heavy body now as he studied them, seemingly trying to make up his mind which he detested most at the moment. Then he grunted.

"With you, Captain," Aimes said curtly.

He swung on his heel and stalked out of the control cabin, to go back to studying the undeciphered writing of the planets they had visited.

Graves let out a single hiss and followed, probably heading for the galley, since it was his period to cook.

Jeremy waited deliberately until the mineralogist's footsteps could no longer be heard, and then turned to leave.

Lenk hesitated far a second, then decided that monotony was worse than anything else. "How about same chess, Jeremy?" he asked.

The other stopped, and some of the sullenness left his face. Apparently the protracted arguments had wearied him until he was also feeling the relief of decisive action.

"Why not?" Jeremy said. "I'll set up the board while you fiddle with your dials."

No fiddling was necessary, since Lenk had never cut them off their automatic detecting circuit, but he went through the motions far the other's benefit. Gra_atic strain came faintly through hyperspace, and the ship could locate suns by it. If approach revealed planets of habitable size, it was set to snap out of hyperspace automatically near the most likely world.

Lenk had been afraid such a solar system might be found before they could resolve the argument, and his own relief from the full measure of cabin fever came from the end of that possibility.

They settled down to the game with a minimum of conversation. Since the other four members of the crew had been killed by some unknown virus, conversation had proven less than cheerful. It was better when they were on a planet and busy, but four people were too few for the monotony of hypertravel.

Then Jeremy snapped out of it. He cleared his throat tentatively while castling, grimaced, and then nodded positively. "I was right, Lenk. We never did explore those other planets properly."

"Maybe not," Lenk agreed. "But with the possibility of alien raiders headed toward Earth…"

"Bunk! No sign of raiders. Every indication was that the races on those worlds killed themselves off—no technology alien to their own culture. And there would have been with aliens invading."

"Time that way? Coincidence can account for just so much."

"It has to account for the lowering cultural levels in the colonizing direction," Jeremy said curtly. "Better leave that sort of argument to Aimes. He's conditioned to it."

Lenk shrugged and turned back to the chess. It was over his head, anyhow.

Men had built only three other cruisers capable of exceeding the speed of light, so far. The first had gone out in a direction opposite to that of the *Clarion* and had returned to report a regular decline in culture as the distance of habitable worlds from Earth increased. The nearest was in a medieval state, the next an early bronze culture, then a stone-age one, and so on, down to the furthest explored, where the native race had barely discovered fire.

It had been either impossible coincidence or the evidence of some law nobody has been quite ready to accept, save for the newly spreading fundamentalists, who maintained it proved that Earth was the center of the universe.

The other two cruisers had not reported back when the *Clarion* took off.

And their own trip had only added to the mystery, and they had touched on four habitable systems. And on each, there had been evidence of a highly developed race and some vast struggle that had killed off that race completely.

The furthest had lain fallow for an unguessable period of time, and in each succeeding one, evidence indicated the time interval since the destruction of the culture had been less. On the world they had left, the end must have come not more than a few thousand years before.

"Suppose one race had gone along in a straight line, seeding the systems with life," Lenk guessed. "Remember, every race we found had similarities. And suppose another race of conquerors stumbled on that line and is mopping up? Maybe with some weapon that leaves no trace."

Jeremy looked at him. "Suppose Graves is right, and his God wipes out all wicked races. He keeps planting races, hoping they'll turn out right, and wiping out the old ones?" he snorted. "Only, of course he thinks Earth is the only world that counts. We're dealing with facts, Lenk, not wild theories. And why should an alien race simply wipe out another race, wait a thousand years or so, and move on—without using the plant afterwards, even for a base for the next operation? Also, why should we find plenty of weapons, but no skeletons?"

"Skeletons are pretty fragile. And if somebody had the mythical heat ray..."

"Bunk! If it would vaporize calcium in the bones, it would vaporize some of the parts of the weapons we found." Jeremy moved a rook, considered it, and pointed. "Check. And there are always some parts of skeletons that will last more than a thousand years. I've got a theory, but it's..."

Pale light cut through the viewing port, and a gong sounded in the room. Lenk jerked to his feet and moved to his screens.

"Maybe we'll know now," he said. "We'll be landing on a planet in about an hour: And it looks pretty much like Earth, from here."

He cranked up the gain on the magnifiers, and studied it again, scanning the surface of the planet below them. There were clouds in the sky, but through a clear patch he made out enough evidence.

"Want me to set us down near a city?" he asked, pointing.

Jeremy nodded. Like all the other planets on this trip, the one below was either inhabited or had been inhabited until recently.

They knew before the ship landed that the habitation was strictly past tense, at least as far as any high level of culture was concerned. The cities were in ruins.

At one time, they must have reared upwards to heights as imposing as those of the free state of New York City or the commonwealth of Chicago. But now the buildings had lost their topmost towers, and the bases showed yawning holes in many places.

They landed in the center of the largest city, after a quick skim over the surface to be sure that no smaller city had escaped. A quick sampling of the air indicated it was breathable, with no poisons and only a touch of radioactivity, too low to be dangerous.

Aimes and Jeremy went out each in a little tractor. While making explorations, they were capable of forgetting their antagonisms in their common curiosity.

Graves remained on the ship. He had decided somewhere along the line that setting foot on an alien planet was more sinful than travel through space, and refused to be shaken.

Lenk finished what observations were necessary. He fiddled around, bothered by the quiet city outside. It had been better on the other worlds, where the ruins had been softened by time and weather. Here it was too easy to imagine things. Finally, he climbed into rough clothes, and went out on foot.

Everything was silent. Grass almost identical with that of Earth was growing through much of the torn pavement, and there were trees and bushes here and there. Vines had climbed some of the ruined walls. But there were no flowers. Much of the planet had apparently been overgrown with forest and weeds, but this city was in a temperate zone, and clear enough for easy travel.

Lenk listened to the wind, and the faint sighing of a few trees nearby. He kicked over stones and rubble where they lay on patches of damp earth. And he kept looking at the sky.

But it was no different from other worlds as far as the desolation went. There were no insects, and no animals stared warily up from the basements, and the grass showed no signs of having been grazed. It was as if the animal kingdom had never existed here.

He made his way back from the section of largest buildings, toward what might have been a park at one time. Here there was less danger of being trapped in any collapsing ruin, and he moved more confidently. The low buildings might have been public sites, but they somehow seemed more like homes.

He stumbled on something, and leaned down to pick it up. At first, the oddness of its design confused his vision. Then he made out a barrel with rifling inside, and a chamber that still contained pellets, now covered with corrosion. It would have fitted his hand oddly, but he could have used the pistol.

Beyond it lay a line of rust that might have been a sword at one time. Coiled over it was a heavy loop of thick plastic that ended in a group of wires, apparently of stainless steel. Each wire ended in a row of cutting points. It might have been a cross between a knout and a bolas. He had a vision of something alien and sinister coming at him with one of those, and shuddered.

There was a ruin of rust and corroded parts further on that might have been a variation of a machine gun. Lenk started for it, to be stopped by a shout.

"Hold it!" It was Jeremy's voice, and now the tank came around a corner, and headed toward him. 'Stay put, Lenk. That thing may be booby-trapped. And we can't be sure here that there has been time enough to make it safe."

Lenk shuddered again, and climbed in hastily as Jeremy held open the door. It was tight inside, but reasonably safe, since the tank had been designed for almost anything. Jeremy must have seen him leaving the ship and followed.

But by noon they had abandoned the fear of booby-traps. Either there had never been any or time had drawn their stings.

Lenk wandered through the section already roughly surveyed, and declared safe. He felt convinced the inhabitants of this world once had been more like men than most other races. They had been two-legged, with arms and heads in a human position on their upright bodies.

Judging from the size of the furniture, they had been slightly larger than men but not enough to matter. The pictures on the walls were odd mostly for the greenish tints of the skin and the absence of outward noses or ears. With a little fixing and recoloring, they might have been *people.*

He came to a room that had been sealed off, pried open the door, and went in. It smelled stale enough to indicate that it had been reasonably air-tight. Benches and chairs ran along one wall, and a heavy wooden table occupied the middle. On that were piled bits and pieces in a curious scramble. He studied them carefully—belts, obviously, buttons, the inevitable weapons, scraps of plastic material.

A minute later, he was shouting for Jeremy over the little walkie-talkie. The xenologist appeared in less than five minutes. He stared about for a second, then grinned wryly.

"Your first, eh? I've found a lot of them. Sure, those were corpses there once." He saw Lenk's expression, and shrugged. "Oh, you were right to call me. It proves we weren't crazy. Wood and some cloth still preserved, but no bones. I've got a collection of pictures like that."

"A corrosive gas—" Lenk suggested.

Jeremy shook his head vigorously. "No dice, Captain. See that belt? It's plant fiber—something like linen. No gas strong enough to eat up a body would leave that unharmed. And they had skeletons, too—we've found models in what must have been a museum. But we can't even find the fossil skeletons that should be there. Odd, though."

He prodded about among the weapons, shaking his head. "All the weapons in places like this show evidence of one homogeneous design. And all the ornaments are in a T shape, like this one."

He lifted a stainless metal object from the floor and dropped it. "But outside in the square, there are at least two designs. For once, it almost looks as if your idea of an alien invader might be worth considering."

The radio at his side let out a squawk, and he cut it on listening to the thin whisper that came from it. Abruptly, he swung about and headed toward his tractor outside, with Lenk following.

"Aimes has found something," Jeremy said.

They found the linguodynamicist in the gutted ruins of a building into which great concrete troughs led. A rusty ruin in one of the troughs indicated something like a locomotive had once run in it, apparently on great ball bearings. The fat man was pointing excitedly toward something on one of the walls.

At first glance, it seemed to be a picture of more of the green people, apparently undergoing some violent torture. Then their eyes swept on—and they gasped.

Over the green people, three vaguely reptilian monstrosities were hovering, at least twice the size of the others, all equipped with the fanged whips Lenk had seen. One of the green men was apparently trying to defend himself with a huge T-shaped weapon, but the others were helpless. The reptilian monsters sprouted great ugly wings of glaring red from their shoulders.

"The invaders," Lenk said. They were horrible things to see. "But their weapons weren't that big..."

"A war poster!" Aimes said bitterly. "It doesn't tell a thing except that there were two groups."

Jeremy studied it, more closely. "Not necessarily even that. It's designed for some emotional effect. But at least, it's a hint that there may have been enemies unlike the ones who lived here. Lenk, can I take the scout ship out?"

"Go ahead," Lenk told him. He frowned at the poster. "Jeremy, if that means the human race is going to have to face an alien invasion from monsters like that..."

"It means nothing!"

Jeremy went off, with Aimes apparently in agreement for a change. Lenk stood studying the poster. Finally he ripped it down, surprised to find how strong it still was, and rolled it up to carry back to the ship.

Each world had been razed more recently, and each with the same curious curse. The race had risen to a high culture, and then had seemingly been wiped out in a few brief years. The destruction had accounted for all life on the planet, other than vegetable—and had wiped out even the bones. All that had been left was a collection of weapons and relics of more doubtful use.

The pattern was the same. The direction was steadily toward Earth, leaping from planet to planet at jumps of thousands of years apart, or perhaps mere hundreds. This planet must have been attacked less than five hundred years before, though it was hard to tell without controlled study of decay here.

Even now Earth might be suffering the invasion! They had been gone nearly three years. And during that time, the monsters might have swooped down hideously out of space.

They might return to find the Earth a wasteland!

His thoughts were a turmoil that grew worse as he stared at the poster. The unknown artist had done his job well. A feeling of horror poured out of it, filling him with an insensate desire to find such monstrosities and rend and maim them, as they had tormented the unfortunate green people.

Graves came stomping up to the control room, carrying lunch, and took one look at the picture. "Serves the heathens right," he grumbled. "Look at them. In hell, suffering from the lashes of the devils of the pit. And still holding up that heathen charm."

Lenk blinked. But Graves' idea wasn't too fantastic, at that. The creatures did look like devils, and the T-shaped object might be a religious symbol. Hadn't some faith or other used the taucross in its worship? And those objects on the third world back had resembled swastikas, which were another religious symbol on Earth.

That part fit. During periods of extreme stress or danger, man sought some home in his faith. Was it so unnatural that alien races might do the same?

"Isn't there anything hopeful in your religion, Graves?" he asked bitterly, wondering what the man had been like before his conversion to the rigidity he now possessed. He'd probably been as violent an atheist. Usually, a fanatic who switched sides became doubly fanatical.

The revival of religious devotion had begun some fifteen years before, and from what Lenk had seen, the world had been a better and more kindly place for it. But there would always be those who thought the only true devotion lay in the burning of witches. Or maybe Graves needed psychiatric treatment for his morose moods were becoming suspiciously psychotic, and his fanaticism might be only a sign of deeper trouble.

The man went off muttering something about the prophecy and the time being at hand for all to be tried in fire. Lenk went back to staring at the poster until he heard the scout come back. He found Aimes and Jeremy busy unloading what seemed to be loot enough to fill two of the scouts.

"A whole library, almost intact," Aimes spoke with elation. "And plenty of it is on film, where we can correlate words and images! In two weeks, I'll speak the language like a native."

"Good." Lenk told him. "Because in about that time, we'll be home on Earth. As long as there's any chance that our people should be warned about invaders, I'm not delaying any longer."

"You can forget the alien invaders," Jeremy objected.

Then he exploded his thunderbolt. The horrible aliens had proved to be no more than a group of purple-skinned people on the other side of the planet with a quite divergent culture, but of the same basic stock as the green skinned men. They also exaggerated in their drawings, and to about the same degree.

Fortunately the treasure-trove from the library would give the two men enough for years of work, and required the attention of a full group. They were eager now to take off for Earth and to begin recruiting a new expedition, taking only enough with them for the first basic steps.

Lenk headed directly for the control room. He began setting up the proper directions on the board while Jeremy finished the account.

"But *something's* hitting the planets," he objected. His hand found the main button and the *Clarion* began heading up through the atmosphere on normal gravity warp, until she could reach open space, and go into hyperdrive. "Your monsters prove to be only people—but it still doesn't explain the way disaster follows a line straight toward Earth! And until we know..."

"Maybe we'd be better off not knowing," Jeremy said. But he refused to clarify his statement.

Then the hyperdrive went on.

The homeward trip was somewhat different from the others. There were none of the petty fights this time.

Aimes and Jeremy were busy in their own way, decoding the language and collating the material they had.

Graves was with them, grumbling at being around the heathen things, but apparently morbidly fascinated by them.

Lenk could offer no help, and his duty lay with the ship. He pondered over the waves of destruction that seemed to wash toward Earth, and the diminishing cultural levels on the planets beyond. It couldn't be pure coincidence. Nor could he accept the idea that Earth was the center of the universe, and that everything else was necessarily imperfect.

Surprisingly, it was Graves who gave him his first hopeful suggestion. A week had passed, and they were well into the second when the men really caught his attention. Graves was bringing his lunch, actually smiling. He frowned.

"What gives?" he asked.

"It's all true!" Graves answered, and there was an inner glow to him. "Just as it's prophesied in *Revelations*. There were times when I had doubts, but now I know. God has set the heathens before me as proof that Armageddon will come, and I have been singled out to bring the glad tidings to His faithful!"

"I thought you, didn't believe God would have anything to do with heathens," Lenk objected. He was trying to recall whether a sudden phase of manic joy was a warning symptom or not.

"I misunderstood. I thought God had forbade space flight. But now it is proved how He loves us. He singled us out to teach us to fly through space that we could learn." Graves gathered up the dishes without noticing that Lenk hadn't touched them and went off in a cloud of ecstasy.

But his point had been made, and Lenk turned it over. Then, with a shout, he headed toward the headquarters of the two, remaining scientists. He found them sitting quietly, watching a reel of some kind being projected through an alien device.

"I hear it's Armageddon we're facing," he said.

He expected grins of amusement from them—or at least from Jeremy. But none came. Aimes nodded.

"First progress in all directions. Then a period when religion seems to be in the decline. Then a revival, and a return to faith in the prophecies. All religions agree on those prophecies, Lenk. Revelations refer to the end of Armageddon, when the whole world will wipe itself out before the creation of a better world, in one planet-wide war. The old Norse legends spoke of a Fimbulwinter, when the giants and their gods would destroy the earth in war. And these green-skinned peoples had the same religious prophecies. They came true, too. Armageddon. Contagious Armageddon."

Lenk stared from one to the other, suspecting a joke. "But that still leaves coincidence—the way things move from planet to planet..."

"Not at all," Jeremy said. "These people didn't have space travel, but they had some pretty highly developed science. They found what we thought we'd disproved—an ether drift. It would carry spores from planet to planet—and in the exact direction needed to account for what we've seen. Races were more advanced back that way, less so the way we first went, simply because of the time it took the spores to drift."

"And what about the destruction?" Lenk asked woodenly. Their faces were getting him—they looked as if they believed it. "Is there another disease spore to drive races mad?"

"Nothing like that. Just the natural course of cultures when they pass a certain level," Jeremy answered. "I should have seen that myself. Every race follows the same basic pattern. The only question is how much time we've got left—a week or a thousand years?"

They turned back to their projection device, but Lenk caught the xenologist by the shoulder and swung him back. "But they didn't have space travel! That doesn't fit their pattern. Even if you're right..."

Jeremy nodded. "We don't have the secret of immortality, either. And this race did. But, damn it, I'd still like to know what happened to all those skeletons?"

Lenk went back to his control room. And perversely, his thoughts insisted on accepting their explanation. It would be like man to think that important things could only happen on his own home planet, and prophecy an end for his own race, never dreaming it could happen to others.

It would be normal for him to sense somehow out of his own nature what his inevitable end must be—and then to be completely amazed when he found the same end for other races.

But...

Space travel—travel at faster than light speeds—had to make a difference. There were the other worlds on the other side of the sun, where men were already planning to colonize. Even if a world might normally blow up in a final wild holocaust, it would have its whole racial pattern changed when it began to spread out among the stars. It would have to have a revival of the old pioneering spirit. There had been the beginnings of that when they left. And with that, such a war could be prevented forever.

He heard Graves moving about in the galley, singing something about graves opening, and grimaced.

Besides, Jeremy had admitted that they didn't have all the answers. The mystery of the vanished skeletons remained—and until that was accounted for, nothing could be considered explained.

He forgot about the skeletons as he began planning how he'd wangle his way into one of the colonies. Then, even if catastrophe did strike Earth in another thousand years or so, the race could go on. Ten more years, and man would be safe...

He was feeling almost cheerful as they finally came out of hyperspace near Earth...and landed...

The skeletons—lay scattered everywhere.

THE END

Made in the USA
Middletown, DE
21 January 2023